8/23

A LITTLE LIKE WAKING

ADAM REX

ROARING BROOK PRESS
New York

Published by Roaring Brook Press
Roaring Brook Press is a division of Holtzbrinck Publishing Holdings Limited
Partnership
120 Broadway, New York, NY 10271 • fiercereads.com

Our books may be purchased in bulk for promotional, educational, or business
use. Please contact your local bookseller or the Macmillan Corporate and
Premium Sales Department at (800) 221-7945 ext. 5442 or by email at
MacmillanSpecialMarkets@macmillan.com.

Library of Congress Cataloging-in-Publication Data is available.

First edition, 2023
Book design by Aurora Parlagreco
Printed in the United States of America
The art for this book was created in Adobe Photoshop.

ISBN 978-1-250-62191-7 (hardcover)
1 3 5 7 9 10 8 6 4 2

For Marie

ONE

A BELL RINGS.

Zelda slaps everything on her bedside table until the ringing stops, finds her glasses (which are fine, despite some light slapping), and rolls gently back onto her pillow.

Daylight slips in through the drapes.

She'd been dreaming she was drowning. Fun. It wasn't the water that worried her, though—in her dream, in that brittle logic dreams have, the water was her home. It was when she discovered the water had a surface—and something more beyond—that the cold came in. A cold that had always been there but she'd never felt before.

There was someone above the surface of the water, wasn't there? Holding out their hand. Already she can't remember who it was. Their face was foggy. Maybe their face was fog.

It made Zelda anxious and foggy until she woke, but now that fog is lifting and Zelda smiles as relief warms her body. She doesn't have to remember the thing that worried her. She doesn't need to worry about the thing she can't remember. Zelda blinks away the sleep that pricks at her eyes and stares awhile at her bedroom ceiling.

The morning light casts shadows in the plaster. There are pictures—like inkblots—in the shadows. She found them when she was young, and gave them names. Her constellations. Every morning, Zelda studies them like a sailor. She's looking to see if she's where she's supposed to be.

Now she's up and yawning. Her house is yellow, sunny. She brushes out her dark hair and ties it back, changes out of the shirt and shorts she sleeps in and into the shirt and shorts she runs in.

Dust motes linger in the light overhead as Zelda laces up her running shoes. She watches them a moment and breathes the day in.

She doesn't know we're here. She can't tell that we're thinking about her.

Then she's out the door. She doesn't turn to lock it because her running shorts don't have a pocket for keys, and besides, in this town, why bother? Why. Then she's down the steps to the gate with the creaky hinge, which she means to fix but never does because it sounds like a cartoon frog.

"*MOR*ning," creaks the gate as it opens, a throaty singsong.

"Good morning, gate," Zelda answers.

"*GOOD*bye," says the gate as it closes.

"See you," Zelda tells it as she jogs away.

She worries sometimes she might be cute.

Here's what Zelda's town is like:

Small yards;
actual white picket fences,

or else fences of wrought iron as curly as cake icing.

Zelda runs.

The air out here is tender and kind. The sun is a blush on her cheeks. There's a sympathetic breeze like a hand on the small of her back as her limbs loosen.

This sidewalk was flat and straight once, but tree roots have pushed it out of plumb like a crooked smile—she has to mind her step as she waves at the paperboy, and says hi to Clara the mail carrier ("Hi, Zelda baby"), and nods professionally to the clown at the laundromat.

She climbs the library steps and slides back down on the handrail. She cuts through the skate park to admire the skaters, watches them all botch their tricks and get back up again. Then she turns into the town square to circle the courthouse a few times, and that's when it hits her.

"Ohmygosh," she huffs, grinding to a stop. "Oh *no!*"

There are a couple of guys playing Frisbee nearby, the kind who are all muscly arms and haircuts. "What?" one of them asks her, stepping close. "What is it?"

"My final," says Zelda, and she glances up at the courthouse clock. "My geography final. It starts in five minutes!"

"Dude! That sucks!" calls the other Frisbee guy. "Well at least . . . ha! At least you're already dressed for running!"

Zelda smiles wanly and raises a hand as she sprints off in a new direction.

"Good luck, Zelda!" say the Frisbee bros, in unison.

Zelda leaps over a little red fire hydrant and veers around the café. The flower cart woman calls, "Zelda, here!" and hands her a daisy as she passes. "Go get 'em, Zelda!" cheers the tattoo guy with his baby. There's a funny tangle of leashes and legs as Zelda tries to get past that one old man with his three tiny dogs. It's just the kind of lively moment you'd expect if Zelda's life were a movie, and these the opening credits. A little snapshot of people and place.

"Whoop, sorry."

"*Yip-yip-yip!*"

"Oh dear."

"I think this belongs to you."

And so on.

Finally, Zelda recovers and dashes past the boutique and bookstore and bakery. Runs under the jewelry store clock on the following block. "Four minutes," she huffs. "Hey! Kid!"

There's a girl with a bicycle, a beautiful blue bicycle with a banana seat and a backrest.

"Kid!" Zelda breathes. "Can I borrow your bike?"

The girl's freckles are a constellation. Her gap-toothed smile is as crooked as an old sidewalk. "Sure, Zelda!" she answers, and hands over the handlebars. Just like that. Zelda mounts the bike at a run, leaping onto the seat and settling into a coast with one breathless sweep of her leg.

"Didn't know I could do that," she whispers absently.

"Atta girl!" shouts a meter maid.

Her feet touch the pedals. In that moment, her ears pop. Like something has changed in the air. A sudden shift in pressure. Or maybe not—no one else seems to notice it.

Three minutes.

Zelda pumps her legs and settles into a groove. She's going to make her test in time. This bicycle has a bell—she rings it. Its tone is perfect and clear, like a drop of blue water, and as it fades she tries to quiz herself with geography words. *Isthmus. Peninsula. Bismarck, North Dakota.*

Then she takes a turn a little wide, and there's an oncoming car, and her heart sinks. Time slows down.

Still, Zelda has enough time to feel every bump in the road, hear the scream of tires, see the startled face of the driver that's about to hit her. It's that woman who's always selling Girl Scout cookies outside the Sav-Mor. Zelda sees her mouth a word she probably doesn't use in front of the Girl Scouts. Then someone somewhere shouts, "Loooook ouuuut!" and Zelda brakes, the car brakes, their brakes catch and they grind like glaciers toward each other in dilated time, patient but inevitable.

Actually, not so inevitable—they both stop, hardly more than a meter apart. A bird sings, *whit-whee*. The woman behind the wheel finishes the word she'd been saying, the crisp *T* of it fogging a little spot on her windshield. Then: time speeds up again as a third person— some boy—lurches across the road between them, trips over a curb, does a header over a railing, and disappears behind some bushes.

It seems like a good moment for someone to say, *Ta-da!* Nobody does.

Zelda's chest thumps, and her head goes light. She's standing in the middle of the street. The car stands in the middle of the street, facing her.

The driver's-side window opens, and the woman sticks her head out. "Sorry, Zelda!" she shouts.

"No!" says Zelda. "Don't apologize! It was me—*I'm* sorry!" She can't remember the woman's name.

"You okay?"

"Yeah, you?"

The driver's okay. Zelda jerks her head at the flowery hedge on the side of the road. "Who was *that* guy?" she asks.

"I think he was trying to save you!" shouts the Girl Scout woman.

Zelda squints at the bushes. "He missed."

She wheels her bike toward those bushes and waves to the driver as she leaves. She doesn't have time for this. She has, in fact, two minutes.

"Hello?" she calls to the guy. "Was that you who shouted, 'Look out'?"

"It was just a suggestion," says a voice on the other side of the flowers.

"Are you hurt? I have to go."

"You go on ahead, then," says the flower boy. "Having a lie-down."

"All tuckered out from the big rescue attempt," says Zelda, trying to get a look at him. The branches are too thick to see.

"*Rescue?* Nah. I was just rushing to get a good spot in the hedge before it filled up."

"Hmm." Zelda bumps the bike up onto the curb and leans across the fence, cranes her neck over the hedge into someone's front yard. A little garden and a crab-apple tree. "Okay," she says. "Thank you for—"

That's when she sees him.

She looks away quickly. As if she'd happened upon something *scandalous*. But it's nothing of the sort. Just a boy. A *cute* boy, her age, his long body draped over the wet grass.

She's afraid to look at him again, but she also really, *really* wants to look at him again. How can it be both at once? She wants to cover her face and peek out at him through her fingers. *Jeez*, she thinks, *get a hold of yourself.*

It probably seemed weird to him, anyway—her looking away like that.

So she quiets herself, collects her features, and leans once again into the yard.

"Sorry," she tells him, "I—"

But there's no one there.

Zelda straightens. She looks all around. There's no one there.

He's gone.

"Well," says Zelda. "Fine. That's fine."

She checks again. To be sure.

"I have a geography test anyway," she tells herself. "In one min-ute. So." She gets back on the blue bike and rings the bell.

The school bell's peal is just fading when, in the classroom, she takes her seat. "Sorry I'm late," she says.

You didn't see her get to the school or watch her come in— just a cut to the classroom, like they do sometimes in stories. The light outside was honey, but here it's like the inside of a refrigera-tor. Zelda's sitting at her desk, panting, the only student in running clothes. She tries to silently scooch her chair forward but makes sort of a trumpety elephant noise instead.

"Almost got in an accident," she explains. "And there was this boy."

It occurs to her that she didn't know him. The boy in the hedge. This morning—this morning alone—she knew Clara, and the clown at the laundromat, and all kinds of people on the street. She recog-nized the Frisbee bros and that guy with the dogs and the little girl who lent her the bike. She'd seen that bike before. She'd seen that girl. Though it comes to Zelda that she has no idea what her name is, or where she lives, or how to get the bike back to her.

"Also, I think I stole a bike," she says.

It's a small town; she knows everyone. Their faces, if not their names. But the boy in the bushes—his was a face she had never seen before. Like an impossible shape. And yet the memory of just a moment with him feels more real to her now than every other student in this class.

Those other students are quietly test-taking. There's a *skritch*ing all around her of lead against paper. The room smells like pencils.

How can Zelda be expected to take a test *now*? There was a boy—she should get excused. When the teacher asks why, Zelda will say, *Boy*, and get a hall pass with the word BOY on it. Go and solve the mystery of him. Maybe if she gets done early . . .

Zelda looks down. There's a piece of paper—her test. In the cold, flickery light, she looks at her test, but it's just a blur.

Everything else in her line of sight is fine. But the exam in her hand . . . she squints—did she lose her glasses?—and taps at her face, but there they are.

"Something's gone wrong," she whispers. "Something in my brain." Her head feels heavy and empty at the same time. And hot. Heavy and hot, while the desktop is so cool. She rests her head to feel that coolness on her cheek. Fresh, like green grass.

"Everything feels different."

She won't fall asleep. She isn't the type of student who falls asleep in class, she thinks, as she waits for the bell to ring.

TWO

A BELL RINGS.

Zelda stirs, slaps everything on her end table, finds her glasses. The world leaps into focus. She rolls onto her back, blinking, to look once more at her bedroom ceiling.

The morning light casts shadows in the plaster. There are pictures in the shadows. Constellations. She found them when she was young, and gave them names. Stare long enough and maybe you'll see what Zelda sees: a brimmed hat and a squiggly mustache that she calls Mister Mayor; the fat fenders and tacky tires of the Little Car. There's the Happy Grandma—follow her line of sight past the ceiling fan and you'll see what she's so happy about: the King of Sandwiches, resting just offshore of a blotch that Zelda thinks looks like Cuba because she doesn't know what Cuba looks like.

When she was little, and would wake from yet another nightmare, these ceiling pictures would be her first glimpse of the civilized world. Like a sign with a map and a friendly YOU ARE HERE. They're illusions, of course. In a different light, or to anyone else, they wouldn't be there at all. It's like Zelda conjures them every morning when she opens her eyes.

Her lashes flutter.

She can't remember what she'd been dreaming about, but she senses she had weird dreams. Exhilarating and debilitating dreams. Like they kept her busy all night so she never got a chance to rest. There was a person, wasn't there? A person in her dream that surprised her, only she can't remember his face. And even though she can't remember his face, she feels a flush of warmth all the same, right down to her toes.

Her mattress is just a little deeper today; the air in her bedroom is a blanket, impossibly soft and thick as the sky.

Quiet.

"Maybe'll just lie here a minute," she tells her ceiling.

Grandma looks really jazzed about it.

She could stay in bed forever, maybe. Sleeping and waking until she forgets which is which. She releases a slow breath as her eyes close and the world deflates like a hot-air balloon.

"*Wake up*," says a voice.

Zelda's eyes are open now. Very open.

"*Wake up. Please.*"

It's a man's voice—gentle and deep. Zelda cringes a bit beneath the bedsheet and says, "God?"

"*Just wake up. Wake up and come back to Daddy.*"

"O-okay," says Zelda. "Sorry."

She does get up, too quickly. Dandelion-headed, clumsy puppet legs.

She's frozen a minute as she waits for further instructions. She hears a machine hum, a passing car, the backyard sound of a mourning dove mourning.

"Hello?" says Zelda. "When you said, 'Come back to Daddy'... what did you mean exactly?"

No answer.

Zelda's shoulders unwind. Suddenly, talking out loud in an empty room feels like talking out loud in an empty room.

"... Okay. If you don't have anything else for me, I'm gonna go for a run."

No instructions seem to be forthcoming. Zelda brushes out her dark hair and ties it back, changes out of the shirt and shorts she sleeps in and into the shirt and shorts she runs in.

They're almost identical, these outfits. She got both shirts free for being the first person on two separate occasions to finish the sentence "104.5 WKZZ Plays Today's Greatest *what*."

The answer was Hits.

Dressed, finally. Shoes laced, she heads out for a jog, pausing at the gate. A long pause. Her bones feel older today. The day feels thicker.

A little car passes, and honks hello.

Her town. Her town is like ... a life-sized model. That's a funny thought. Like a perfect set of miniatures, the sort you'd collect in pieces and display at Christmas. Except not miniature. She's not sure how to put it. A perfect model, like a ship-sized ship in a colossal bottle, corked off from the real world.

No, not like a ship in a bottle. That's not right. Her town is great—she doesn't know why she thought that.

"Hi, Zelda baby," says Clara as she comes up the sidewalk, mailbag bouncing against her hip.

Zelda shakes some of the fuzz loose and gives Clara a smile. "Hey. Hey! Clara—you deliver mail to everyone in town, right?"

"Sure do," says Clara.

"Do you know a . . ." Zelda trails off. She was about to just say *boy*. But it *was* a boy, wasn't it? In her dream. Maybe she was dreaming about a real person—wouldn't that be something? She asks, "Are there any new . . . people in town?"

Clara blinks. "New people?" she says. "What do you mean, *new people?*"

"I know," says Zelda, waving the thought away. "You're right. It sounded ridiculous to me as soon as I said it. How're things, Clara?"

"Can't complain," says Clara. "Finally finished my barbecue pit—you're invited this Sunday!"

"Oh, good!"

"Speaking of home improvements," Clara says, and eyes the fence. "You ever going to fix that squeaky gate? It sounds like the door to Hell, is what I'm saying."

"Ha. It *sounds*," Zelda informs her, "like a cartoon frog."

Clara smirks to show she disagrees, agreeably.

"Heeey, speaking of Hell," Zelda says in what she hopes is a breezy, conversational way, "I . . . think I heard the voice of God this morning?"

Clara stares, so Zelda shrugs to show her what an ordinary voice-of-God situation it is.

"How about that," says Clara. "What did he want?"

"Um. Okay. He definitely wanted me to wake up," Zelda begins, and again she mulls over the *come back to Daddy* bit. "And maybe start going to church?"

"Well," says Clara. "That *does* sound like something he'd say." Then she reaches into her mailbag and hands over twelve greeting cards and a catalog. Zelda takes them, glances carelessly at the catalog, the dresses and girls. Same paper dolls as always.

"You take care of yourself, sweetie," Clara tells her with a creased brow. She turns and continues on her way. "Don't go getting sick, now."

"Just didn't sleep well!" Zelda explains. "I guess."

Another moment, and Clara's gone. Zelda looks down at the gate.

She's suddenly fearful of the sound it'll make. The door to Hell— why did Clara have to say that? Zelda resolves to pull it quickly, like a Band-Aid.

"*MOR*ning," creaks the opening gate.

She sighs happily as she passes through. "Hi, gate."

"This *WORLD* is a *lie*," it groans as it closes.

Zelda stands like a bent needle, her hand over the latch.

Slowly, she pushes the gate and it *cre-e-eaks*; pulls it back again and it *cre-e-eaks* and closes.

She breathes, in and out.

You think you know this next part—you've seen it before. She'll tell herself she was hearing things, maybe, that it was all in her head.

But no, actually—she just *forgets*. It sinks back below the surface like a dream. Her mind idles; her head is a quiet house. She stares absently like people do in the early morning, and tries to think about what she'd been thinking about.

The grass grows a little. Fat, dirigible bees mess around in the flower bed.

She gives her head a toss—*Whatever, it couldn't be that important.* She stuffs the mail into her own mailbox and sets off on her run. The wind pricks at her eyes.

What a curse it is, she thinks, *to dream.* What is it even for? You spend all your waking hours fitting together another pretty little day, only to tear it apart, scramble it up with the other days, spend all the anxious night trying to make sense of the pieces.

She says hi again as she passes Clara. She waves to the paperboy. When she greets the clown at the laundromat, we see a slight misgiving on her face.

"Laundromat clown," she whispers.

She shakes it off.

Dreams: They used to seem like such a dirty trick—her own mind jinxing her with a restless night for each restful day. Or, when she was feeling optimistic, she supposed a person might need a little bad with the good, some thunder and lightning to appreciate the sunny skies, blah blah bloo.

Thunder and lightning, ha, she thinks. *I don't even know what those are.*

Of course she's kidding. Kind of. But there's been such a streak of nice weather that thunder and lightning seem only distantly worrisome, like the measles. The summer sun shines down on small yards, white picket fences, wrought-iron gates as curly as cake icing. This whole town is a cake. A cake with too much frosting. Showy— a feast for the eyes. A cake not made to be eaten.

A cake not made to be eaten.

She runs the next two blocks with a wobbly frown, her mind

empty of all but the jetsam of that single thought, rolling in and out, in and out.

"Everything feels different," she says absently. And she's jolted by the sense that she only recently said those words. Those words exactly.

Up ahead there's a skeleton. This is not a surprise—there is always a skeleton. *It is a truth,* Zelda thinks, *universally acknowledged, that every neighborhood has to have one yard where they never take down their Halloween decorations.* So a skeleton. Old webs. Funny gravestones, too—the sort to say,

DEAR
LEE DePARTED

or whatever. As she draws alongside the yard she turns her head to read them. And finds she cannot.

Are they blurry? Maybe they've faded in the rain, she thinks, before reminding herself there hasn't been any rain. Besides—they're *not* blurry, exactly, just . . . hard to read. All she manages to make out before passing is

HERE
LIES.

And that's it.

Here Lies. It strikes a chord in a way she can't really pin down.

Anyway.

She'd been thinking about dreams.

She's less dramatic about them these days. A dreaming brain is just an empty stomach—with nothing to feed it, it can't help but growl. It can't help but eat itself.

Like, a few nights ago she dreamed she was trapped in a city of stones. A henge that scraped the sky and a pale eye where the moon should be. What did it mean? Nothing. The night before that, she'd been buried alive by her old Girl Scout troop—they were the same little girls she remembered, but their hands were strong. She kept screaming, "I'm not dead," but they didn't believe her. They sobbed as they put her in the ground. Then they made camp around her grave, keeping watch to make certain she stayed where she belonged.

They got badges for it.

Sometimes, after a certain sort of dream, Zelda wakes and she can't move. *Sleep paralysis*, that's the technical term. She's trapped for a spell. The Girl Scout morning was one of those. It's like her mind escapes, but her body's still buried. Buried in the dream. It took twelve seconds to come out of it, that time.

Bluh. Anyway! She can't remember anything she dreamed last night, so that's an improvement. Obviously. None of the usual cages and claustrophobia. Binding ties and prying eyes.

Zelda climbs the library steps and hotfoots it back down. *Free as a bird!* she cheers, in her mind. She makes a spectacle of herself, throwing punches, flexing and relaxing everything from her shoulders on down to each fingertip and toe. Just relishing having control. She vaults the handrail like a champion, she sprints like a cheetah, she slows and turns into the town square to circle the courthouse a few times like a jogger.

That's when it hits her.

"Oh no!" She skids to a halt. "My high school geography final! It starts in five minutes!"

Then she stands a moment, her mouth like a shut purse.

"Doesn't it?"

A Frisbee sails overhead. The line in the sky that it traces is as predictable as a signature.

Her heart starts racing. And not from the jog—something's off.

"Dude," says a voice. It's one of the Frisbee guys—they look concerned.

"*Dude*," the other one agrees sadly.

"Are you all right, dude?"

"I'm fine," Zelda says. "I'm just . . . I'm having this weird feeling of déjà vu."

"Déjà vu, dude?" asks one of the bros.

"From the French," explains the other, "meaning 'already seen.'"

"Dude."

Zelda turns in circles, taking in all the pieces of the town square. All the shops ringing the courthouse in their familiar places, like the properties in Monopoly. The usual people, out enjoying the day. She's had a strange sensation, and she's trying to hold on to the feeling of it, but it's a cloud. She wants to speak it aloud, but it's cotton candy, melting on her tongue. It occurs to her she might just be searching for a surprise. She might be looking for something—or someone—new. Out of the ordinary.

What a sad thought, she thinks. *There's no such thing.* Only in dreams is there ever a new boy, a boy her age, his long body draped over the wet grass.

As if she needed another reason to hate dreams. Here comes one to remind her how hollow they can be. Like a commercial for something delicious—something faked and fluffed and sprayed with glycerin that'll *never* be as good in real life. Empty calories. But my God, is she suddenly hungry.

She doesn't have time for this, of course. Her geometry final starts in five minutes.

Geography, not geometry.

Geometry or geography?

Then she hears that voice again. "*It's time to wake up,*" says the voice. That deep and gentle voice that sounds like it's nowhere and everywhere at once. Like it's reverberating off the sky. It doesn't get a reaction from the Frisbee bros, anyway, *or* the other people on the lawn, but it was *so clear.*

"I *am* up," Zelda whispers back.

Everyone's staring at her—what else is new, everyone's always staring at her—but she's finding it harder than usual to ignore. That couple on the picnic blanket. That baby in the stroller. Oh man, the birds. Are the birds watching her, too? Do they always and she's just now noticing it? Wait, is that what bird-watching *is*? Birds watching you? She thought it was the other way around—*You know what, it's fine. Everything's fine. Why isn't everything fine?*

"*You're okay,*" that voice tells her. "*You're going to be okay.*"

"I just need a minute," Zelda mumbles, breathless.

"But shouldn't you get going?" the guy holding the Frisbee asks. "Your geometry final starts in five minutes!"

"And you didn't study!" says the other guy. "Or remember to go to class all year!"

"Right!" says Zelda, tensing. She frowns. "Right!" she says again, and hustles off.

In school, she stares at her final.

"It's just . . ." she begins to say. "Isn't it summer? And didn't I graduate? Why am I in school at all?"

The paper on her desk is a blur. It's being difficult. She wills it to stop—and it does, in a way. The blur focuses into something that's sharper but not any easier to read. Words and figures are all a scrawly riot, like a swear word in a comic strip. Overlapping circles. Triangles. Vectors and charts.

"I've dreamed of this," she remembers. "Of not being able to read. I've dreamed of this exact problem before, but now it's real. Now it's *really happening*."

She exhales and squints hard until the first question comes into focus:

A RISOCERES TRAMMANKLE—

No. What the heck. Is that word rhinoceros *or* isosceles? She squints.

AN ISOSCELES TRIANGLE—

Okay.

—WITH ANGLES ABC—

Got it.

BOARDS A TRAIN TRAVELING AT AN AVERAGE SPEED OF 100 KM/HR TOWARD CINCINNATI.

What

WHEN YOU WERE A KID YOUR FRIEND MATT ROUSE MOVED TO CINCINNATI.

Matt who?

MATT ROUSE SOUNDS LIKE RAT MOUSE. THAT'S WEIRD.

Zelda stares for a bit, then writes TRUE.

Good, she tells herself. *Strong start.*

But the second question is just

MUHLISIANA PURCHASE?

and she's not sure what it wants from her. Should she raise her hand? No one else is. But they must have the same test she does, and the whole back half of it doesn't seem to be in English.

Also it's mostly pictures of haircuts.

A yellow cat brushes against her leg.

"Wh—*Patches!*" she says, angling over to look at it. The cat stretches up to meet her. The jowly face, the exact collar . . . she picks him up, and it's really him. "I thought you got run over when I was a kid!"

"I did!" says Patches.

Zelda nuzzles his purring tummy, and puffs air up at her face to clear out the cat hair, and grins at him hanging from her hands. His big sad eyes, his saggy mustache face. Warm little furry little body. She'd really thought he was dead—why did she think that?

There's an unpleasant thought crowning in her head, like a wisdom tooth coming in, and she can't stop touching the tip of it. So by the time her grin fades, it's clear she's looking past Patches, through him at the gauzy middle distance of her thoughts. He squirms. Zelda puts him in her lap, whereupon he takes up her pencil.

"What's the Pythagorean theorem again?" the cat asks.

"Just a second, Patches. I'm thinking."

A guy behind her says, "Pssst! Zelda!" She turns to look. He's in his underwear, but all of her classmates are in their underwear. "Only ten more seconds to finish the exam!"

"You may count on me," says Patches, briskly circling haircuts.

"Okay, but . . . didn't I take this test already?" asks Zelda. "Like yesterday?"

Silence.

"Hey . . . hey, yeah," says a student.

"I think I took it yesterday, too," says another.

"*I* didn't," says a girl. "Yesterday I had a, you know, teeth-falling-out-of-my-mouth dealie? So I mostly did that."

"Weird," says a boy.

The teeth girl scowls and covers her mouth with her hand. "It's a pretty common problem."

"I didn't mean your teeth—I meant about the test."

Everyone looks down at their papers for a second. A girl coughs.

"Now my test is a signed photo of Billy Dee Williams," she says. So is Zelda's. So is everybody's.

"There's never much geography on these geography tests, is there?" Zelda says. "I mean, there should be"—she struggles to picture it—"questions about, I don't know, maps? Other places?"

"What other places?"

"Yeah, what other places?"

Zelda waves this off. "Never mind that," she says. She looks nervously for the teacher (was there ever a teacher?), but no one appears to be in charge. "Something else has been bugging me. Why is there always a clown at the laundromat?"

"What do you mean? That's the laundromat clown."

"Yep—laundromat clown," says everyone, and it's hard disagreeing with a whole room full of people. It's hard when every little window of clarity seems to fog over the moment she tries to catch her breath.

"I'm only saying," she tries, slowly, "that, you know, creepy clowns . . ."

"Yeah?" says a classmate.

". . . and test anxiety . . ."

"Right."

". . . and missing teeth and underwear . . ."

"Uh-huh."

"That it's, like . . . all *dream* stuff," Zelda says. "This is like we're in a dream."

It's *so* quiet after she says it.

Zelda has a few well-earned moments of worry about how a statement like this is going to play with the rest of her classmates. It feels real, though. It feels *right*. Just saying it is a swift broom through the cobwebs in her mind.

She's always thought of herself as brave, so she turns and looks her half-naked classmates in their entirely naked faces. They look right back at her. One of them shyly raises her hand.

"If we *were* in a dream, we could fly."

Patches floats by. "We can!"

Someone squeals. Patches rises like a little astronaut, languid as a lava lamp. Now everyone but Zelda is getting up—some stand atop their chairs or push off from desktops—and they take to the air like swimmers. Exactly like swimmers—they paddle and kick, cupping great handfuls of air and tunneling through. None of them is terribly good at it. But they're ecstatic anyway.

"I forgot I could fly," says a breathless girl. She flaps and yaws. "Why did I forget I could fly?"

The classroom is tangled with bodies now—bodies and Patches, bodies in underwear making clumsy water ballet over Zelda's head. Pinwheels, pink ankles. They struggle to get higher (it's harder, higher), and since there's no ceiling (was there ever a ceiling?), they wriggle free from geography (and physics), and now the whole town is spread beneath them like a diorama . . .

And all the while, Zelda is sitting tight as a fist in her chair.

So I guess that's it, she thinks. *I'm still dreaming. What a nightmare.* She must be stuck in one of those dreams where you think you've woken up but you haven't—she has a lot of those. Okay, fine—soon she'll wake up and things will be back to normal. Blue skies. Friendly faces. Every face familiar.

No. *No.* Not every face. It comes back to her now, comes back completely—she met someone new. Yesterday, when she was biking to class. There was a car, and someone tried to save her. She spoke to him. He was funny. And she only got a glimpse, but his face was like a color she'd never seen before. Then he was gone.

This world was a child's toy: a peg for each hole, a hole for each peg. Everything in its place until the unexpected shape of *him*. Like a hook. A question mark. This life was a children's book, but now there's a boy, and he's the question mark at the end of every sentence.

He started this. He planted the seed of doubt.

Zelda winces inwardly.

Oooh, she thinks, and wiggles her fingers. *The seed of doubt. What dramatic thoughts you're having, Zelda. Does the seed of doubt sprout into the . . . into the incredulitree? Does it have disbeleaves on it? Shut up, Zelda.*

The point is, he was new and then he disappeared and now she's asking questions. Because before yesterday everyone was her regular neighbors, the butcher and baker and laundromat clown.

Laundromat clown.

Was that normal? Do laundromats have clowns?

Some fast-food restaurants have clowns. As mascots. Commercial spokesclowns. So whatever, the laundromat has one, too. Maybe the customers think it's fun! A clown who's always there, who never speaks. Watching you while you do your laundry. Just watching and grinning like a broken window and pinching the cheeks of your children.

Huh.

The clown is definitely just a dream thing, she thinks. It'll be gone when she wakes up.

Zelda had a weird geography test today, and yesterday, too; so maybe that's all been the same dream, a dream with a boy and strange voices and laundromat clowns. But the day before that she went to the Astronomy Picnic, and she remembers passing the laundromat clown to get there, too. On Monday, there was the St. Valentine's Day Pet Wedding and Lasagna Cookout, and of course she saw the clown then because everyone went to the laundromat afterward to wash their lasagna bibs.

She gasps. *Oh no,* she thinks with a shiver. *None of those sounded like a real thing.*

So she probably dreamed the cookout, too. How long has she been at this? Could she have dreamed the whole past week? The whole past month? She searches her memories. Last Christmas . . . last Christmas, every man, woman, and child in town gave her a present. Even the rabbi—and that didn't sound very likely, did it? In September, she played a sold-out hoobaphone recital, and that was mostly her explaining to the audience that there's no such thing as hoobaphones.

"They gave me a standing ovation anyway," she reminds herself. "I got a record deal."

This town. *Her* town. Where everybody knows her name. Friendly people, always smiling, asking about her day, watching and waving.

It's nice here, she tells herself. *But Here Lies.* What if the place that seems too good to be true is too good to be true?

Zelda frowns. And races from the room.

THREE

OUTSIDE, IT'S ALREADY NIGHT. THAT makes no sense. But as with all the things recently that make no sense, Zelda can only take note of it; brush it off in her mind and put it with the others.

She backs up against the side of her high school—feels the cool painted-cinder-block brick wall. She looks up and sees moths rave around a yellow streetlamp. She breathes in the parking lot smell, hears the distant shush of cars. *This is a lot of sensory input for a dream*, she tells herself. Touch, sights, smells, sounds—everything but taste. It's not realistic. Or, rather, it's *too* realistic.

She must be mistaken.

She's still looking skyward when a raindrop lands on her nose, trickles around her nostril to the corner of her mouth. She licks it away. She tastes its crispness and the salt of her own skin.

Another raindrop now, and another. They polka-dot the sidewalk. In moments she's soaked. Thunder and lightning do their thing in the distance—Zelda is flabbergasted. Like other towns and distant countries, weather is something Zelda has only read about in books.

She's dressed for running so she runs, thinking only to get home again and take a quiet moment to sort this out. And maybe a bath. Rain pastes her shirt to her skin. Her sneakers slap against fresh pools on the pavement.

In the traffic circle ahead of her a little car with fat fenders veers and skids into a signpost. The airbag blooms. A man steps out of the car and looks skyward, goggle-eyed and gaping.

"What *is* this?" he wants to know.

"Rain," says Zelda.

"*Rain*," he whispers. He's still looking directly into it when he spots a flock of geography students, flying south.

"There are people flying!" he says, pointing. "And a cat! There are people and a cat *flying*!"

Zelda stops. "I know," she says. "It's okay. It's just . . . This is a dream. I think. We're in a dream."

"WE'RE IN A DREAM?"

"We're in a dream."

"DOES THAT MEAN I SHOULD TURN INTO A BIRD AND ALSO FLY?"

Zelda scowls. "What? No. Why would it mean—whoop, okay, he's doing it. He's a bird. There he goes."

"Zelda!" someone calls, and Zelda turns to see the old man with his little wet dogs crossing the street toward her. "Did that man turn into a bird?"

"Uh-huh, yeah. He did."

The old man raises his parched face to the sky and marvels. "THAT MAN TURNED INTO A BIRD!"

"THAT'S MESSED UP!" says one of the dogs.

"Zelda!" shouts a passing librarian. "DID THAT DOG JUST *TALK*?"

"I think we need to take it down a notch," says Zelda, backing up to find a dry spot under an awning. She shivers there a moment, looking to escape before anything else astonishing happens. But the moment she sets off again, the Mayor's black limousine pulls up in front of her. Busy intersection tonight.

"Zelda, thank goodness," says the Mayor as he exits the back seat of his limousine and smooths his sash. "How about this weather, eh? Flying people, and also something my advisors are telling me is rain."

The stuff his advisors told him was rain is swashing festively off the brim of his hat. Zelda steps clear of the splash zone.

"A recent poll reveals that eighteen percent of townspeople are *freaking out*," adds the Mayor. "That's an eighteen percent increase over a previous poll taken three minutes ago."

Zelda retreats back under the awning, and the Mayor follows. The people and dogs have joined them, and everyone's crowding around. "Can you all back it up a little?" Zelda says. "Let me think."

"Back up and let her think, everyone! By executive order!"

The crowd attracts a crowd. A yoga class lets out, and now there are a dozen new people with rolled-up yoga mats. They, too, cluster under the awning. There's a gang of kids up past their bedtime. The kids attract an ice cream truck, and now "Teddy Bears' Picnic" is playing on a loop from the curb. The group of old-timey Christmas carolers who go a-wassailing each December in their top hats and muffs—they're here, too. The buzz spreads.

"What's going on?" asks a latecomer.

"Zelda says our lives? The ones we're living right now? Aren't real."

"Aren't real?"

"Zelda says they're a dream."

"That's ridiculous."

"You take that back!"

"Don't you *talk* about Zelda like that!"

One of the carolers throws the first punch. A top hat flies through the air.

"Goodness!" says the Mayor, shuffling Zelda out of the way. "Stop! The street is no place for street fighting!"

An epic brawl is breaking out by the fountain in the center of the circle. The wassailers in particular seem to have a lot of bad blood between them, and now they kick and pitch, punch and piledrive.

"They're not so much wassailing as *assailing*," Zelda says proudly, but nobody hears her.

It's too warm for snow, but it starts snowing all the same. Now the traffic circle is a terrible snow globe of crisp white drifts and fat flurries and carolers trying to bite one another.

"Someone needs to take control," says the Mayor. "Deliver a strong message of hope to the town."

"Like a town meeting," says a girl with a kite.

"Oh, I love town meetings!" says the Mayor. "I get to stand on a podium. Zelda? Do you agree we should have a town meeting?"

"Uh, sure, I guess."

At least the brawl doesn't seem to be amounting to much—blows land and make a lot of noise, but they're all sizzle and no steak. Zelda breathes slowly. She wills herself to be calm. If she's calm, the dream will be calm.

Now all the brawlers are making out. "I guess that's better," says Zelda.

Gosh. She shouldn't be staring, but Zelda can't look away. This is a lot of big feelings on display. This is not the behavior of people who know they're being stared at. Part of her wants to laugh and part of her wants to say *Ew* like an eight-year-old and part of her wants to watch it like a nature documentary and part of her wants a closer look.

But does any part of her want to join in? That's what she's wondering. Does any part of her want to find her own person to kiss? It would be her first—except for a spin-the-bottle game when she was thirteen, and that doesn't count. She's never felt that way about anyone. She's maybe never felt that way, period. But she didn't used to like olives, either, and now she does. So.

She's had dreams about forgotten doors. It's her house, but there's a door in the back of the closet, a door behind her headboard, a door in the floor. She dreams she opens a door and remembers all the excellent rooms—whole wings—beyond it. Beauty and space. So much to explore. So much wasted potential.

This feels like that. Like Zelda might also have wasted wings.

She's wondering how she might go about spreading her wings when the Mayor leans in and makes her flinch. "Zelda? Could you call it? Everyone always listens to you."

"Um. Call what? Sorry."

"The town meeting," says the Mayor.

Zelda sighs. "Fine. I call a town meeting."

"Louder, please. Speak into the megaphone."

"I CALL A TOWN MEETING!"

FOUR

IT'S LATER, AS SHE SITS all alone on a bench outside the court-house, that Zelda wonders how everyone knew to come. Sure, she'd shouted into a megaphone; sure, she'd said *I CALL A TOWN MEETING*, but her voice couldn't have carried all that far in the rain. Yet half the town is packed inside the courthouse behind her. She can hear their murmurations through the masonry. They're getting ready to start. They're waiting for *her*, most likely.

"Doesn't *make* any *sense*," she says carelessly, ruefully. Like those words lost their meaning a while back and she's only saying them to make fun of herself. But she *does* mean it—she can't stop feeling in her heart like some sense should be made.

This is a dream.

She's been playing the Game of Life when she could have been playing pretend. She's been moving her little car around the spaces, and there aren't any spaces. She's been following the rules, and there aren't any rules. But those rules, the reassuring knowledge that there *could be* rules—you can't just stop believing in them overnight.

"It's all rigged anyway," she says aloud, to the sky. "People treat me like a champ, but I've been playing everything on Easy Mode. Baseball tees and bumpers in the gutters."

Now that she knows, what fun is it to keep playing? What other choice does she have until she wakes up?

In a minute, she'll stand, move along the marked sidewalk spaces to the courthouse doors, join the meeting. She could *probably* just snap her fingers, zap herself inside with a magical *poof.* She could probably make the whole courthouse building hike itself up and settle back down around her like a hen. She knows she won't, though. She'll follow the rules of Life.

If it were really the Game of Life, she could have a cat sitting next to her.

Patches jumps up onto the bench and rubs his cheek against her fingers.

"Oh," says Zelda. "Ha. Good to see you, Patches. You're done flying?"

"A mistake on my part," says Patches. He has a nice speaking voice, apparently. Like a fancy waiter. "If cats were meant to fly, then whither the birds? And what would become of the cat's famous modesty," he adds, "if not even the angels could look down on us from on high?"

"Is this you being modest right now?" asks Zelda. "I'm just checking."

"Besides, it wasn't even fun. It was swimming through syrup, so to speak."

"So to speak," says Zelda. "But maybe we shouldn't use metaphor?"

she adds. "'Cause if I think too hard about swimming through syrup I might dream we're actually swimming through syrup."

"I see you have anointed yourself dreamer—now who's being immodest?"

"Whatever," says Zelda. "I just wonder if we should choose our words kind of carefully."

"I am a poet—I choose my words *exquisitely*."

"Do poets like having their ears scratched?"

"Some do. Lord Byron didn't."

They sit in friendly silence for a spell while Zelda scratches Patches on the head and neck. The warble of courthouse voices is growing louder, but Zelda tunes them out. This is nice. Sitting with an old friend on a bench in the park. Everything behaving the way it's supposed to, plus or minus one talking cat. She looks at the stars.

"When did it stop raining?"

"It didn't," Patches tells her. "When you called your meeting the rain tried to enter the courthouse with everyone else. But they wouldn't let it, so it's sulking out in front of the juice bar."

Zelda grimaces. ". . . What?" She cranes her neck to look across the square, and sees a little black cloud sobbing and drinking a smoothie.

She sighs. "Oookay. I better get inside. I'm the one who opened this can of worms."

"So to speak."

"So to speak."

She stands and sneers at the courthouse. She could turn into a bug and fly in through the keyhole. She could be a giant and wear the place like a hat.

After a moment, she moves along the sidewalk spaces to the courthouse doors.

Everyone's at the meeting: Clara the mail carrier, the guys with the Frisbee, the students, the laundromat clown, the flower cart woman and the old man with the dogs and everyone, everyone. Kids are on laps and shoulders, people are standing in the back. The courthouse hall is way over capacity, and it's a beehive of fidgety whispers.

The Mayor has given Zelda the podium, but he hovers like he wants it back.

Zelda grips the lectern and looks out at all the faces. She tries to get a handle on the butterflies inside her. She says, "Ladies and gentlemen and . . ."

She locks eyes with the laundromat clown. She's realized mid-sentence that she doesn't know if the clown is a lady or a gentleman or neither or both.

The clown is smiling at her. Really, really smiling.

". . . and nonbinary friends and animals and everyone," Zelda continues. "The Mayor asked me to call this emergency meeting because I've discovered something . . . something weird."

People are nodding at her encouragingly. Or else frowning little *oh no, honey, what is it?* frowns. It's an easy crowd; this is going to be easy.

Nonetheless, now that she has everyone's attention she's reluctant to dive in. She's still wearing her running clothes. Her hair is wet.

"It's hard to know how to start."

"Is this about the new trash collection schedule?" asks the owner of the Mexican restaurant, who's at every town meeting trying to get people talking about the new trash collection schedule.

"It's not about that."

"Because they're not picking up the recycling often enough—"

"Everyone knows how you feel, Carlos!" says the Mayor.

This must be one of those lucid dreams, thinks Zelda. She's heard people talk about those. You're dreaming, but you know you're dreaming. You can take control of the dream. Other *people probably have lucid dreams that are* fun, thinks Zelda wryly. *Okay, here goes— time to take control:*

"This is a dream!" says Zelda, and the townspeople flinch. "Boom! There. This . . . all of this, right now. Your whole lives, this town . . . it's just a dream I'm having. I'm sorry. But it is."

Someone coughs. The cough rises, scrabbles like a mouse in the rafters, the vaulted ceilings, and dies. Zelda shifts from foot to foot.

Then the whole hall is quiet. Quiet apart from the sound of a cricket. But then the man in the seat next to the cricket gives the cricket a meaningful look, and after that it's entirely quiet.

Finally, murmuring. And not the thoughtful kind. Scoffing.

"Is this a joke?" asks the scuba instructor.

The housepainter says, "I thought you were going to play us something on your hoobaphone."

Zelda droops over the lectern. "I spent *forty-five minutes* telling you hoobaphones don't exist."

"Wait," says the dog man, looking around. "Does she really think she's dreaming or is she being poetic?"

Okay, she's losing them. What did she expect? She just told them reality isn't real. Zelda raises her hands against the rising hum of voices. "I know how it sounds, but it's true!" She points a finger at the kids in the back. "Ask my classmates! Who are in their underwear, might I add."

The students all look down at themselves. "Ohmygosh," says one.

A girl from geography stands up. Which is brave of her, considering. Zelda wants to say her name is . . . Stuffy? That doesn't seem right. "I think Zelda's telling the truth," says Stuffy. "We all flew today. Seriously. *Flew.*"

She shifts.

"But if it's a dream, then I'm pretty sure it would be *my* dream."

Well, thinks Zelda. *Obviously not.* That's ridiculous. She's embarrassed for her.

Patches has claimed a seat in the front row. He raises a paw.

Zelda says, "The chair recognizes Patches."

Patches stands up in his seat and steadies himself against the backrest, which is adorable.

"Good people," he says in his sonorous baritone. "I have known Zelda all my life. I hope I won't embarrass her when I say that she is a girl who knows how to pet a head. The sort of person who would let you have the last bit of yogurt in the yogurt container before she threw it away—little things, my friends, I *know*. But they add up to a most pleasing sum. If this girl says our life is but a dream, then I believe her. Also, I suspect it's actually *my* dream. Also, I'm a talking cat."

Lots of chatter now, people saying, "The cat makes an important point," that kind of thing.

One woman is quietly shaking her head, though. When she finally speaks, her voice rises above the rest. It is definitely the voice of a person who has sent food back in a restaurant. "I think I would *know* if this were a dream," she says. "Quick—somebody pinch me."

There are children in the chairs on either side of her, and they can't believe their good luck. They reach for her arms with greedy fingers, pinch, pinch, pinch.

Everyone tenses for a second, watchful. But nothing happens, so the woman folds her arms and says, "*See?*"

"'See?'" says Zelda. "See what? So I dreamed a woman got pinched—what does that prove?"

"Good point!" shouts the Mayor, behind her. "Perhaps there should be more pinching? Just to be scientific?"

Zelda turns to frown at him. "That wasn't what I was say—"

"Someone could pinch *me!*" the Mayor continues. "If they wanted!" And he phrases this like he's asking everyone generally, but he's staring directly at the Deputy Mayor with a hopeful look on his face.

The Deputy Mayor says, "I believe I made myself clear about this at last year's Christmas party."

"Ow!" says a dad in the crowd. He's been pinched by his son. "Tyler, too hard!"

Zelda can see the idea taking hold. People smirk at their neighbors, shrug little *why not?* shrugs.

"Uh, wait," says Zelda.

And now the whole town is pinching one another. All of them. That takes a minute to sort out.

"Whoa!" Zelda shouts. She briskly sidesteps the Mayor, who has been nudging his way back into the podium's airspace for the last five minutes. "Whoa, whoa, whoa! Hey!" she shouts again, but she doesn't have the benefit of a microphone anymore. "Come on, everyone! Knock it off!"

A hairstylist pinches the local newscaster, and flinches as she's pinched by the mortician, who is then pinched. The carpenter pinches the meteorologist, and the pinch is passed like a bucket brigade between every member of the volunteer fire department. The little kids are really going for it. It's like a wonderful Technicolor door has been opened and they're trying to pinch as many people as they're allowed before they're back in Kansas again. Several of them are trying to pinch the scuba instructor through his wet suit, and Zelda realizes, suddenly, that real scuba instructors probably don't always dress for scuba.

She rushes the podium with a *you better not* look on her face, and the Mayor steps aside, hands up. She seizes the microphone.

"You feel better?" she says. "Got that out of your system? Okay, maybe I'm wrong, but what if I'm right? Anyone think for a second about what's gonna happen to everybody IF YOU WAKE THE DREAMER UP?"

A jolt goes through the room. It clutches at every heart.

Only the kids are unaffected, and soon even they're reined in by the sudden hush. Parents pull them close without a fuss.

The silence of five hundred people is a terrible silence. It makes Zelda weak in the knees.

"But . . ." says a man. "It isn't *really* a dream. Right? That's silly!" He forces a laugh to show everyone how silly it is. The laugh comes out panicky and shrill like it's fleeing a burning building.

A man that Zelda sometimes sees at the library stands up. "Excuse me?" he says. "I have something to say."

The Mayor leans into the mic. "Go ahead."

"Last night? I was in a play?"

There's some nodding—a lot of people saw this play.

"And I didn't know any of my lines," he says, clearly troubled. "I hadn't even been to rehearsal! It was awful." He turns to the theater director. "Why wasn't I replaced if I hadn't been to rehearsal?"

The director shrinks in her seat. She doesn't seem to know the answer.

"You shouldn't have made me go onstage," the actor mutters. "*Death of a Salesman* doesn't even need a pantomime horse in the first place."

"Interesting," says the Mayor, nodding. "Interesting. Anyone else?"

The greengrocer raises his hand. "Ooh! I didn't have this mustache yesterday!"

A fisherman with a lot of babies stands and says, "I keep finding babies!"

"*I* keeb forgedding I'm vegedarian!" says a woman eating a ham sandwich.

"Sometimes I have more hair than usual!" someone shares. "Or not enough!"

"You wanna know maybe the weirdest thing of all?" asks the librarian. "Just a little bit ago, Zelda said, 'I CALL A TOWN MEETING,' and *now we're having one.*"

"So?"

"So does anyone remember how they got here?"

Huh, thinks Zelda. *Good point.*

"I bet we all have questions," Zelda says. "Existential questions! Am I using that word right?"

Patches nods.

"Questions about, you know, the very nature of . . . of . . ."

"The shifting sands beneath this sleepy simulacrum?" the cat suggests before licking his tummy.

"Sure, that," Zelda agrees. "But . . . since I have everyone here, I just want to say, thank you for a nice dream. I hope my real life is a lot like this. Every one of you has treated me like a sister, or a daughter."

At this, she loses her train of thought. Or, rather, her thoughts once again barrel like a runaway train back to the make-out party earlier at the fountain. Because what she said is true: Every person in town has treated Zelda exactly like she was a sister or daughter. There has never been any romance in her life. She has never been in love. Which was fine—she's never had chicken pox, either—but if there was one thing she had learned in the last forty minutes, it was that there were a lot of pent-up feelings around here. None of it bothered her before. But then yesterday there was a boy in the bushes.

He's not here. She checked, the moment she came into the courthouse, and she's beginning to feel foolish and moony. *It's not about the boy, though*, she tells herself, *it's what he represents.* He was like a stone. Hard and heavy and real. She got the briefest glimpse of him, and now the rest of the town is like papier-mâché. He's torn a hole right through everything, and she can't even tell him about it. All she wants to do is talk. She hardly wants to kiss him. Hardly at all.

Shouldn't she want her first kiss—at least her first dream kiss—to be with one of these papier-mâché people? She's known them her whole life, or at least she's dreaming she has. She scans their faces and feels nothing. A couple of the underwear boys from her geography class are objectively nice-looking, but no, nada. She's certain kissing any one of them would feel robotic and cold, and that's the worst first kiss she can imagine.

Actually, the worst would probably be the clown. What if it didn't stop grinning, but you went ahead anyway and kissed its tiny teeth. *Oh, look, the clown is winking now. Cool.* Zelda isn't feeling so romantic anymore.

"Um, I . . . think about it," she presses on, "and it's like: Of course this is a dream. Of *course.* I think we're all basically happy, aren't we?

Or we thought we were.

"No crime here. We have what we need. And I think we all feel appreciated? What a perfect dream we've been given."

Perfect as an empty cup.

"What a miracle. It makes me almost not want to wake up! Is that weird?"

She catches her breath, and tries to look at each one of their faces.

These are not the faces of people who've just had their hearts warmed, actually.

"The only thing 'weird,'" says a Pilates instructor covered in tiny rabbits, "is you thinking the dreamer is *you*! When it's obviously me!"

This really rouses the crowd. Suddenly, everybody's talking over one another.

"*You're* the dreamer?" says the radio DJ to the nurse. "Please."

The nurse looks offended. "I think I am."

"I *know* I am. All my life I've had this feeling? This feeling like other people weren't as real as me? And finally I know why!"

"That doesn't make you the dreamer, it just makes you a terrible person."

Zelda's saying, "People. People. People," with her palms up. "Look, I think it's natural that you'd all want to believe you're the dreamer, but it's clearly me."

"Oh, of *course* it's Zelda. Everything's *always* about Zelda."

Zelda stiffens. "Uh, what? What does that mean."

The baker leans forward and gives her a smile. "Oh, don't get the wrong idea, Zelda—we think you're wonderful."

"Wonderful," the tailor agrees.

"But you do just sort of . . . get your way, don't you?"

"Maybe that's our fault."

The Pilates instructor breaks in. "Remember when she was seven, and she was like, 'Everybody! Step on a crack, break your momma's back!'"

"So we all stop stepping on cracks—"

"Which is *not* easy—"

"And as soon as we got used to that rule, she started making up new ones."

"'Step on a tree, break your momma's knee.'"

Zelda's incredulous. "Okay, but you didn't have to . . . it's not like it's the *law*."

The Pilates instructor waves pointedly at a pair of stone tablets in the corner:

1. STEP ON A CRACK, BREAK YOUR MOMMA'S BACK
2. STEP ON A TREE, BREAK YOUR MOMMA'S KNEE
3. STEP IN THE STREET, BREAK YOUR MOMMA'S FEET
4. STEP ON A HOSE, BREAK YOUR MOMMA'S TOES
5. STEP ON A BOULDER, BREAK YOUR MOMMA'S SHOULDER
6. STEP ON A DALMATIAN, BREAK HER CONCENTRATION
7. STEP ON A SHOELACE, BREAK YOUR MOMMA'S POO FACE

Zelda hunches her shoulders. "I was seven," she mutters.

"Meanwhile, we have to carry skateboards everywhere so we don't step in the street!" shouts the Pilates instructor. Everyone in the crowd has a skateboard.

"You definitely didn't have those a second ago," says Zelda.

"It's been very hard on my momma," says the geologist. "I have to step on boulders for work."

"I've been so worried about *my* momma's poo face."

Zelda's getting a headache. "Okay, but . . . all the more reason to think I'm the dreamer, right? I don't mean to be in charge, but I'm obviously in charge. I have the podium. I got everyone to drop what they were doing and join me in town hall, just because I shouted—"

Patches yells, "CONGA LINE!"

Boop, everyone's in a conga line. Zelda is wearing a ruffly shirt. Everyone is in rumba clothes and big hats; there are flowers everywhere, rum punch, a man on stilts with maracas, the whole deal. There's a party-sized Cuban sandwich. The Mayor has a steel drum. One, two, three, kick, and then Patches yells, "TOWN MEETING!" and it's a town meeting again.

The last note of the steel drum still thrums the air, though the drum itself is gone. A few orphaned orchid petals settle lightly to the floor.

"All right, point taken," says Zelda.

Some of the townspeople still have their drinks. But only some of them. They're getting glances from the people who lost their drinks, and so they're sucking them down with the light-headed abandon of people who are afraid their drinks might disappear suddenly for any number of reasons.

A lot *of things might disappear suddenly*, Zelda thinks. *It* all *might.* A clock is ticking. A metaphorical clock, counting down the seconds of their metaphorical lives, but a real clock, too—as real as anything here—in the tower above them, clucking its tongue. Zelda shouldn't be able to hear it, but the room's gone so quiet. Quiet apart from the sound of a cricket, getting to the bottom of his rum punch. But then the man in the seat next to the cricket gives the cricket a meaningful look, and after that it's entirely quiet.

The librarian raises her hand. The chair recognizes the librarian. She asks how long has the dreamer been dreaming—

Yes, exactly, thinks Zelda—she'd been wondering the same thing.

—how long, if the librarian can remember her whole life in detail down to the last Dewey decimal point?

I do not know a single one of these people's names, Zelda realizes with a pang.

The chair recognizes the pizza chef, who wonders if dreams are maybe a place, a shared place everyone visits when they sleep, and that remains there after you wake. Maybe they're *all* dreamers, sharing that place.

The chair recognizes the air conditioner repairman.

"Barry?" the chair asks him. It gallops over on its metal legs. "Barry Lee?"

Okay, thinks Zelda. *I guess that guy's Barry.*

Barry and the chair reminisce awhile about high school. They used to sit together at lunch.

"We should get back on track," says the Mayor.

The petsitter wonders why she herself sleeps, and dreams, if she's only a character in a dream. Is the dreamer dreaming of her dreaming?

The carpenter raises a hand and wonders, aloud, if they could all just keep living quietly as they had done, before they knew.

"If we do that," says a woman, "the world will still end. Someday. Maybe *we* won't see it, but we'll know our children might, or our grandchildren."

"Uh-huh," the carpenter answers. "But didn't we know that already? Before?"

For a moment, everyone's lost in thought. Again Zelda steps up to the lectern.

"I think this just means we all ought to treat each passing second as a gift," she says. "A precious gift. Because I . . . because the *dreamer* could wake up—jeez, it could happen at any time, couldn't it? *Now*," she adds, and the people flinch. "Or *now*. So . . . I guess I'm just saying we should all do the most, the very *most* we can with what little time we have left," she finishes with a smile. "You know?"

It turns out to be the worst possible thing she could have said.

FIVE

ZELDA THOUGHT SHE LIKED THIS town. The dogs at the dog park. The wooden roller coaster by the reservoir. The big water tower out by the buttes—the graduating seniors decorate it every May. She loves the old man who greets people at the Sav-Mor and who always calls Zelda "Brown Eyes." This same old man is standing on top of his chair now. He's inflated himself a Superstars of Wrestling body and is declaring himself the god-king of all he surveys. That's upsetting. The Mayor is shouting. A whole lot of people are shouting.

Now they're all up out of their seats, pushing, grasping for loved ones, screaming at one another to calm down and stop screaming. The hall itself spends some time changing into everyone's middle school gymnasiums before settling down into a courthouse again.

Of course, Zelda's classmates are trying to fly, and soon there's a lot of that going around. And if there's one rule in this richly textured imagination-land, it's this: Everyone sucks at flying. They flail and waffle and bonk heads. The Girl Scout woman and one of the members of the city council are kissing like they've been dreaming about it their whole lives. The owner of the comic book store has a grappling gun—actually, he might have brought that from home; who knows—but he wasn't wearing a cape and unitard a second ago, and neither were all those other people. Reluctantly, Zelda remembers that when two comic-book superheroes meet for the first time, they usually get into a fight over some misunderstanding—ah, look, there they go.

"I am the vengeance of the night!" announce three different people at the same time. And as the superheroes prove Zelda right by fighting, she can't tell if she thought of it because it's true, or if it came true because she thought of it.

"I'll save you, Zelda!" shouts a person in a cape.

"I'll save Zelda from *you*, villain!" shouts a different person in a cape.

"All right." Zelda sighs. "I'm out."

She might need some help getting through the crowd, actually. She looks for the Mayor, but he has his hands full of trophies. One of them just says PRETTIEST. At least two are full of ice cream.

"Thank you!" shouts the Mayor to the crowd. "Thank you! I won't let you down!"

So much for the Mayor. There's a gavel on the lectern—Zelda bangs the gavel. She tries to call everyone to order, but her voice is a bee in a blender. She can just barely hear herself, and the sound of someone calling her name, and the Mayor screaming, "Crocodiles!" because some of his trophies have turned into crocodiles.

"Zelda!"

There it is again.

Through the swell of bodies, Zelda squints, and hears her name, and now Patches is bounding off a hockey goalie and onto the lectern in front of her. She scoops him up and hugs him close.

"You okay?" she asks.

"Nothing hurt but my pride," says Patches. "And my tail and my paw."

"Aw, which paw?" asks Zelda as a man dashes past, covered in bees.

"This one. Kiss it."

She kisses it, then searches the room for exits. "I want to get out of here," she says. "Off to someplace less . . . stirring."

"Ah, quite. What I hear you saying is that I, the dreamer, may be jostled awake by my proximity to this surly hurly-burly."

"That's not what I'm saying, no."

"Why are you holding a turkey leg?" asks Patches.

Zelda drops it, and wipes her hand against her shorts. "It was a gavel a minute ago," she explains.

They fight their way to a side exit, and push through the doors to the outside. On the square a number of impossible weird things are happening. It is once again raining, really raining. The storm cloud has left the juice bar behind and grown huge overhead; it really seems to be taking out its hurt feelings on the town. The rain tastes like mango and tears. People's favorite grandmas are back from the dead, and at least one of them is as tall as Godzilla and doddering down Main Street.

"I SAVED AN ARTICLE FROM THE PAPER FOR YOU," bellows the giant grandma.

Other townspeople are piloting impossible automobiles—cars you have to drive from the back seat, dashboards you can't see over—but they are zooming around with go-cart abandon.

"Look out!" calls Patches, and Zelda lurches just in time—a unicorn has nearly trampled them beneath its delicate sparklehooves. It looks back to give Zelda a "Sup" before disappearing into a crowd of cheerleaders.

"Jeez," says Zelda as she tucks herself and Patches under an oak tree. Between the carolers and the superheroes, there's an awful lot of fighting. "Real mature!" she shouts, but it just bounces off them. They have force fields. "Why is everyone being stupid? It's like the whole town is going through puberty."

Patches says:

> *"Fine faces, like asylums, hide*
> *Untidy tides of lives inside.*
> *Mere anarchy doth swarm and teem*
> *When e'er we sleep, and, sleeping, dream."*

Zelda locks eyes with Patches as lightning arcs overhead and wind shakes their tree.

"What was that from?" she asks. "Who said it?"

The cat sniffs. "*I* said it. It is a Patches original."

"Sorry. I gotta get used to you being this . . ."

"Erudite?" asks Patches. "Cultured? Intellectual?"

"I was going to say *snooty*. I do remember one time you played with a piece of popcorn for twenty minutes."

"I remember that, too," he says fondly.

"Hey. Kid," says someone. It takes Zelda a second to realize it's the tree. "This is my hiding place. Go find your own hiding place."

"Your . . ." Zelda frowns. "How are you hiding, exactly?"

"I'm pretending to be an oak tree."

"Okay, fine," says Zelda, getting up with Patches. "Whatever."

She's resolute as they stride past a crowd congregating around a bear that sneezes money.

"Hey, it's Zelda!"

"Zelda, come see! Money bear!"

Zelda avoids eye contact. "I shouldn't have called the meeting," she says to Patches. "I shouldn't have told."

"You would take it all back," says Patches, "to spare good people the torment of this hideous freedom."

Actually, Zelda had been thinking more that she could have spared herself all this bother. For a second, she sees her town clearly. She called it a miracle, and it's like a miracle—childish and unbelievable. A life surrounded by anonymous people, all of them treating Zelda like she's the star of the show. Everyone always up in her face, standing too close. Binding ties and prying eyes.

There's a moment in a girl's life when she's just old enough to see everybody's been letting her win, Zelda thinks. *And afterward, the game will never be fun again.*

"That moment should have happened to me a long time ago," she says, and looks around the town. "I think I might actually hate it here."

But her heart softens when she spies Clara the mail carrier, who's standing by the statue of Plato and smiling up at the skyline. Clara always was her favorite. The only other person who got a name.

"Clara!" she shouts into the wind. The square is full of strange wind. It pushes phantom sheets of howling rain. Zelda and Patches come alongside the mail carrier and try to figure out what she's staring at. "Clara? Is that giant woman your grandma?"

"My gran-gran," says Clara sweetly. "Haven't seen her since her funeral."

"She seems like she's . . . Is *rampaging* the right word?"

Clara's gran-gran pushes over a broadcasting tower.

"REVERSE MORTGAGE!"

"Rampaging," Clara repeats with a chuckle and a shake of her head. "Not with *her* hips, poor thing."

Zelda smiles and puts a hand on the mail carrier's arm.

"Good night, Clara."

"Good night, Zelda baby."

Out the corner of her eye Zelda sees all the cars crashing, small fires breaking out, celebrities giving people perms. The bear is trying to get its money back. Something or someone is stumbling like a newborn colt toward the parking lot—a minute ago, it looked like the unicorn, and in a few more it'll look like the man who runs the plumbing supply, but right now it's in a halfway place with none of the charms of either. Clara's grandma has swung her cane at one of the superheroes and cracked the water tower instead. Everyone's soaked. Probably some kind of metaphor. A fireplug sends a geyser of confetti into the air.

"Is this really what people dream about?" asks Zelda.

"I always dream that I'm naked," says Patches.

In the road ahead, the shimmering host of cheerleaders grow ever closer, each one of them baring her perfect teeth. They aren't smiles, exactly. Slick white, pink gums. Chanting, *RAH RAH RAH RAH*

"Um. You're blocking the road," says Zelda.

RAH RAH RAH RAH RAH RAH RAH RAH RAH

"Just . . . back off a little."

RAH RAH RAH RAH RAH RAH RAH RAH RAH RAH RAH RAH RAH RAH RAH

"Okay," says Zelda. "Playtime's over." She shuts her eyes and tightens her fists.

"TOWN MEETING! TOWN MEETING AGAIN!"

Boop, everyone's back in the courthouse hall.

Everyone's breathing hard, or dripping, or still wearing their superhero outfits, or covered in confetti.

There is very little eye contact.

"All right, work it out amongst yourselves," says Zelda, already halfway out the door. "Good night."

Patches follows, and Zelda scoops him up. She hears the courthouse doors open again behind her and sneaks a glance. Everyone's going home.

"Thank you for the lift," says the cat.

"Don't mention it."

For a while, they have company on their walk. Zelda hears the slap of the scuba instructor's swim fins behind her for two blocks before he peels off onto Third Street. The high school marching band is marching home together in the shape of a giant square—but silently. The sight of them in those outfits, in quiet retreat, is just about the saddest thing Zelda has ever seen. One by one, neighbors decamp without a sound until it's just Zelda and the cat. The carolers are the last to go, turning down an alley in their muffs and top hats as they take up the first verse of "Silent Night." By the middle of the second "sleep in heavenly peace," Zelda can't hear them anymore.

Sleep in heavenly peace, Zelda tells herself, in her mind.

"Hmf," says Patches. "They weren't acting so heavenly before."

"You saw that, too?" says Zelda. "That was crazy. I said something funny—I was all, 'They're not so much wassailing as *assailing*,' but nobody heard—"

"People heard," said Patches.

Well, thinks Zelda. *So now what?* What does she do with her so-called life, now that she knows what she knows?

She remembers the feeling she got, briefly, when she realized it was all a dream and she didn't have to keep worrying about her geography grade. She has a real test on her hands—couldn't she just flunk it and wake up? Maybe her waking life is better.

Now, she thinks. *I could wake up now.*

Now.

Now.

Then again. Then again, when she wakes, she'll lose this warm, purring friend in her arms. She wasn't wrong about him getting run over. She dreamed him back to life, too, like Clara's grandma.

Clara! If Zelda wakes up, Clara will just . . . cease to be.

And so will I, she thinks.

Zelda is startled by her own thought, but it's true. *Whether I'm the dreamer or not, when it ends . . . this me—this version of me right here, right now—dies.*

It can't be helped, of course. Zelda is going to wake up eventually, and this abundant dream of years will shrink down to a pinhole memory in her mind—just a faded photograph of one weird night, a single fervid sleep.

"Probably ate some cheese before bed," she mutters.

"I beg your pardon?" says Patches.

"Sorry, nothing. I was just thinking . . . We should make the most of this. I don't know if the rest of the dream will feel like three seconds or a thousand years, but I want to do more with whatever we have left."

"To suck dry the marrow!" says Patches. "To run unencumbered through fields of dream with blood in our teeth!"

"Um," says Zelda, "sure. Because I met someone—briefly—and it got me thinking there must be more to see. There's . . . *definitely* more to feel," she adds, as a few of these bright new feelings swim circles inside her.

She catches her breath.

"So. A good night's sleep," she says, "and then we figure out what to do. And how to do it. If only . . ." she adds softly. "If only there were some expert. To help me understand all this. I need a genius professor, a wizard, a . . . *something*."

"Mayhap you require a poet," says the cat, "and that is why I came back to you."

They're home, and Zelda pauses once again at her creaky front gate. She sets her hand atop the crown of it, like she's feeling for fever.

"Hello, gate," she says. She winces and pulls it open.

"*HELLO*," the gate replies. A cartoon frog. Zelda exhales.

"You know," says the cat, "Homer wrote that dreams pass through gates of either horn or ivory. And through the former passes the truth, whilst the latter admits only lies and dashed hopes." Patches squints. "What . . . what is this one made of, exactly?"

Zelda walks up the path and lets the gate swing shut behind her. "I dunno. I pass through it all the time; it doesn't mean anything. It's just a gate."

The gate makes no comment at all as it closes and clicks.

SIX

A BELL RINGS.

Zelda lurches for her alarm—but it isn't her alarm. Patches stirs at the foot of the bed and says,

> *"Twas no alarm ding-donging,*
> *but a pealed appeal belonging*
> *to a caller who is longing,*
> *longing at your cottage door."*

"Whazzat?" says Zelda.

"Doorbell," Patches answers.

Zelda staggers to her feet, finds her glasses. At the bedroom door, she pauses and looks back.

They look the same, her plaster constellations. She thinks they look the same.

She shambles down the stairs, the carpeted steps so plausibly shaggy between her toes. If last night at the courthouse was all a dream, then maybe the dream is over. Maybe these steps, this house, this world is the waking world. She tenses and turns, about to run back up the stairs to ask her talking cat what he thinks of this.

"Oh," she whispers. "Right."

Zelda answers her door. It's Clara with a package.

"Hello, sweetie," says Clara. "Did I wake you?"

This question makes Zelda want to sit down. The gravity of it.

Clara raises the package, a clean brown box. "I'll be by with the regular mail later, but this one needs your signature."

"The mail," says Zelda. She looks up. "The mail? You're delivering the mail."

"Only for my whole adult life, yes."

"But . . . the *mail*. After all that happened last night . . ."

"What happened last night?" Clara says, all smiles. "I may have missed it. My gran-gran and I took a walk and turned in early."

"Huh. And your grandma's well?" asks Zelda. "Well and . . . appropriately sized?"

"'Appropriately sized'?" says Clara. "What kind of . . ."

Clara lets her smile down gently. She's used to being careful how she carries things. Her eyes unfocus, and it's like Zelda can see the events of the previous night descending on her, but slowly. Behind her, Zelda hears Patches descending slowly, too, and pausing to test his claws on the third stair like he used to when he wasn't dead.

"Clara?" says Zelda. "Are you okay?"

Clara's eyelids dip for a moment, as though touched by fingertips. Then she sucks in air.

"Last night!" says Clara.

"Yeah."

"Last night, at the courthouse!"

"I know. Had you forgotten?"

Clara looks like she might cry. "I'd forgotten," she admitted. "But then *you* reminded me." It feels like an accusation.

Patches bunts his head against Zelda's ankle before coming to sit beside her. It's reassuring, like she called for backup.

"I'm sorry," she tells Clara. "Forget I said anything. Forget about the . . . whatever. Everything."

"It's a dream," says Clara, her face a tangle. "My whole life. Not real."

Zelda puts her hands on Clara's shoulders as if she might be able to hold the woman together. "That's not . . . quite true," she says. "It's a life, right? It is if you think it is."

Clara looks lost. "It is if I think it is," she mutters. "Been with the post office twenty years. I swear I have. I've almost finished deciphering the zip codes."

Zelda forces a smile. ". . . Oh?" she says. "Wow."

"Uh-huh. And when I do, I'll get promoted in a big ceremony from Postwoman First Class to Priority Female. It takes two to three days."

Patches coughs politely.

"There you go!" says Zelda. "Look, really, I'm sorry. If you want to talk about it—"

Clara looks afraid—like it's avalanche season, and Zelda won't stop shouting about avalanches. "No, thank you. You know something? This morning, I woke up and I had breakfast with my grandmama and I didn't remember a thing until you answered your door. I've been out on my route, and I'll tell you, it's the same all over town—everybody

ADAM REX · 73

going about their business like it didn't really happen." She studies Zelda. "And if you're right ... well, then I guess it didn't." She pushes the package into Zelda's hands. "Sign here."

"But—"

"You tried getting people to talk about it last night," says Clara, "and you saw what happened. Go ahead and make your plans. I plan to *forget*. Maybe I'll round out a nice little lifetime before it's all over. Maybe I'll die of old age and it'll all go on another thousand years without me—you don't know. You don't know how it works any better than I do."

After a moment, Zelda nods. "Okay." She signs for the package. "Hey, speaking of your grandma—"

Clara tenses. "*What?*" she says, and her eyes are begging. "What *about* my grandma?"

"Nothing," says Zelda. "Just tell her hi for me."

Clara relaxes and smiles. "Surely will," she says. "She always did like you."

She holds her smile, her stare, just a little longer than seems customary.

"I'm sorry," Clara finally says. "You're going to think me so rude, but what were we just talking about?"

"The weather," Zelda answers.

"*That's* right."

Clara squints up at the sky.

"It's sunny. Okay, back to the grindstone."

"So to speak."

"Uh-huh. You have a good day for me, Zelda baby." In a moment, Clara's gone.

After a longish silence, Zelda looks down at Patches and says, "You've been quiet."

"It didn't seem like the right moment for a talking cat."

"Yeah. Well. We know Clara isn't the dreamer. She obviously doesn't know a thing about the postal service."

"Perhaps she only dreams of carrying the mail," says Patches. "Perhaps in sooth she is a *queen*, and the crown weighs heavily on her scented brow."

Zelda bobs her head. "Sure, maybe."

Patches is rolling around on his back. "I'd like to go outside," he says, the very moment the door is closed.

Fine, then, thinks Zelda as she closes the door a second time. *Everyone's forgotten—except me and Patches. Everything's back to normal. So to speak. I tried to be real with those people, but being real only made them* aggressively *imaginary, so whatever.*

Better they forget.

Zelda draws back a curtain and watches the street. People pass, wearing backpacks, smiles, summer dresses. Patches is stalking a puff of dandelion—a pretty scene. Very realistic.

What do you all think about, Zelda wonders, *when I'm not thinking of you?*

The town feels like a puppet show now. She wonders if the puppets are out there, all of them—each silently in place like a clown outside a laundromat, waiting for Zelda to come watch the show. It makes her shiver.

Patches's tail twitches as he nears his dandelion. The seedhead looks like a little firework. Frozen in time, stuck in place. Sleeping. It needs a good push to roust it. Patches gives it a good push—at the window, Zelda whispers, "Bang"—and the seeds explode forth. They catch the breeze and drift up and away until Zelda can't see them anymore. Those seeds get to move on to the next chapter of their lives.

She's trying to feel happy for the dandelion seeds, but the truth is she's getting pretty mad at all the suburban sunniness out there. And why not? She's just lost her life. She's lost the illusion that it was a good one. Everyone has always been so kind to her, *so* interested, and now she knows it was only because she, dreaming Zelda, was genuinely the most important person in the world. It only strengthens last night's resolution: she needs to make a change. A big one. She needs to find a new way to be a part of this world. How can she go back to pantomiming a real life, with only imaginary friends?

If you had asked her a couple days ago, she would have said her town was too good to be true. She would have had a laugh about it, and felt lucky. She would have said her *life* was too good to be true.

And what about my real life? she thinks as she bites at a nail.

What if it's too true to be good?

She's a little confused about where it ends and the dream begins. She has a whole lifetime of memories inside her. She *thinks* she does. What's the regular amount?

Some of these memories are totally suspicious. She has a hunch, for example, that she didn't really help Santa Claus save Christmas that one time. But so many of her memories are so perfectly ordinary that she can't tell if she's remembering her dream life, or her real life, or both.

Here's what she figures: that in reality she lives in a town a lot like this one—only not made of paper and not full of paper people. A town where strangers *don't* cheer, "Go, Zelda!" when she has exact change for the bus. She is looking forward to this.

But—she probably lives in this house, because she has so many memories of this house. She probably went to that high school, because she remembers that high school. She really used to have a cat named Patches. She remembers when he died.

So probably she's mostly remembering real things from her real life, and if there's some normal stuff she's forgetting and some abnormal stuff she's remembering, then whatever—dreams are weird.

What really rattles her is all the other possibilities. Like maybe she only dreams of this house because it's her childhood home—she could live in a totally new town now, one she can't currently remember. Couldn't she? In stories, people are always waking up places and—for a second—not knowing where they are. Like their last dream before waking prepared them to expect something else.

Maybe all her memories—everything, going all the way back to childhood—are false. Stuff she's only dreaming that she remembers. Maybe it really has all been the same dream—almost two decades of life, crammed into one night's sleep.

Her whole life here could be just an overcrowded metaphor.

So could she.

With a start, she wonders, *Do people ever dream they're someone else?* Then she stares, stares at nothing as that thought runs through her.

Well. I'll find out when I wake.

For now, her arms are tired? She looks down at them, confused.

"Oh, right—I have a box," she says. She sits down on the floor with it.

It's a perfect cardboard cube, very nicely made. There's no tape, but nonetheless the seams are square and tight. There's no return address, either, only a recipient. She prizes up a flap as she reads,

"I want to come back inside!" Patches calls from outside.

"Just a second!" Zelda calls back. "Oh!" She flinches because the box flap has sort of exhaled and unfolded, revealing hidden origami insides. It's jutting its lip out like the spout of a milk carton. And is there music? She swears there's music coming from deep inside the box—something with a sad clarinet.

"Zellllda—I want to come in now!"

"Guh," says Zelda, getting up again. She stamps to the foyer and opens the door, but there's no one there. Back in the sitting room, Patches is on the coffee table.

"Window," he tells her.

The cardboard cube, meanwhile, is now an eight-sided diamond, posing like a dancer on tiptoe.

"Were you going to open that?" asks Patches.

"I was trying to."

They hunker down with it between the sofa and the davenport. The box is bigger now. More like the size of an end table, if the end table was an eight-sided diamond. So not a very good end table.

"I don't get this thing," says Zelda. "It had seams when it was a cube, and now it doesn't."

Patches bats at the box, his ears flattened back. "How did you change it from a cube to an octahedron?" he asks, then rolls onto his back to fuss at it with his claws.

"An octoheedrum? What?"

"*Octahedron*," says the cat. "That's what it is now. A polyhedron with eight sides."

Zelda wrinkles her nose. "If I'm the dreamer," she mutters, "how do you know things I don't?"

"You didn't answer my question. How did you—"

"Oh. Well, when I went to the door *to let you in*, it was a cube. When I got back, it was an ectoheadron."

Their eyes meet, each thinking the same thing.

A minute later, they're sneaking back into the sitting room and peeking over the sofa at it. Zelda slumps.

"Still an actiheadroom," she laments.

"Is it playing music?" asks Patches. "Sounds like Artie Shaw."

In a pique, Zelda exhales and spins the box like a top.

"Oh, hey!"

Spinning the octahedron causes both pyramidal halves of it to open up like flowers: pop-up petals within petals that gape and yawn their way into a box with thirty-two sides shaped like triangles and pentagons.

"Okay, then, smart guy," says Zelda. "What do you call this?"

"An idosidodecahedron? No. An ikoikoundaydecahedron."

"Ha! You don't know."

Patches bristles. "I most certainly *do* know, madam. It is an ivodeododecahedron."

"You keep saying different things"—Zelda pokes her finger at her own head—"because *I* don't know what it is. I'm just *dreaming* of a cat who does."

"This is fruitless," says Patches. "So to speak. I am unquestionably the dreamer, and *that*"—he swishes his tail at the box—"is an icosidodecahedron."

Except it isn't. They turn away from their argument to see that the box has become a hundred-sided geodesic sphere the size of a washing machine. Zelda clucks her tongue.

"We're either really good at this or really bad at this."

"If a box you're unpacking has more sides to open than when you started . . ." Patches says.

After several minutes of picking and spinning and peeking and pawing, it's still a geodesic sphere, and the cat has wandered off.

Zelda rocks backward onto her butt and blows the hair out of her eyes. The giant cardboard sphere sits there in her sitting room. Sitting there, it looks about as natural as a giant cardboard sphere. She sighs and gets up.

Later she'll say it was inspiration. The truth is she just steadies herself on the sphere as she stands. But now that she's pushing instead of pulling, the whole thing flattens out into a saucer. Zelda backs away as it wobbles and tips up onto its edge, and in a moment she's standing in front of a wide cardboard disc with a cardboard knob in its center, rimmed by a faceted cardboard frame.

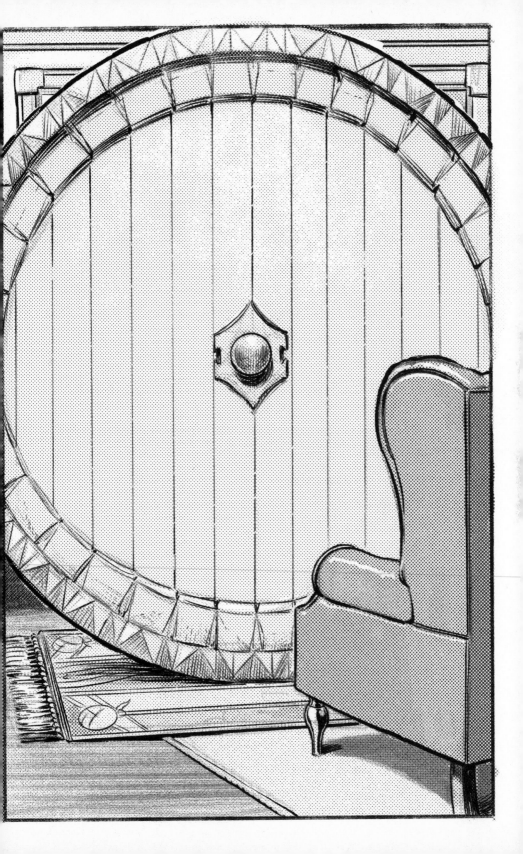

Aha.

Okay, then! Finally, adventure! She can have a stupid fun adventure, and the story will end with, *And then she woke up, and it had all been a dream.*

"Always hated stories like that," she whispers.

Then she shouts, "Patches?" Because if she's going to be Dorothy, she may as well have her Cowardly Lion. "Patches, I think it's a door! Should I open it?"

Patches's toenails click on the hardwood as he steps back into the room. "Did you say something about opening the door? I'd like to go out. Oh."

They stare at the door a moment. There's still clarinet music playing on the other side of it. That is, there's nothing on the other side of it but the other half of Zelda's sitting room, but she's read enough stories to guess how this is going to go. She'll open the door and step into a snowy forest or whatever, and before long they'll be having tea with a hedgehog in a vest.

She reaches for the knob when Patches says, "Best to knock. We're not housebreakers."

"You're barely house*broken*. Ha. Okay."

Zelda raises her hand, holds her breath. Blows it out again and knocks three times on the cardboard. It's a surprisingly rich, resonant sound.

The music abruptly stops. Then they can just make out a voice, drawing closer, saying "Coming, coming," from beyond the door. Finally, it opens, and a baggy, pill-shaped head pokes through. A pale head with plump blue bags under watery eyes. It's wearing a felted hat crowned with three different kinds of antler. A cobwebby beard like an overstretched Halloween decoration waves coquettishly in the draft from the air conditioner.

Oh, perfect, thinks Zelda, *a wizard. I was just wanting one of those.*

The wizard flinches and blinks at the sight of her sitting room— it's obviously not what he expected to find outside his door. But most of all he seems surprised by *her,* like a girl in her pajamas is some ridiculous spectacle. Which seems unfair—he is *literally* wearing antlers.

"Ah," says the wizard. He looks concerned. "This is . . . Hm. Hello. Can I help you?" His English accent is creaky, as if there isn't as much pip-pip in his cheerio as there used to be.

Zelda isn't sure what to say. She had been waiting for the wizard to take a stronger hand in the conversation than this. "I . . . got a box?"

"Oh yes?"

"And it turned into your door?"

"Did it, now."

"I assumed you sent it."

"No," says the wizard, "not I." But he nods in resignation, like this is just one of those things that happens sometimes, like this is the butt-dial of the wizarding world. "Well, come in, come in."

The wizard shuffles deeper into the interior. Zelda lingers on the threshold. She *could* follow the strange man inside. She *could,* although she once watched a safety video in PE that said not to do this very thing. Not this *exact* thing, of course—in the video, the magic door was a cargo van and the wizard was a man who said he had a box of puppies. But the argument was the same.

And yet. She's obviously bothering the wizard. He seems not entirely happy to see her. Somehow that puts her at ease.

"If he were in the mood for hasenpfeffer," says Patches, "he'd be more pleased to meet a rabbit. So to speak."

"Meaning what—I should go in?"

Patches shrugs, sort of. He doesn't really have shoulders.

"Better hop to it, then!" says Zelda. "Because rabbit." She looks back. "Patches? Did you hear what I—"

"I heard."

SEVEN

THEY STEP INSIDE, AND BREATHE in the earthy, oaken smell of the place. It's a vast room, amoebic in shape with red clay walls that slope upward into a narrow spout. There's a leaning tower of dusty light coming down through that spout, and it falls directly on the shiny bald head of the wizard, who has removed his hat.

"Welcome to my frightful, smelly house," he sighs.

Zelda wants to say something nice, but she hesitates too long. The moment passes. She's thinking, kindly, that it's sort of like living inside one of the lumpy pinch pots she made in art class as a little girl—crafted with love, and awful.

It's also crowded. The pinch-pot house is stuffed with benches, tables, rickety ladders propped against tall racks of shelves; a hanging garden of swooping plants, fungi, mobiles, improbable kites; and one giant dangling glass globe packed entirely with a writhing knot of glistening snakes.

"Seems a weird place to keep that," Zelda whispers.

On the tables and shelves are scrolls, bottles, crucibles, maps, and clockworks. Models and dioramas. Zelda *does* find a hedgehog in a vest. It's stuffed and mounted under glass.

"He has a little teacup," she tells Patches wincingly.

A blue fire is prowling across the floor on red legs, like a cat. Patches hisses at it; it hisses back.

"Would you like the tour?" says the wizard, replacing his hat. "My name is Erx, by the way."

"Zelda. This is Patches."

"Yes, I know."

Erx sweeps his arm like a disinterested spokesmodel. "So: This is my home and atelier. It is built in the ancient hollow of the largest tree in the Forest of Hands and Feet, formerly known as the Candy Cane Forest before all of the candy canes turned into hands and feet. This is my Magic Mirror, which can gaze upon any open place in all Creation, and this is my regular mirror for bathroom things. Beside you on the table is my Very Accurate Model of the room in which we are currently standing."

Patches jumps atop the table beside Zelda, and they both have a look. It is indeed an exquisitely detailed model of every curve and shelf and thing.

"Ohmygosh, look," says Zelda, squinting. The model even has a tiny Zelda and a tiny Patches, bending over *an even tinier model of the model*. And inside that . . .

"Um," Zelda says to the wizard. "Are those—"

"Exceedingly small people looking at a model that's inside the model inside the model?" Erx says. "Yes. The answer to any additional question along that same line is also yes."

"Uh-huh. And . . ."

"You're about to ask if it's possible that we ourselves are merely figures inside a model, contemplated by larger figures inside a larger model, and I would consider it a great favor if you didn't."

"Oh," Zelda says. "Okay." She and Patches squint a while longer.

"The cat in the model is a calico," Patches complains.

The wizard sniffs. "I said it was a Very Accurate Model, not an Entirely Accurate Model." He gestures toward a few more objects of interest. "This is a kettle. This is a tortoise who either moves very slowly or is dead. This is a marble glass, and this is a glass marble. This is a ten-thousand-year-old scroll of papyrus upon which is written the world's first swear word."

"Ooh, what is it?"

"*Genk.* These here are bottles containing interesting sneezes I've collected. This is a small but magnificent canopic jar containing the Ashes of the Phoenix, Who Will One Day Rise Again. This is a bag of sand that will make one sleep forever, and this is a potion of invisibility. This is a spoon. This is a bowl of duck food I keep meaning to throw out because the duck ran away, *this* is a bowl of super-growth pills I keep next to the duck food, and in the corner is a perfectly ordinary boy."

Zelda flinches. In the shadows, something flinches back. It steps forward on hesitant feet. Then it comes into the light, and Zelda blushes from head to toe.

"It's *you!*" she says. She hears the sound of her own voice, like a kid meeting her favorite Power Ranger. She immediately dials down her enthusiasm. "It's you."

"Uh, hey," the boy says with half a wave. He seems to try out a couple expressions, fumbles them, puts them away again.

He's about Zelda's height. His brown limbs are long, loose. The only thing "perfectly ordinary" about him, in Zelda's estimation, is his clothes. His simple T-shirt and jeans and Chuck Taylors seem like a mistake next to what Erx is wearing, which looks mostly to be a stack of old horse blankets.

"You're the boy," says Zelda. *The flower boy*, she thinks, and is hugely relieved when she doesn't say it out loud.

"You're . . . the girl," he answers.

And it's funny to hear it put like that, like the two of them are the only girl and boy in all the world.

But also, maybe they are?

Do the walls melt away? Is it just the two of them on the floor, in a spotlight, squared off as if they might dance? Or duel. Or dance-duel! *Oh my God, yes*, thinks Zelda, and she tries to convince the dream: *Dance-duel! Dance-duel!*

But no, the walls haven't really melted, and they're not really alone. They *are* being looked at by a weird old man and a cat.

The boy closes the distance between them in faltering fashion and offers his hand. Zelda shakes it, and it shakes her. "I'm Langston," he says.

"Zelda."

"He knows," says Erx.

Zelda's pajama shirt is kind of V-necked. She pulls it closed.

"You disappeared," she says. "I came over to see if you were okay, and when I looked you just . . . disappeared."

He's still holding her hand. He clears his throat and gives it back to her. "It's funny, I remember it more like, you looked at me and then looked away real quick? Kind of like people do when they get to the scary part of a movie or whatnot."

"Oh, what? No," says Zelda, waving this aside. "I mean, I looked away for a second, but then I tried to look back at you and you weren't there. So."

Patches eyes Langston. "You are Erx's apprentice?" he asks.

Erx seems taken aback by this. "Oh no. Langston is . . . well, you're just Langston, aren't you, lad. He merely showed up . . . at some point," says Erx, frowning at his own uncertainty. "Well. Langston likes to use the Magic Mirror. Watches all the goings-on in your little town."

Zelda can see her town in the mirror now, as if the wizard's made it so. It's like a window looking out at the town square. And the courthouse. One of the Frisbee bros chases after a Frisbee, but oh, look—someone's dog has caught it instead. Everyone laughs. A man on bended knee is actually, this very moment, proposing marriage to the scuba instructor on the courthouse steps. As if either of them has a future to share. Applause. Starlings pepper the sky.

Then the images fade, and all that remains in the mirror frame is a rosy, shimmering twilight.

"I saw you in the Magic Mirror, on that bike," Langston is saying. "I saw the car coming. And I wanted so badly to save you that . . . boop, I was just there." He folds in a little, remembering. "You . . . know how the rest of that went. Which is good! I'm glad you and the car stopped. Obviously. But without even meaning to, I teleported back here."

"Teleported," Zelda says.

"*Teleport* is a nerd word," Patches says. "It means the same thing as *boop*."

"I've just never heard it in conversation before."

"Even Erx doesn't know how I did it," Langston notes. "The teleporting. He thinks it means I could be a wizard, too."

"I never said that."

Zelda has a question to ask, but after the high spirits of the previous night, she thinks she ought to tread lightly. "Do you . . ." she says to Erx. "Do you—with, like, your magic powers—know hidden truths about the world?"

"You mean that it isn't real?" asks the wizard. "Oh, of course, dear. It's nonsense. Bunkum. Case in point: I am a wizard."

Zelda waits for him to continue. "Yes?"

"Well, that doesn't seem very realistic, does it? Heavens, look at my hat."

Zelda shrugs politely.

"Darling girl. If any of this were *actual* life, then I wouldn't be standing before you. I would instead be no place, not talking about how real it isn't."

"I guess."

"I've been studying this!" says Langston. "The world being kind of off—I've been studying it." He veers off to a bench and comes back with a fat notebook, swollen with loose leaves. He opens it, and several of these swish to the floor. "I think the town is at the center of it," he adds, "so I watch it all the time, taking notes."

And what notes they are. Pages and pages, all written in the same blocky hand. Do they look like the handwriting on the package Clara delivered? A little. But that package was a snap to read, whereas Langston's notes are as slippery as her geography test. Zelda squints and concentrates and is just able to make out the phrase, *lasagna cookout???* circled in red ink. On a loose page on the floor is a drawing of the laundromat clown, scribbled out, and a drawing of what could conceivably be Zelda herself. A sort of manga Zelda with stars in her eyes. Langston sees what she's looking at and stoops to cram all these refugees back in his book.

"Anyway," says Langston. "Been studying it."

"'Studying it,'" Zelda repeats. "It's not an asteroid, it's a town— why not just live here?" Zelda asks him. "Not . . . here in Erx's laboratory, I mean, out *there*," she adds, waving at the door, assuming the view outside that door is still her sitting room and not the White Cliffs of Dover or whatever.

Langston looks toward the door. "Live in your house?"

Great Scott, she thinks. "I *meant* the town in general, but . . . sure . . . you could stay awhile. On the couch. Until you find your own place, *the point is*, I'm just saying, why not get in the thick of it, if you want to study it so much." She holds back a smile. "You could swing all over town, protecting girls from their bike rides."

"Ha. Well. You know, I don't want to get . . . attached to my subject. Impartiality," he says. "Science."

Erx inclines his head and says, "Tell her the other reason."

Langston's shoulders clench. "You said you wouldn't talk about that."

"Oh, go ahead—it's cute."

Langston sighs, shifts his eyes, rubs his neck.

"Also . . ." he says, "I . . . don't really care for the—"

"He is terrified of the laundromat clown," says Erx.

Zelda tries not to react to this. Which is itself a reaction, in a way. Patches just goes ahead and laughs.

"Aight." Langston sighs, nodding and twirling his hand. "Let it all out. Don't hold back."

"Ho HO!" Patches finishes.

"I'm not ashamed—she's creepy."

She, Zelda thinks. *Is the laundromat clown a she? Maybe.*

Langston lifts his head. "But! The important thing is I was watching you last night." He locks eyes with Zelda. It makes her feel weird. "You know, watching the town meeting, I mean. I used to think maybe it was all a simulation. Like a virtual reality Matrix thing. But then I started thinking it might be a dream, and now here we are actually meeting the dreamer . . . I think that clinches it."

They're narrow, his eyes, with thick black lashes and creases underneath. Like he's halfway to a smile. Zelda would like to see him smile. All at once, she's imagining ways she could make it happen.

She's getting a little lost in that train of thought when the full weight of what Langston just said catches up to her. She looks at him and Erx both.

"Neither one of you thinks you're the dreamer," she says.

"Naw," says Langston. He shrugs like it's a perfectly normal thing to shrug away. Like his status as an NPC should be plainly obvious to anyone.

"It does not seem likely," says the wizard. Again, he points out his hat.

"It's just you're the first people I've met who don't. Even Patches thinks he is."

"Not *even* Patches," sniffs the cat. "*Especially* Patches."

"Um, so, wait," says Zelda to Erx. "Where did you say we were? The Forest of Hands and Feet?"

"Indeed."

Zelda steps over to the mirror. There's a chair set in front of it, so she sits down. "Can I see it?"

"Certainly," says Erx, and he places his speckled hand on the mirror's black frame. "Normally, I would simply invite you to peek outside, but as my front yard is currently busy being your sitting room . . . Magic Mirror! Forest of Hands and Feet."

The fizzy pink nothing inside the mirror instantly changes and becomes a perfect window into a different world. Zelda grimaces.

"I . . . guess that's why they call it the Forest of Hands and Feet."

"Quite."

"I don't know what I was expecting."

Langston comes to stand near her, and suddenly Zelda feels lit like a Christmas tree. What is this blazing brilliance between them? It's as if their bodies are reaching out for each other across the gap, and now every part of her is awake; her shoulders are awake, her elbows. Who thinks about their elbows? She's suddenly aware of the weight of her own hands. They nest like doves in her lap.

He's so *warm*. Is anyone else in all of dreamland this warm? She's never felt that warmth of another person, this closeness. She certainly doesn't remember if she has. That's a *tragedy*.

I must have had close relationships, she tells herself. *Parents, at least, and friends. But the dream isn't letting me remember.* She studies the mirror again.

"So . . ." Zelda continues, eyes forward. "This forest. How do I not know where it is? Is it close to town?"

"We think it's pretty far away, actually," says Langston. "It's somewhere else entirely."

Oh, right, she thinks. *Geography.* "Somewhere . . . *else*."

He's the sort of boy best described with double negatives, Zelda thinks. *He isn't frail. He's not* not *handsome*. She supposed the term she was circling was *average*, but how could that be? How could that possibly be?

Patches hops into her lap. "There are many worlds, of infinite variety," says the cat. "Imagine a universe like a vast bowl filled with different shapes, each with a different flavor—"

"You're describing cat food now," says Zelda. "Are you hungry?"

"Yes. But my point stands: There are many worlds, and I have walked many of them in my many, many lives."

"I thought the dream was just the town," whispers Zelda, feeling foolish. Even worse—she may well have thought *everything* was just the town. Not consciously, of course—that would be ridiculous. She knew there were other places; she'd occasionally learned about them in school. But she didn't . . . *know* there were other places. She is realizing, to her embarrassment, that she hadn't believed anything else really existed.

Beside her, Langston is scribbling in his notebook of crinkly paper.

"So, like, this is the dream," says Langston, presenting Zelda with the circle he just drew. For clarity, he takes it back and writes *THE DREAM* inside it, like it's a pie chart that's all pie. "I think the town is here, right in the center. The town and everything in it."

Zelda can tell Langston is thinking of the laundromat clown by the way he shivers. Also by the comic-book thought bubble of a laundromat clown that appears briefly over his head. Erx nods at it.

"He's been doing that," he whispers to Zelda. "The bubbles. I believe it to be a by-product of a number of amusing magical accidents that have befallen him recently."

Langston looks up from his thoughts. "Doing what? What are we talking about?"

"Nothing."

"Well, if the town is in the center," says Langston, "and I think it is, then I think the forest is out . . . *here* somewhere." He makes another dot. It's a terrible map.

Like a computer going to sleep, the Magic Mirror has faded once again to the same warm pink screen saver. It's a dusky pink, but it's not just that. There are pinpricks of every other color, firing and fidgeting inside it. It reminds Zelda of something. She can't decide what.

"This mirror," she says to Erx. "Is it always this color when it's . . . off?"

"No. At times it grows quite dark, and stays that way for some time before brightening again."

Zelda lowers her head and glances slyly at Langston. His head is eclipsing a hanging lamp behind him, making his ear burn red and fuzzing out the side of his face into soft pinks and golds. Like any eclipse, Zelda doesn't want to look away, but knows she must or she'll go blind. Then Langston catches her looking—their eyes meet. *Oh.* He jerks his head a couple degrees and pretends to examine an Erlenmeyer flask nearby. As if to say, *I wasn't staring! I was just taking inventory of all the girls and flasks in the room.* Zelda smiles.

That fuzzy color of the lamp behind Langston's cheek reminds her of the mirror, actually. "Wait," she says. "What was that about it getting dark and brightening?"

She glances guiltily at Erx. She can tell from the wizard's exquisitely tiny smirk that he understands exactly why Zelda wasn't paying attention. "The mirror sometimes grows slowly dark. It just as slowly brightens again. This dimming and brightening is a cycle that repeats over the course of hours, I believe," adds Erx, "though I have not timed it. It's just one of the mysteries of the glass. It also does this cool thing when you ask it to look at itself—watch: Magic Mirror, show me the Magic Mirror. Whoa, look at that. Freaky."

"Remember that time it got real bright?" says Langston. "Like, hard-to-look-at bright. But that was only for a second before it faded to pink again."

"So, okay," says Zelda. "It gets dark for a while, light for a while? About half and half?"

"About."

Zelda rises suddenly, evicting Patches from her lap.

"Sorry, Patches."

She strides over to the brightest lamp in the room, an oil flame inside a great glass globe, and puts her face as close to it as she can stand. Her nose tingles; it's hot. She closes her eyes.

"There it is," she says. "The same dark, fizzy pink. Little specks of other colors—this looks just like the mirror."

"What does?" asks Langston. "Your eyes are closed."

"Exactly."

She crosses the room again as Langston frowns and passes her, going to the same lamp to see if she's right.

The mirror has finished its infinite recursion and gone pink again. Erx looks at it with fresh interest.

"And so . . ." says Erx.

Patches is atop the chair again and squinting. "*So* . . . if this Magic Mirror can see what the real dreamer can see," he says, "then when it's not focused on the dream . . ."

"Then it's just looking at the inside of my eyelids," finished Zelda. "Ta-da."

"*Your* eyelids?" says Patches, turning. "Now, why would I be dreaming about your eyelids?"

"They're . . . nice eyelids," Langston mumbles.

Zelda does her best to ignore this and says, "But the dreamer— whoever she is—"

"*He* is," Patches corrects her.

"—she's in a room—"

"*He's* in a room."

"—where it gets bright, then dark, then bright again? Over and over?" Suddenly, her heart is in her throat. "Why . . . why would that be?"

She realizes she must look desperate, because she's hoping someone will give her an answer, any answer other than the obvious.

"I . . . suspect, dear girl," says Erx, "that we are seeing the natural cycle of daytime and nighttime—"

"*No.*"

"—and that the dreamer has been asleep for—"

"Don't say it."

". . . days."

"NO," Zelda answers. "No no no. Time works *different* in here. Don't you think? I mean, just because the mirror gets light and dark once a day in dreamland doesn't mean it's a day . . ." She gestures vaguely to indicate the Real World. ". . . out there."

Langston's whole body is a shrug. "Occam's razor tells us the simplest explanation is usually the right one."

"Oh, *sure*," says Zelda, and she gives a thumbs-up. "Occam's razor. Simple explanations—those definitely work in a dream. Hey,

Patches, remind me what all those people were lining up for last night after the meeting?"

"A bear who sneezes money."

"A *bear* who *sneezes* money. Simple!" says Zelda.

"Hey, I'm on your side!" says Langston. "I just . . . We gotta explore every possibility—"

Zelda leaps up and starts pacing the room, weaving in and around the wizard's weird belongings, her fun-house reflection springing up the sides of brass instruments and rippling through bottles and vials. "Days. My God. How many days?"

Erx folds his hands. "I do not know."

"If I have been asleep for days but *dreaming*," says Patches, "then that would seem to augur well." He picks his teeth with a claw. "Dreaming means brain function."

"And yet Zelda is perfectly justified in her concern. The prognosis for such a sleeper would only worsen over time."

"Does that mean what I think it does?" says Zelda. "The longer I'm asleep, the less likely it is I'll ever wake up?"

The wizard's white-faced silence is answer enough.

Days. Dreaming for days. Zelda doesn't want to admit how well this fits. Even if time does pass differently here, still—the dream seems to have such deep history, and so much detail. Like it couldn't possibly be the work of a single night. But what could have kept her asleep for so long?

She looks around the room at all the people, cat included. "We're all smart, right? We can figure this out—why would I be asleep so long? Did I get hurt? Am I sick? Did I get cursed by a wicked fairy? I don't think the real world has wicked fairies, but I'm open-minded."

Zelda stops pacing, and the instant she stops, it all catches up with her. "Something's wrong with me," she whispers, her hands tented over her face. The glass globe of snakes slithers and slithers above her. "Ohmygosh, something's really wrong."

She's still looking at their faces—Erx, Patches, and Langston—when she tells herself, *No—stop looking at them. It's a Band-Aid. Rip it off. Rip it off quick before you start liking them any more than you already do—this isn't going to get any easier.*

Zelda takes a breath,

takes her arm-skin between her fingers,

("Wait," says Langston)

thinks of every face in town,

and pinches.

Ow.

A second later, she tries it again, but harder. Nothing.

She slaps her own cheek. She slaps it again as the others look stiffly on. "Wake up!" she pleads, and pinches herself up and down. "Wake *up!*"

She's hyperventilating a little. The room fogs over. The edges of her vision seem to effervesce with a scintillating light. *Wouldn't it be something*, she thinks, *to faint in the middle of a dream?* No—she refuses. After a moment, her breathing slows, and with titanic effort she once again makes eye contact with the other people in the room.

Which is awkward. It's like she's just tossed a grenade at them, only she forgot to pull the pin so now she has to make small talk.

"I . . . guess pinching is like tickling," she says with a weak shrug. "Can't really do it to yourself."

This makes a light bulb go on over her head. An actual light bulb—she swats it away, and it breaks somewhere in the corner.

"*You* can pinch me!" she tells Langston as she crosses toward him.

Langston appears to have complicated feelings about this. Like his face is trying to make every kind of expression at once. Patches steps in the way.

"Zelda."

"People are not supposed to sleep for days!" she says, crouching down to the cat's level. "Dreamtime's been fun and all, and I'm very sorry, but now I need to figure out how to fix this!"

Langston screws up his face and says, "We shouldn't read too much into the mirror—"

"Ah, good," says Patches. "Everyone put in a penny. Mr. Occam has some thoughts."

"Okay, yeah," says Langston. "I said that about Occam's razor because . . . I'm one of those guys who likes to talk about Occam's razor."

Zelda knits her brow. "Is that a thing?"

"It's a thing," Erx says with a sigh.

"But let's not be too quick to put all our faith in the *Magic Mirror*," Langston adds, and crosses in front of it. "You know? I just don't think we can trust an instrument *inside* the dream to measure anything *outside* the dream. They're separate things."

"Not wholly separate," says Patches. "If a phone rings in the waking world, can I not hear it in my dream, and dream I answer it?"

"Yes. *Sure.* And after you wake up from a nice dream conversation with the President of Mushroomland, you'd be a fool to think you learned anything real about mushrooms."

"Not so! Such a conversation would be symbolical. It would be lyrical. Were I attuned to the abstract poetry of the subconscious, I would learn what I *think* about mushrooms. How mushrooms *feel*."

"Okay," says Langston. "But—"

"The dreamer knows they are asleep," Patches presses. "Zelda is our proof of that. They know they sleep, and they sense how long they have been sleeping. They sense that something is *wrong*. Now they are ringing the dream-phone to tell us and we would be fools, sir, *fools* to ignore it."

Langston and Patches both seem to have reasonable points. Zelda looks to Erx to break the tie, but the wizard waves her off. "Leave me out of this," he says. "The President of Mushroomland is a personal friend."

Zelda breathes. "Langston," she says, and hugs herself. "Show me that map again."

Langston holds it up. It's really just a circle with dots in it, but still.

"This circle has an edge," says Zelda. "There's a part that *is* the circle, and a part that isn't. Does the dream have an edge?"

"We think it does, yeah."

"The edge of consciousness," says Erx. "No mind is infinite."

"No human mind," Patches agrees.

"Magic Mirror," says Zelda as she once again takes her seat. "Show me the edge of the circle."

The mirror zooms in on Langston and a corner of his drawing. He flinches and waves at himself.

"Okay, no. Magic Mirror, show me the edge of the dream."

But now the view just fades to that same fizzy pink.

"I have sat where you're sitting and tried the same thing, many times," says Erx. "But in this task and this task alone, the mirror fails."

"We met a family of pinecones once that'd been there," says Langston. "To the edge. They said it's really cloudy. But they also said if you look through the clouds long enough you can see a person. In a *bed*."

"Seriously?" Zelda straightens. "Like, the dreamer?"

"Perhaps," says Erx. "But when asked to describe this dreamer, they could not. The smallest pinecone said, and I quote, 'All humans look alike.'"

"It's sadly true," says the cat.

"Well . . . still!" Zelda leaps to her feet. "There's an edge! There's a literal *end of the dream, get it*? The dream has an *end*. I'm going."

Langston says, "I don't know if that means what you think it—"

Zelda wheels around with her finger in the air. Right away it feels like too much, but she decides to commit to it. "I have to do something!" she shouts. "I have to wake up! If I don't wake up soon, I will probably die! A *wizard* said so!" Zelda circles the room with her hands on her cheeks. "I'm a ticking time bomb."

"So to speak," Patches says—quietly, because it's not really the time for it.

"Langston—you said there were pinecones who told you the dream has an edge." Zelda falters a bit—this isn't the rock-solid testimony she wishes it were. "If the dream's so thin there that you can see the actual dreamer, then it's as good a place as any to try waking me up again."

"Or Patches," says Langston. "Or whoever you see when you get there."

"Right," says Zelda. She has to wrestle for a moment with the implications of this. "Of course. They . . . should get to wake up. Whoever they are."

Even if they aren't me, she thinks. A second later, she says it out loud, just to see how it sounds.

Couldn't hurt to just have a look, though. First. If they can. If they can can see through the fog to the dreamer in the bed, then they can know what's what before anyone goes and does something rash.

She frowns and nods resolutely. Then she strides out of the wizard's workshop and back into her own sunny sitting room. She has every intention of getting dressed, so she's pleased to see she's suddenly wearing a cute denim romper and yellow sneakers.

Patches is hot on her heels as Zelda climbs the stairs to her bedroom. "Care for company on your quest?" he asks.

"Man, really? You still want to be my cat after how I behaved in there?"

"I am my own cat. But I am *your* friend. And what are friends for, if not to forgive when one friend tries carelessly to murder the other by pinching their whole world into nonexistence."

Zelda pauses her packing and looks the cat in his little face.

"I'm sorry it's like this, Patches."

"With respect, you do not know what it's like. You dreaming me, me dreaming you, the king of Spain dreaming us both, who knows. One thing remains consistently true."

"And what's that?"

Patches purrs. "According to the novelist Erich Segal, 'Love means never having to say you're sorry.' Which is idiotic, but still: forgive the lack of poetry when I say quite plainly that I do love you, Zelda."

Sure you do, thinks Zelda. *But not on purpose. You're just a character in my dream—I* made *you to love me. But love doesn't work like that.*

They're interrupted by the sound of a wizard knocking over a coffee table.

"Zelda?" calls Langston. "Are you still here?"

Zelda shoulders her backpack and finds Langston standing outside Erx's door in her sitting room. The wizard himself is sitting on the davenport.

"Sorry about your coffee table," says Erx. "Sometimes I forget the volume of my preposterous clothing."

Langston has his own backpack. He steps forward.

"I'm coming with you," he says.

"Um," Zelda answers. "Are you?" She's about two parts elated and one part annoyed to be spoken to like that.

"Oh," says Langston, shrinking. "I don't know. Can I? Sorry, in movies people say that, and it's always fine."

"Mm. So why do you want to go to the edge?"

Langston starts saying a number of things very quickly, about discovery and science and the landscape of the mind, but all the while he's making another thought balloon. It's an image of Zelda wearing a princessy getup. Surprisingly puffy. Something she'd never wear in real life. She blushes and does her best to ignore it.

"...And with any luck you can bring all that knowledge with you," Langston continues. "You know, when you wake up."

Zelda smirks. "You mean when Patches wakes up. He says he's the dreamer." She leans in close to Langston. "I don't really look good in pink," she tells him.

Langston pulls back and—pop—the thought bubble's gone. Erx chuckles.

"Wh-why did you say that?" asks Langston.

"Just in case you were thinking otherwise."

Erx slaps his legs and stands up. "I'll leave you kids to it, then." He moves back to the cardboard door and studies it a moment.

"You won't come with us?" asks Zelda.

"To do what?" Erx answers without turning. "Chaperone?"

Zelda's a blusher, apparently. She's never had the occasion before, but now it's the Fourth of July, and this year they've decided to light all the fireworks at once. Patches rolls his eyes at her.

"I will escort you to the edge of town," says Erx. "But no, I will go with you no farther, though I wish you well. You see, I'm not so certain this is all a dream—I think it might just be a story *about* a dream. And if it is a story, then I trust I am not the protagonist."

This seems like a comment Zelda's supposed to disagree with—*Do these jeans make me look like a supporting character?* "Nah," she says. "Why . . . would you say that? You could be the main character. Easy."

"You are the main character, dear," Erx says to Zelda, and it's jarring to hear someone state so bluntly what she's kind of always believed in her heart. "Because other characters are more or less oriented toward helping you realize your journey, and because you're the one with a talking animal friend."

Patches saunters up. "Perhaps *I* am the main character," he says, looking at Zelda, "and *I* am the one with a talking animal friend."

"Hey, buddy," says Zelda.

Erx ignores this. "I fear that makes me the wise grandfatherly character who dies in the second act to signify the end of innocence or some such." He opens the door wide and steps away from it. "I'd just as soon stay home and listen to records. But I will grant you a boon on your quest: Each of you may take one item from my workshop. Choose well, for—"

Langston's eyes are saucers. "Dibs on the sword!" he shouts, before leaping past the wizard and through the door. If it were a cartoon, he would have left a Langston-shaped cloud behind him. But it isn't a cartoon, it's a dream, so instead he leaves a swarm of hummingbirds and three bars of the Canadian national anthem.

Patches bats at the hummingbirds.

"Well," says Erx. "It would seem Langston has been window-shopping for some time. Patches? Young lady? Anything catch your eye?"

"Iw dake dis hunninggird," Patches says with his mouth full of hummingbird.

Zelda says thank you, but no. Because the truth is she's already taken something from the wizard's workshop. She doesn't want to be *greedy*.

EIGHT

THEY'RE STROLLING THROUGH HER OWN neighborhood, and at first Zelda feels staggered by the awkwardness of Erx, like a stone in her shoe. *What must we look like*, she wonders, *walking alongside this D&D character down the sidewalks of Everytown, USA.* He creaks as he walks—she can't figure why—and trails a sulfurous mist behind him. He seems to be lit more distantly by a colder, insidious sun.

No one gives him so much as a second glance, though. A teenager points to his staff and says, "Cool stick." Clara even—somehow—has a letter for him when they pass.

"From a mortuary," Erx announces as he examines the envelope. "Advertising cremation services." He holds the letter by its corner in his outstretched hand, and it disappears in a flash of pink flame.

"Doesn't mean you're going to die!" says Zelda. "You're just walking us to the edge of town!"

"And not a step farther." Erx sighs. "You children can learn your life lessons some other way."

Zelda gives Clara a hug. "Better stop my mail for a while," she whispers, and Clara says *fare thee well*.

"By the way," she adds with a smirk, "who's the cute boy?"

"That's Erx," Zelda answers. "He's a wizard."

Clara hitches her smirk up another rung and swats Zelda play-fully on the arm. "Okay, then. You be good, Zelda baby."

And they're on their way again.

She sneaks glances. At Langston's chin, his ear. At that muscle in his jaw that flares when he grits his teeth. Why does he grit his teeth? She knows he glances at her, too—she can feel his eyes like a hand on her cheek.

They walk for some time without speaking. Zelda tries to give the breezy impression she is enjoying the comfortable silence of old friends. She isn't, though; it's terrible. She spends the first five minutes trying to think of something to say, the next five wondering if it's been too long to say something. After that, she starts wishing maybe an airplane would fall on them so they'd have something to talk about.

They've actually been going in the wrong direction, purposefully so. If town is the center of the dream, and the courthouse is the center of town, then to find the circle's edge they need only walk in a straight line away from the courthouse. Or so their theory goes. "If you're at the North Pole, there's nowhere to go but south," Langston said, back when they were all still saying things. It's taking longer than Zelda thinks it should, and making her anxious. She's usually a bit of a jaywalker. But Langston's taken the lead, and the faithful way he waits for every walk signal, checks and double-checks every crossing, has Zelda feeling like a delinquent. So she waits, too, like it's what she's always done. Even though in her mind she's scream-ing, *Let's go let's go let's go.*

This is what happens when you meet someone new, she thinks. *You pretend to like whatever they're into.*

So they've only now reached the square, and they turn away from it onto Beeline, the straightest avenue to the sticks. Everyone around here will tell you: If you want to get out of town, you take Beeline. They just couldn't tell you where it goes, exactly, if you asked.

"Hey, Zelda!" one of the Frisbee bros yells after her. She waves back, happy just now for the attention. Can't hurt to have Langston see all the attractive men about town calling her name.

"Hey, Zelda dude!" calls the other bro.

Well, that's less good.

"Don't you have a geography test?" the first bro shouts.

"Not today!" Zelda answers. "Playing hooky!"

"Dude! Outrageous!"

"*So* outrageous!"

"You're like the funny kid sister I never had, Zelda!"

Oh*kay.*

Langston sucks air sharply. *Here we go*, thinks Zelda, and she readies herself for some conversation at last. But no, he lets the breath back out again. He was just breathing. False alarm.

She circles her neck around like she's stretching it, and steals another look at him. Tries to gauge what he's thinking.

Is this what it's like to like someone? It's kind of exhausting, actually, Zelda thinks. Her brain keeping constant tabs on every little thing. The shape of her. The shape of him. The exact shape and size of the space between them. She likes the swing of his walk. It looks like it should be set to music, a loungy bass. She suspects her own walk has more of a fidgety kazoo quality to it, and she tries to relax. It's a challenge to walk and think about how to walk at the same time, and she stumbles over a crack in the sidewalk.

"You okay?" Langston asks her.

"Yep!"

They spoke! To each other! Finally. It wasn't much of a conversation starter, but Zelda implores herself to keep it going.

"Speaking of those Frisbee guys," she says, though they absolutely hadn't been. "I have never seen them in another context. It's like I can't imagine them doing *anything* if they're not also giving or receiving a Frisbee."

"Whipping a Frisbee around the produce section as they shop for groceries," suggests Langston.

"Gently lobbing the Frisbee before a roaring fire as they celebrate their first Christmas together," says Zelda with a sigh.

She makes Langston laugh. It's great.

"You know," Zelda says, "those Frisbee guys, and Clara, and *everyone* in town last night . . . they each thought *they* were the dreamer of all this."

Langston huffs and shakes his head. "That's silly."

"Is it, though? Seems to me it should be kind of . . . hard to think of yourself as an extra."

Langston smiles a tight smile and shrugs in a *what can I tell you?* kind of way. "I manage," he says.

When Zelda knits her brow at him, he adds, "I mean, who are the townspeople kidding? I've watched this place. You're queen bee around here. Everyone else is a drone. An unmanned drone, I guess."

"Yeah," says Zelda, with a twinge in her gut. "I feel weird about that . . . Until a couple days ago, it seemed so natural."

"What happened a couple days ago?"

"Dunno!" she answers, kind of loud.

"And anyway, isn't that just like a dream?" Langston continues. "Until a couple days ago, it felt natural. Natural that you'd be the center of everyone's attention. Because, like, don't we all have a map of the world in here?" He taps his own head.

"One of those really good maps," Patches agrees. "Like a circle with dots in it."

"A mental map," Langston says, ignoring Patches. "It's covered with all our markers and monuments, all the stuff we think is important, but always with a big YOU ARE HERE right in the center."

Zelda thinks about her plaster constellations.

"Like a big ol' statue of ourselves," Langston continues, "because our sense of self has to be the biggest landmark of all. And when we dream, we go and mistake our map of the world for the *world*," he finishes. "Or you do, anyway. I assume."

"You don't dream?" asks Zelda.

"I dream all the time. Usually remember them, too. But if I'm not the dreamer, then I guess when I dream that's really . . . you dreaming of me dreaming." He bites his lip. "You're right: It is hard to think about."

After a few seconds, she gives him a side-eyed glance. "Do . . . *you* feel like an unmanned drone?"

Langston considers this. "No," he admits. "I don't. As nice as that sounds."

Zelda blanches. *"Nice?"*

"Okay, no—too far," Langston says, and shakes the thought free. "I don't want to be an unmanned drone. But wouldn't it be great to have, like, a GPS, but for life?" He looks at her to see if this lands any better. "A little mental assistant, helping you steer in the right direction. They could play Cyrano, you know? The smooth-talking poet, feeding you lines, helping you know what to say to classmates and . . . baristas and whatever."

Zelda laughs. "You are so weird."

"It could be an app on your phone: Sirino. She whispers clever conversation into your earbuds so you don't sound like a dum-dum all the time."

"Why do you even think you need that?" asks Zelda. "You're talking to me just fine. You sound great."

"A veritable mock-Socrates," says Patches.

"Mockrates," says Zelda.

"You *did* just call me weird," Langston reminds her.

"Whatever. I don't think you need an app. You're a . . . charmer."

He smiles a wriggling half smile, like he's fighting to keep it in its cage. *More*, thinks Zelda.

"I'm doing better than usual," he says. "I guess because now I know I'm only saying what your brain is telling me to say. I'm only doing what I'm told. *You're* playing Cyrano, even if it doesn't feel that way."

Zelda knows this is true, but still she says, "Maybe not! Maybe this is all you. You know, you . . . *could* be the dreamer."

She tries to follow how this idea plays out on his face. He purses his very nice lips at it, tries to dismiss it out of hand.

"No," he says, shaking his head.

But. But then she'd swear he grows into it. He looks at her squarely—his stride slows. He looks at her *deliberately*. There is nothing casual about this glance. He's drinking in all the light of her, and it opens him up like a flower.

That distance between them—of which Zelda had been so acutely aware—seems to vanish. She'd swear he doesn't move, but she's moved by him—by the sudden closeness of him, humming on her skin.

He says, "When you look at me, I feel real."

It's barely a whisper, before he turns his head and a subtle kind of panic sharpens his face.

"Zelda?" says Patches. He's suddenly underfoot. "May I speak to you a moment in private?"

"Um," says Zelda.

"Forgive the interruption," the cat says to Langston, "but I need to discuss with Zelda a veterinary concern of the most personal nature."

"Uh, yeah," says Langston, his train of thought derailed. "Of course." He slows to walk alongside Erx as Zelda picks up Patches.

"What are you *doing*?" the cat whispers to her.

"About what?" Zelda whispers back. "What do you mean?"

"You know full well. Why on earth would you even *suggest* to this boy that he might be our fantasist beyond the veil?"

"'Fantasist beyond the veil'? Do you hear yourself?"

"It's cruel, Zelda."

"Wh—He has as much chance at being the dreamer as anyone else. C'mon."

"Oh yes? How egalitarian. Why not tell yonder solicitor *he* is the dreamer, too?"

Zelda looks and sees who Patches means—there's a man on the sidewalk, handing out flyers. Zelda takes one as they pass. Takes one and *doesn't* stop to tell the flyer man he might be the somnambulant god of all creation. Patches pretends to be confused by this, and looks to her for an explanation.

"It didn't come up," Zelda mutters.

She examines the flyer. It seems to say **GOBING**

OTTABEEZUS!! 40pees in block letters across the top. Below is every kind of punctuation. "Can you read this?" she asks Patches.

"It is a flyer, advertising a flyer advertising service."

"Hm. Interesting."

Actually, one small line at the bottom of the flyer jumps out at her with perfect clarity:

YOU'LL FALL FOR HIM IN THE END—BUT HE WON'T FALL FOR YOU.

She reads it a second time, and a third. It refuses to say anything else. "Psh," Zelda huffs. She crumples the flyer and throws it aside. And hits a woman coming out of the bakery, actually. "Sorry," says Zelda. She moves to pick up her trash.

"I'll pick it up for you, Zelda!" says the woman, and she does. She beams and holds the wad of paper to her heart.

"Okay . . . thanks."

"Thank *you*!"

A moment later, Patches says, "I notice you did not grasp that woman's hands and tell her the good news. So just Langston, then? Will you be telling Erx he, too, might be the dreamer?" Zelda glances backward at the wizard. At the wizard and Langston.

Erx hums atonally as he walks. It's possible he doesn't know he's doing it. Langston waves a tiny wave.

"Okay, you got me," she says to Patches. "I guess I have an . . . interest in Langston particularly. I don't like him thinking he's a puppet. I don't like thinking it, either."

She remembers a girl back in fifth grade—what was her name, Shellifer? Chinny?—who drew a boy's face on her own hand, and was caught kissing it behind the portables.

"I don't want to kiss my own hand," she finishes.

"What a curious expression."

"But anyways, it's not *cruel*. You can't worry about cruelty *and* say Langston's not real at the same time. He either matters or he doesn't."

"I worry not for Langston but for *you*. Cruelty takes its toll on cat and mouse, both."

"Or it might take its toll on you," says Zelda. Patches squirms, so she sets him down. "*Your* mind, because either *one* of us might be the dreamer. Right?"

Patches coughs. A hairball noise. "Of course," he answers, after a moment. "That is precisely what I meant."

Zelda watches him. *He doesn't really believe he's the dreamer*, she thinks. *He's just saying it to be difficult, because he's a cat.*

Before long, the four of them have more or less clustered together again. Zelda gives Langston a little smile. He gives her an absent smile in return—his thoughts appear to be miles away.

The sun is warm. The sun is always warm. The breeze is cool. Ditto about the breeze. Zelda tries to remember the last time it rained.

Oh, right, she thinks with a shiver. *Last night. It rained last night.* She'd forgotten.

"If this were my dream . . ." says Langston.

"Which it most likely is not," says Erx.

"Yeah. Okay. I was just going to say it's pretty different from how my dreams usually work. Lotta anxiety stuff, usually. Sports." He trails off a little. "Trying to find a bathroom that locks."

"I had a dream once," says Patches. "I was chasing lizards, but couldn't catch one. My paw would pass right through, and there the lizard would be atop my paw, like a projection. I suspect it has something to do with that laser pointer Zelda tortured me with when I was a kitten."

"Sorry," says Zelda.

"Regardless. I remember it because it was one of those dreams within a dream. I awoke, but I was not awake. And I did not know I was still dreaming until I tumbled off the bed and woke up properly. And now I learn I may be dreaming still."

"Or being dreamed of," says Langston.

"Yes, yes—or being dreamed of," Patches groans. "Pedant."

Langston is making another thought balloon. He's apparently thinking of dunking Patches into a bucket of water.

"You're making thought bubbles," Zelda tells him. "I should have told you sooner."

"I'm . . . what?"

"Making thought bubbles," says Erx. "Forgive me, lad. They started happening shortly after that day, some time ago, when you were electrocuted."

Langston frowns and says, "I don't remember being electrocuted."

"That is often how it works, yes."

"And after getting electrocuted he made thought bubbles?" asks Zelda.

"Possibly. Possibly it was after he drank a bottle of ghosts. That was a busy day."

Zelda looks at Langston. "Why did you drink a bottle of ghosts?"

"My fault," Erx explains. "I shouldn't have kept it inside the Cabinet of Delicious Sodas."

Langston has followed all this like Ping-Pong, but now he has his hand up. "Wait. Zelda. Do you mean thought bubbles like in a comic book? Like you can read what I'm thinking?"

"See it, not read it. But sometimes, yeah."

"Oh," says Langston, and then he quails. "*Oh*. Am I . . . doing it now?"

"Depends. Are you imagining me in a prom dress?"

"I'm trying not to."

"Don't think of me in a frog costume!" Zelda says, and so of course he does. "Don't think of yourself holding a leopard! This is fun."

"I'm glad. I'm glad you're having fun. What am I thinking of now?"

"Well, that's rude."

"My turn, my turn," says Patches. "Don't think of yourself as Baby New Year."

"Don't think of yourself with muttonchops!"

"Don't think of yourself as a hopeless, noodle-armed nerd boy. I mean," says Patches, scoffing, "what would that even look like, right?"

"Don't think of yourself dressed as a cowboy!" says Zelda. "Aw. You have low self-esteem—you'd make a prettier cowboy than that."

"Ffft," says Patches. "This has lost its appeal."

"Wait," says Langston. "What street is this?"

"Beeline," says Zelda. "Remember? We agreed, we'd take the straightest route from the courthouse."

"Yeah, but . . . is this the street . . . is this where . . . ?"

He's worried about the laundromat clown. Zelda likes to think she knows him well enough by now to guess this, but also he's making a neon-bright thought bubble of the laundromat clown.

"Oh God," he says, and draws his sword. "That's the laundromat up ahead. Cross the road! Cross the road!"

He herks and jerks between cars and bicycles to the opposite side.

"That wasn't even a crosswalk," says Zelda, impressed. The rest of them follow.

"You can just stay where you're at!" Langston calls over to the other side of the road, and the laundromat. The clown is there. The clown is always there.

It lifts its head. Its smile, already an inch too wide, widens.

"COO?" says the clown.

"Huh. First time I've ever heard it speak," says Zelda.

She's never been the afraid-of-clowns type, but there's something about having visitors that helps you see your town through fresh eyes. The clown, with its shrubby orange hair. Orange pantsuit. Too many little brown teeth, packed in like matchsticks. A face that could be makeup, or could be a bad allergic reaction to something, or both.

"COO COO KISSY?" says the clown.

"Is that really how it talks?" says Zelda.

It wants to cross the road, but traffic has gotten thick just now. It reaches for him. It hooks its fingers and strains its arms.

Its arms are—maybe?—getting slightly longer. Very slightly, very slowly. If at all. They probably aren't. Zelda winces.

Langston walks briskly past and waggles his sword at it.

"You . . . just . . . you . . . gonna . . ." He caps off these stirring words with another swing of his sword. "Try it and find *out*! Cut that hair for you."

"Roll your twenty-sided die!" suggests Patches.

Langston is still making a thought balloon of the laundromat clown. Which makes sense—what *else* would he be thinking about right now—but it's weird to see one clown across the street and a second one hovering over his head. The two clowns appear to notice each other and strike up a conversation.

"COO COO AW COO BABY KISSY COO?"

"KISSY BABY WUDDA WUDDA COO COO KISSY!"

Langston loses it and starts slicing the air above his head, but even a wizard's sword can't change his mind.

"Use the ring, Frodo!" says Patches. Zelda wheels on him.

"C'mon, man, give him a break. He has a phobia. You're not perfect."

"Perfection is subjective. But I may thank the gods I am un-burdened by silly pho—"

Zelda points and shouts, "VACUUM CLEANER!"

Patches starts, scrabbles, folds himself in half, and clambers up Erx's robes. He perches in the wizard's crown of antlers, back arched and electric. Erx flinches ever so slightly.

"Ow," he says.

Patches looks all over for the vacuum. After a moment, under-standing sets in and he shrinks. "I regret that mistakes were made," he mutters.

Zelda moves to catch up with Langston. *He could use a friendly distraction*, she thinks, as the traffic has cleared and the laundromat clown is just now leaving the laundromat.

"COO *COO!*" it cheers as it starts stiffly walking across the road at him. Its shoes squeak like dog toys.

"COO COO!" answers the clown in Langston's thought bubble encouragingly.

Langston shouts the loudest swear anyone's ever heard.

That clown only has eyes for Langston, thinks Zelda with the weird-est pang of jealousy. But . . . what is she jealous of, exactly? Does she resent the clown for having Langston's attention, or Langston for having the clown's?

This town has messed her *up*, she thinks—she's gotten so used to playing center stage. And she can say she doesn't want that anymore, but here she is feeling ignored the moment the spotlight shines on anyone else.

She jogs ahead of Langston and pivots to walk backward so they can look at each other. "Hey, Langston," she says. "Quest is going pretty well so far, don't you think?"

She's just helping out a new friend, obviously. Obviously she isn't trying to center herself in a situation that isn't about her.

She leans and looks around him at the wizard. "Erx!" she shouts, and points to the clown in the street. "Anything you can do about that?"

Erx seems unnerved by the clown, too. He's putting as much distance between himself and it as he can, which mostly means pressing himself up against the sides of all the businesses across the street from the laundromat in turn. He accidentally falls in through the front door of the mini-mart with a DING, and emerges a few seconds later with sunglasses and a thirty-two-ounce soda.

"Erx?" Zelda shouts again.

The old man nods, and his knotty fingers sign a kind of double-jointed alphabet. "Laundromius Connectimento!"

"Okay, *again*," Zelda calls to Patches. He's still atop Erx's hat. "How can I be dreaming in Latin if I don't know Latin?"

"That wasn't Latin," Patches assures her.

Whatever it was, it has an effect. The laundromat clown comes to a halt in the middle of the road, though its ridiculous body continues to strain and stretch. It's like it's changed from clown to mime—walking in place as though pulling against invisible chains.

"The clown is now restrained," says Erx. He sighs, like it's not the first time he's had to say this. "It is bound by the unbreakable Chains of Zirconia to the laundromat it calls home."

"Great!" says Zelda. She tries to catch Langston's eye. "See that?"

The clown heaves with a lusty "COOOOOOOOOOOOO!" and the whole laundromat tips forward, wrenching free of its foundation. The noise is teeth-chattering, like the whole world is clearing its throat.

"Whoop, okay," says Zelda, "let's hustle!" They all pick up the pace.

Cars are honking because there's still a clown in the street, but it's only inching along. The whole laundromat inches along behind it—it sounds terrible.

"AW, COO," says the clown in Langston's thoughts, and it reaches for its compatriot in the road. Then an idea lights its face, and it casts its arm down at Langston instead. Like it's fishing—it wants to hook a glinting finger in his mouth.

"Uhhh, okay, don't look up," says Zelda. "Look at me. Hi. It's a nice day for a walk, isn't it? I . . . *am* glad you decided to come with me."

That's gotten Langston's attention. They lock eyes, and she gets a little defibrillator jolt to the chest.

"I'm glad I came," he says. "Or, at least, I was. I will be!" he adds in a hurry. "It's just . . ."

"It's just that you're still thinking about the clown. I get it. But think of me instead. That's better, isn't it? Think of me."

He is thinking of her now—her and the clown, both. The two of them jostle for room in the thought bubble, but the laundromat clown is smaller than it was.

Meanwhile, they've left the actual laundromat clown behind. They've speed-walked over a ridge, and it isn't visible anymore. The cooing and the grinding and honking all seem like things that are happening to other people now.

"Imagine if I just . . . picked up that laundromat clown and threw it into the Grand Canyon," says Zelda. "That'd be funny."

And now Langston can't help but imagine it, and it *is* funny. Zelda can see it play out in his thoughts.

She gives him a big smile. He smiles, too—finally—and, my God, it's stunning. It's like his teeth are some brilliant display he's been keeping under wraps until mating season. For the first time Zelda understands profoundly how a good set of tail feathers might really get a peahen going.

Langston's whole body unclenches, and his thought balloon abruptly fades.

And that's probably for the best. Zelda might not be ready to see what he thinks of next.

NINE

THE WHOLE SHAPE OF HIS face changed when he smiled. From the eyes down, he was like a valentine—the corners of his mouth pushed his cheeks into round peaks and sharpened his chin. She thinks about that smile. She tries to think of ways to make it happen again. Then she pivots to walk beside him and crams her hands into her pockets because she wouldn't know what to do with them otherwise. She might just reach out and rest one in the hollow of his collarbone, or in the scoop of his skin where his biceps ends. He's this whole collection of shapes and lines. Ridges and hills and valleys, soft skin over lean muscle over hard bone. And so is everyone else she's ever met, but it never mattered before.

Her brain is all hamster wheels again.

"Well!" says Langston, after a spell. "So much for first impressions."

"Ha!" She recovers. "What, because of the clown?"

"The clown, plus the real cool-guy way I reacted to the clown."

"Hey, look," says Zelda. "I get it. I mean, I never thought about the clown much until recently, but, hoo! Sure gave me a lot to think about today!"

"You thought it was scary?"

"I thought it was totally scary."

Patches has climbed down from Erx mountain, and he inserts himself between Langston and Zelda as they walk. "What's more," he says, "we felt but the liminal heat of the clown's fiery affection. Langston was its laser focus."

Affection? That seems like a funny word for it, but Zelda is nonetheless happy with Patches in that moment. He's making nice with the new kid.

"I guess . . ." says Langston. "I guess that's weird for you both, right? Having that proof I'm the dreamer."

Zelda blinks. "Um, proof of what now?"

Langston looks apologetic. Actually, he looks hammily apologetic, like a bridesmaid who just caught the bouquet at the end of a wedding. "We just passed a nightmare, and it was made especially for moi," he says, and shrugs.

Zelda laughs. "*Ohh*kay. You just got through telling us this is not the kind of thing you usually dream about."

"And then a minute later, a clown tries to eat me!" Langston points out. "It's pretty compelling."

Erx grunts. "It is likely you were in no real danger. I'd have sacrificed my life to save you, your guilt would mark this as the day you finally became a man, yadda yadda," he says drowsily.

"You're not going to *die*," says Zelda.

"I'm just saying," says Langston. "In a nightmare, you're the victim. Nobody's ever had a nightmare where somebody *else* is the victim. Right? There was a clown, and she only wanted to eat *me*. Sorry y'all don't look as tasty as I do."

Zelda snort-laughs. Patches gives her a *told you so* look. "All right, I get it," she tells him under her breath. "I made a monster."

"What?" says Langston. "Now I can't be the dreamer?"

Zelda realizes she's been wanting exactly this: sparring, playful banter. After a life like an elementary school play, she finally meets someone who seems like a real person, and it spoils her fun if he doesn't agree. But Patches had a point. She's going to need to tamp down his expectations if she doesn't want to see him get his imaginary heart broken later on.

"Remember what you said about me," she tells Langston, and points two fingers at her own head. "Queen bee. You found the *one person* in town who doesn't think I am an extra slice of birthday cake, and you think that makes you the dreamer."

That very second, a family of three passes by on a tandem bicycle. "Hi, Zelda!" they shout, and ring their little bells. Zelda motions as if to say, *See?*

"You know who they were?" she asks Langston.

"No. Who—"

"*Neither do I*," says Zelda. "That's what a celebrity I am in this town. For God's sake, look at Erx's drink cup! It has my picture on the side of it."

It's true: It does. There's a photo of Zelda playing basketball she doesn't remember taking. She's dunking a cherry into a bucket of ice.

"You and Erx don't even live here. You live in the Forest of Hands and Feet, but you still knew who I was."

"I even sent you a present last Christmas," says Erx.

Zelda turns. "Did you? I'm sorry, I don't remember—I got so many gifts."

"It was an enchanted chicken's foot floating in a jar of vitreous gelatin."

"Okay, now I remember."

"Whoo. An extra slice of birthday cake." Langston whistles. "What kind of metaphor is that?"

"The amazing kind. So, no offense, but I'm the dreamer," Zelda tells them as they near the edge of town. "Because last night I wished for a person to help me, and the very next morning the postwoman delivered one. I said . . . Patches, what did I say? I said I needed an expert, or a wizard or genius professor. And boom, I met a wizard."

"And a dream expert," says Langston, presumably referring to himself.

"Sure," says Zelda, just to be agreeable. "And why *else* would I suddenly have someone new in my dream if I hadn't conjured you up?"

"Hmm," says Langston. He's swinging his new sword around. Thoughtfully, though—if one can thoughtfully swing a sword. He seems to be trying to give the impression that he's learning valuable sword facts instead of just playing with his new toy.

Patches purrs. "I take Zelda's point—why, indeed. And I think I might be ready to concede that I am not, myself, the dreamer," he says to Langston. "For if I were, why would I ever invent *you*? Unless you're my subconscious's way of scolding me for living too magnificent a life."

"Thanks," says Langston. "Thank you. Maybe you're also not the dreamer because you're a talking cat? Because I don't think there's supposed to be talking cats."

"Perhaps he is only dreaming he can talk," says Erx.

Langston makes a face. "Is that ... possible? That a cat could dream in English?"

"Unless he *isn't*," says Zelda. "Unless he's dreaming in *cat* about people who *think* he's dreaming in English. Or maybe ... ooh, *maybe* he's just some guy *dreaming* he's a cat."

"Either way," says Langston, "it's probably fine that I rubbed his belly, right?"

"Stop talking about me like I'm not here," says Patches.

Langston returns the sword to the sheath on his back. "Well, anyway—is it really that weird?" he asks. "Me being a stranger, I mean? Do you only dream about people you've already met?"

Zelda thought. She did, didn't she? Didn't everyone? "I mean ... yeah, basically. I either dream about people I know or else some totally made-up monster like a witch or whatever. I don't dream about a ... strange boy." She doesn't even know why she's blushing now.

"I used to have a lot of dreams about witches," says Langston. "When I was a little kid. Sometimes my grandma would watch me, and the only DVD she had was *The Wizard of Oz*, and I wore that thing *out*."

"I've never actually seen it," says Zelda. "I only know it by reputation."

"You'd like it. It's about a white girl who doesn't realize she's having a dream."

"Oh, it's a documentary!"

"She has a little dog."

"That doesn't sound very realistic," says Patches.

"Anyway, I was over there one day, maybe six years old, sweating through my least-favorite scene where the witch burns the scare-crow, and meanwhile my grandma decides today's the day I need to learn about the Klan. So she's telling me about that in one ear, and the movie's going in the other, and I think they got kind of mixed up in my head. Fire. Pointy hats. Gave me the worst kind of nightmares for two or three years."

"God," says Zelda.

Langston shrugs and rolls his eyes, as if he's trying to shake off the cowl of his own seriousness. "Funny I ended up with a wizard, right?"

"Hilarious," says Erx behind them.

"That's the only reason we haven't met before. I've been with Erx, learning what I can through his mirror. I mean, I mostly studied the town, but sometimes I'd have the mirror show me the forest. You wouldn't believe the stuff I've seen."

"So tell me. Tell me what you've seen."

"There was . . . there were these big-headed guys and this . . . kind of sideways building? That was weird. And these cool bugs that were like . . ." Langston tilts his head around as he speaks, like his thoughts are a little silver ball he's trying to steer through a maze.

"There's an old adage about other people's dreams being boring," says Patches, "which I mention now for no particular reason."

"Okay, well, the bugs are kind of hard to describe, but you would have thought they were cool if you'd seen them," finishes Langston.

"Uh-huh. So here's what I think about that," says Zelda. "I think, if somehow you *are* the dreamer, then it's awfully strange that you'd whip up the world's cutest town and plunk it down in the very center of your dream and then never spend *any* time there. I think it is un*likely* that you would make all these people and then leave them to have relationships with one another while you go off on your own to look at cool bugs."

For a moment, Langston has nothing to say to this. "I mean," he says finally, "I know you're probably the dreamer. I'm just messing."

Whoops, too far, thinks Zelda. The sidewalk here is like peanut brittle, and it crunches underfoot.

"Sorry," she says after a minute. "I didn't mean anything by it—"

"It's cool," says Langston. He laughs—kind of. A huff and a freighted smile that isn't as much fun to look at. "Everyone else having relationships while I go off alone to look at cool bugs is more or less how I spent high school."

They lapse into silence again. A silence as brittle as the sidewalk. Zelda doesn't know what she ought to be doing.

The knot of them comes undone, and soon they're walking in more of a loose line: Langston, then Patches, then Zelda, then Erx.

Zelda thinks, *I'm being a jerk. Why am I doing that?* She doesn't know what will happen if she's nice, so she's sniping at Langston instead. She's a late bloomer, she reminds herself. She forgot to have crushes on people in grade school, so she's treating Langston like a grade-school crush. She should have gotten this sort of behavior out of her system a long time ago—years of mistakes under her belt, like an operating manual of *don'ts*.

Patches's tail is twitchy. It looks like Zelda feels. There's something about this part of town that seems hollow. The cookie-cutter houses *feel* hollow. Were they to meet a person here—and Zelda sincerely hopes they do not—the person would be hollow, too. Everything's less carefully drawn.

She thinks Langston feels unnerved by it as well. After a moment, he reaches back to touch the hilt of his sword again. He's been doing that a lot, like it's a comfort.

After another minute of walking, Zelda's certain she knows what makes this neighborhood so strange—there are houses and sidewalks and streets but no hydrants or mailboxes. No streetlamps, no stop signs.

But as soon as she thinks it, she glimpses a stop sign out of the corner of her eye—like it stubbed out its cigarette and straightened its octagon and rushed onto set in the nick of time. Zelda narrows her eyes. "I'm onto you," she whispers.

Okay, now the dream is overcompensating—stop signs everywhere. There are three on one street corner.

They're easy enough to recognize by shape and color, but Zelda realizes with interest that she can read the *S* but isn't totally sure what the other letters are. She squints.

Does it really say *spot*? She looks again.

There.

Finally. "This neighborhood is just making it up as it goes," Zelda complains.

It says STOP, so she stops, absently, and in a moment Erx is standing beside her. "You have never been here before," says the wizard. It isn't a question.

"No. I haven't. This neighborhood . . . I guess I've just . . . never had a reason to come here."

"Were you to walk from the courthouse in any direction, you would eventually find a neighborhood like this. Perhaps this neighborhood exactly."

Zelda takes it all in: ticky-tacky houses, indifferent roads. Tree-shaped trees. There are three different tornados skating around on the horizon.

"For the young lady who had all she wanted," Erx continues, "the dreamer is forced now to hastily invent something new. Beyond the borders of town, expect a shambling garden of half-formed ideas and garbled intentions."

Zelda huffs. "'The young lady who had all she wanted.' I should be offended, but . . . before a couple days ago it was true. How sad is that?"

"Don't torture yourself. Whether you are the dreamer, or merely the dreamed of; the storyteller, or only a character; you are, in this place, the figment of a mind—*not* the mind itself. You are a paper doll, and so all you could see was the paper. If now you find yourself yearning for other dimensions, then what a triumph of consciousness."

It doesn't feel to Zelda like a triumph. It feels like a mistake—she got lost and stumbled through a door and found the other side of the stage. The wigs and plywood sets.

"You and Langston have been watching this place," she says. "You know that indoor shopping mall on Broadway?"

She doesn't wait for an answer, but instead barrels on.

"There are birds in it—sparrows mostly. They perch up in the rafters and fly down to finish people's hot dogs for them. I guess some of them come in through the sliding doors and can't find their way back out? But I bet a lot of them are just born there. They hatch in a nest over the food court maybe, live out their lives there, die there. Can you imagine what a . . . spellbinding shock the world would be to one of those birds if it ever found its way outside?"

"Plato's Cave," says Erx.

"What?"

"What you are describing is Plato's Cave," he says.

"Isn't that the name of the adult bookstore on Fletcher?"

"No, it is . . ." Erx pauses, confused, because it *is* the name of the adult bookstore on Fletcher.

Way up ahead, Patches and Langston have realized they're alone, and turn. Langston frowns.

Zelda grabs the cuff of Erx's sleeve, surprising them both.

"It has to be me, Erx," she whispers, even as she looks Patches and Langston right in their distant faces. "It *has* to. Because if it isn't, and I don't get to wake up . . . then *that*"—she gestures behind her—"was all I got. Just half a life in a town full of people with no names."

Erx lowers his voice, too, because Langston and Patches are drawing near. "I suspect you have little to worry about, there. I said already that you are the main character of this story; whoever heard of a person not being the main character of their own dreams?"

"Hey," says Langston, when he's close enough to speak. "What's up?"

"My time as your traveling companion," says Erx. "I was just telling Zelda that I will take this stop sign's suggestion and say my farewells." He seems suddenly agitated, turning and searching his surroundings like he's lost his keys.

"You are going back to Zelda's house?" asks Patches. "Returning to your atelier through the cardboard door?"

"Quite," says Erx, flinching suddenly at a cloud. "It is the only way, unless one of you good people can direct me toward the Forest of Hands and Feet."

"Langston has a map," says Patches. "It's a circle with dots in it. Might it help?"

"Enough about my map."

Zelda is watching the wizard. "You're fidgety because you're worried this is the part where you die."

"It would be narratively sensible, if not trite. Cut down by fate just as I've said my goodbyes and fulfilled my promise. Leaving the three of you with a fresh respect for the fragility of life and so forth."

"You're not going to *die*."

"Please stop saying that. Haven't you ever heard of dramatic irony?" He looks this way and that. For an instant, Zelda swears his head turns just a little farther than it should, like an owl's. "In fact . . . this isn't even a goodbye! I am just walking away rudely." He is, in fact, jogging away. His heavy robes make a *fuppa-fuppa* noise as he retraces their steps, then turns abruptly and hides behind a tree.

The others watch for a moment.

"I think he's going to keep hiding until we're out of sight," says Langston.

They reach the edge of town. Again, Zelda stops. There's no visible line, no sign, but she knows it to be the edge nonetheless by the squeeze in her heart. It's like the tensest point of an invisible tie that binds her, and now she can snap it or let it tug her back home. She has never been this far from her little yellow house.

"All my life, I never really thought about where this town *is*," she says quietly. "I don't even know what state I was in. Ha—an *unconscious state*, I guess. Guys? Did you hear what I—"

"We heard," says Patches.

Was the town still there before she looked at it? Will it still be there if she comes back? It seems suddenly like a leap of faith to suppose a town that has forgotten so much won't simply forget itself.

Patches and Langston are watching her. "You okay?" asks Langston.

Probably! thinks Zelda. *It feels like I'm dying, but in a good way. How are you?*

Ahead is a grassy landscape of gently rolling hills. Leafy trees set just far enough from one another to make each seem like a destination—a place to rest and wait for a falling apple to inspire new ideas about gravity or good and evil or whatnot. It's nice.

Zelda puffs out her cheeks and takes a step.

Nothing really happens. It feels new, though. And exhilarating.

"Free as a bird," she says.

"What?"

"Nothing."

TEN

AS THEY WALK, ZELDA STARES, frowning, at the air right in front of her nose.

"Bubble," she says.

"Did you say something?" asks Langston.

"Shh. Concentrating," she tells him. Then she squints. "Bubble."

Still nothing.

The problem, Zelda thinks, is that she believes in herself. In her heart, she thinks she's real, and she's not. Not really.

What had Erx said? *He said I'm a paper doll, too*, she thinks. *The figment of a mind—not the mind itself.*

Again she says, "Bubble," and holds her breath until a glint and a bit of movement draw her eye.

"Ha *ha*! Look!" Zelda cheers. "I made a bubble! With my brain."

"Where?" asks Langston, and when Zelda tries to point it out she can't find it.

Well, that's what she gets—it probably popped.

"Butterfly," she whispers. And a butterfly flutters past, so rainbow-perfect it makes you sick, but now Zelda can't remember if she said "butterfly" because she saw it or she saw it because she said it.

Regardless, Patches catches and eats it.

"Oh, I know what I should make," Zelda says, first to herself and then to Langston. "I should have a sword, too. Right? Plus maybe mine shouldn't be the sword from *ThunderCats*."

"Heh," says Patches.

"It's real metal," Langston grouses. "A collectors' item. Worth a lot of money, actually."

"Except you took it out of its original packaging—oh no," says Zelda. "Now it's worthless."

A look on his face tells her she's cut a little too close to the bone here—that Langston is absolutely the kind of person who has toys he's never touched.

"What I took it *out* of," he says, "was an anvil on a big stone."

Patches' ears prick. "Did you? Like Arthur and Excalibur?"

"Yeah, but it's not as big a deal as it sounds. The anvil had a hole in the center—Erx keeps umbrellas in it."

Zelda thrusts her arm in the air like she's the Princess of Power and cries, "SWORD!" Her voice is a falcon that soars across the universe.

They're all looking at her hand. Langston says, "Did you mean for there to be a sword there now, or . . ."

"Perhaps she intended only to raise her fist in a hearty salute to swords everywhere."

"Okay, ha ha. Hold on."

I'm not me, she thinks. *I'm a dream—a little dream of me.*

She tries to hold that thought in her mind, and also thoughts about swords, which is hard, but with fresh resolve she strikes another pose, arm in the air.

"SWORD!"

Nope. Nothing.

"What are you doing?" asks Langston.

"Let me answer that question with a question," says Zelda. "Why are we walking?"

"Because . . . we don't move as fast when we sit? I don't understand the question."

"I mean, until Gandalf back there left us, I think we all got caught up in his kind of story," says Zelda. "A real walk-a-thousand-miles-to-Mordor kind of story."

"Wait, you're going along with Erx's idea that this is a story? I thought we agreed it's a dream."

"It *is* a dream. And all the more reason to ask ourselves—again—why are we walking? We could be driving moon rovers. We could be riding kangaroos."

"We could be riding *dirt bikes*," Langston whispers. It's semiromantic, the way he says "dirt bikes." Zelda wonders if she should be jealous.

"Well," she says. "Either way, we need to *move*. Ooh! I can imagine us up a car."

"A car," Langston repeats.

"Yes. It's like a little room full of chairs that rolls. They're something we have in the real world."

"Do you . . . know a lot about cars?"

"Uh, did you hear my amazing car definition a second ago? I could work for the dictionary."

Langston straightens his clothes and looks like he doesn't know what to do with his arms. "I just . . . You couldn't keep tabs on a bubble for ten seconds, but you want to put us all inside a speeding metal cage powered by your self-confidence—do I understand that right?"

"The boy has, loath as I am to admit it, a point."

"Party poopers."

"We're not so far from town," says Langston. "Let's go back and *borrow* a car. You know," he adds. "Something with object permanence. Something that isn't going to turn into a rocketing pile of nonsense."

"Why would a car in town be any more reliable? It's all dreamstuff."

Patches says, "There does seem to be a reassuring *veritas* to things we don't imagine ourselves. Remember the town meeting. Everyone took their flights of fancy—superhero costumes and hot rods and such—but as soon as they were distracted, the dream reverted quite swiftly back to form."

"Everyone took their flights of fancy but me," Zelda grumbles. Which she has to admit was her own fault. If she's going to spend a whole party trying to fight her way to the exit, she can't complain later that she didn't have a good time. "Oh! Flights! We could be *flying*. Couldn't we?" She hasn't tried that yet herself, but everyone else was doing it. Even Patches, sort of.

"Perhaps I'll get better with practice," he says.

"I just want to get to this edge as quick as we can," Zelda presses.

"And that's exactly the problem," says Langston. "Rushing. What if we fly and lose control? What if we forget to believe we can fly for a second, and so suddenly we can't?"

"Then we fall. Falling always takes you out of a dream." Zelda scans the landscape for something she can climb. "Shoot, I should be trying to fall on purpose."

"Unless falling doesn't take us out of the dream. And we die. Does anyone know what happens if you *die* in a dream?"

This takes the wind out of her sails for a moment. And then she thinks, *sailboat*, and then she pushes that idea aside in favor of something a little less ambitious.

"Okay, then," she says. "Get ready for an amazing compromise: bikes."

Langston's face falls. Just plummets.

"We . . . could each imagine our own," Zelda adds.

"I want to ride in a basket," says Patches.

Langston shrinks from this. "Uh, no."

"No?"

"Too dangerous."

"The basket?"

"All of it," Langston clarifies.

He quickens his pace, like the subject is a clown chained to a laundromat that he's trying to walk away from. Zelda hurries to catch up.

"You almost broke into song when you said 'dirt bikes,'" she reminds him, "but regular bikes are too dangerous? They're easy to imagine and—"

"*No*," says Langston. "No bikes." He sends them furtive glances— he realizes he's said this with way too much conviction. "I mean, if that's okay. I said 'dirt bikes' because I've always . . . *admired* dirt bikes, but it wasn't a serious suggestion. They're death traps. And I don't feel good about normal bikes, either."

"Is this why you were so keen on saving me the other day? Are you the sworn enemy of bicycles?"

"Did a bicycle murder your parents?" asks Patches.

Langston gets a queer look on his face and doesn't answer. Zelda dives back in.

"I just figured if a bike, you know, disappeared out from under me I'd probably land on my feet," she says.

"I'd land on *my* feet," announces Patches. "I am famous for it."

"I have a bad feeling about the idea," says Langston. "Which I know doesn't sound very scientific, but . . . I think we should listen to our bad feelings here. Why don't we just go back to town and figure out our next move."

"I don't want to go back to town!" says Zelda. "I'll get caught up in it. That place wasn't good for me—too many yes-men."

"Okay, okay."

Zelda lapses into silence. Hasn't she challenged Langston enough? With all the teasing? That's what her inner voice is suddenly whispering, after a lifetime of her inner and outer voices sounding generally like the same affable foghorn. *Boys don't like too much pushback*, it tells her, in a tenor she's never heard before. She can't help but grimace at it.

Screw it, she thinks, *I'm imagining a bike.*

"Whoa, hey," says Langston. "I thought we agreed—"

"I'm not riding it," says Zelda as she trundles along her cherry-red ten-speed street bike with wide saddle and a horn. "I'm just taking it for a walk. You can check out its amazing attention to detail if you want to."

She honks the horn: a *hee-haw* sound.

Langston's glum expression cracks, and a little light shows through. He does an impression of being impressed.

"*Probably* only the dreamer could whip up such a perfectly realistic bike," Zelda tells him.

"*So* realistic," Langston agrees. He rubs his chin, and Zelda is momentarily arrested by the flex of his arm. "And look at that really real flat tire it got from the imaginary thumbtack I just imagined."

"Wha . . ." Zelda looks down at the mushy tire under her handlebars. "You jerk."

Langston's actually strutting now. "That's the kind of power move you can expect from the boy whose immense brain has conjured up this entire amazing dreamscape."

"Uh-huh." She thinks, then concentrates. "*Fortunately*, thumbtacks are no problem for the *true* dreamer, because . . . this tire is like those trick birthday candles nobody likes."

"Uh, meaning?"

"*Meaning*," says Zelda as the tire reinflates with a *foomp*, "it keeps going no matter how many times it gets blown out, ha ha."

"Must be hard, though, pushing a bike with so many wind chimes hanging off of it."

"I THINK YOU'LL FIND," Zelda shouts over all the jingly tinkling, "THAT THESE TINY HELICOPTERS CARRY AWAY UNWANTED WIND CHIMES."

Patches bats at the helicopters.

"Wait," says Langston. "Do those tiny helicopters have tiny helicopter pilots?"

"Duh. I guess. Why?"

Langston peers into the choppers as they airlift the wind chimes away. "You just *made* people. Do they have whole lives now? Spouses and kids? Are they in the wee army to earn money for tiny college?"

"I don't know," Zelda says. "Does it matter?"

"They're just, like, little toy helicopters," says Zelda. "Little toy people." The topic is making her feel weird. She winces. "Am I crazy or did the dream turn into comics for a second?"

"You're probably right," says Langston. "You know, in the long run—it's just interesting to me. Look at that helicopter Patches wrecked."

Zelda looks. Patches is trying and failing to hide a fiery helicopter crash behind his tail. He looks like he has regrets. "It was an accident," he insists, "during a routine training exercise."

"So ... I made some people!" says Zelda. "Big deal! I made everyone I've ever met! I made you!"

It's a strange thing to say out loud. She made him. She gives Langston a quick once-over, admiring her handiwork without being too obvious about it.

"Or *I* made *you*," says Langston. It isn't quite a challenge—they seem, suddenly, not to be fighting anymore. "Which, now that I think about it, feels a lot more likely," he adds. "To me."

"... Why? Why more likely?"

He stops walking. He rubs his neck. He lowers his head to look at her, like he can't take all of her at once.

"Because," says Langston. "Because you are exactly how you would be ... if I did."

Oh.

Patches groans one long groan that goes on for eight seconds. He flops onto his side and blows a raspberry.

Zelda hasn't any insides. They've been replaced by a fizzy pink. But she's left Langston on the hook too long, and he looks ready to wriggle out of it.

"That came out weird," he says. "What I really meant was—"

If he's about to take it back, then Zelda doesn't want to hear a *word* of what he really meant.

She shouts, "Pizza hat!"

Langston flinches and takes off his pizza hat.

She says, "Baby presidents!"

"Aaa—what?" Langston shouts. They are suddenly surrounded. "This is a lot of babies."

"Oh, please. There's only, like, sixteen," Zelda says. Social Studies wasn't her best subject. "You know what," she adds, and squints. For the third time, she raises her hand in the air.

"SWORD!"

The air bends.

"HA! There, see? I did it!"

It's a little on the simple side compared to Langston's—more like the sword a talented third grader would draw. But it feels solid in her hand; weighty. A shiny, silver, gold-hilted, cross-guarded, beautiful sword with a fat ruby on the end.

"Sword!" Zelda cheers, and she slices a tree in half.

"Truly a grand and terrible instrument of war," says Patches.

"I don't know about 'grand,'" mutters Langston, "but terrible, sure."

"It should have a name that strikes fear in the hearts of your enemies," Patches continues. "As I now find myself something of a traveling bard, it would be my honor to christen it with a stirring sobriquet!"

"Sure," says Zelda. "Knock yourself out. Langston? You have offended my sword's honor, and I challenge you to a duel."

"What? No, I didn't."

"Foecutter!" shouts Patches. "No! Dreamcleaver!" The presidents toddle around on the mossy grass. Baby Warren G. Harding is chewing on the pizza hat.

"You said it isn't grand," Zelda reminds Langston as she slips out of her backpack. "Even though it's totally grand. Draw your sword, sir: I demand satisfaction."

"The Exsanguinator!"

"I just meant it's kind of . . . basic," says Langston, and Zelda gasps, albeit with a smile.

"How *dare* you. Prepare to be chopped."

"Chap-Chopper! No, ignore that. The Thankless Child!"

"'The Thankless Child'?"

"It's Shakespeare."

Langston is smiling now, too, just a little. She wants to see those teeth again, but it's better than nothing. Better than one of his placeholder smiles, subbing in for whatever genuine emotion ought to be on display.

He says, "Your sword looks like a giant emoji, is what I'm saying."

"The Mansprainer!"

"I'd like to see you do better!"

"I already have a sword. I don't need to imagine one."

"Then imagine a shield. You're gonna need it." She squares off against him, happy and weapon at the ready.

"Okay," says Langston. He draws his sword with his right hand and squints at his left. He doesn't have a shield. And then he does.

It's strange—the new objects never really *appear*. It's more like you remember they're there. Just now, Zelda remembers that Langston is carrying—was possibly always carrying—a plain steel shield strapped to his forearm and hand.

"See?" says Zelda. "Not so easy, is it?"

"What do you mean? This is a great shield."

"It's a logo for antivirus software."

Zelda takes a second to remember all the shields she's ever seen, and before long she has a shiny, star-spangled circle. It's a bit wobbly, though—she's holding it by a single metal handle like it's the lid of a trash can.

"Oh, nice one," Langston says. "The small central grip is an odd choice for a parma shield that size—did you mean to make more of a buckler?"

"Okay, dungeon master."

"Just trying to help."

"You can't confuse me with your nerd words!"

"*Nerd words.* You know you're the one who mentioned *Lord of the Rings* earlier, right?"

They crouch and circle each other a couple times, just to enhance the spectacle of it. Mugging and feinting.

"Whoop," says Zelda, raising her sword and sidestepping baby Eisenhower. "I could have timed this better. It does suddenly seem like too many babies."

"Look at that one," says Langston. "That's a lot of mustache."

"That's how you know it's Grover Cleveland."

Then, briefly, the babies give them an opening. Zelda and Langston charge forward at the same time, and their shields collide.

For a second, he's close. A long second. He smells like cedar. She feels the huff of his breath on her lips. The sound of it is the only sound she hears.

They separate with urgency and circle again. Langston grins

and beats his sword against his shield—*clang-clang*. Zelda sticks her tongue out and does the same.

"Nemeslice!" shouts Patches. "The Decapitán!"

"Beedoh!" says baby Franklin Delano Roosevelt.

By now, most of the babies have moved off to either side and plopped down in the grass to watch. Zelda catches Langston's eye.

They step together again, swords crossing like a kiss. She can see Langston's chest rising and falling, pulling at his shirt. Her own chest is rising and falling—they're both breathing way harder than their half-assed playacting calls for, and Zelda's heart is racing. They've drawn so close now—Langston's face reveals all its finely tuned features. His trim jaw, how it flares out as he clenches his teeth behind plum-colored lips. Those *eyelashes*—she wants to pull him closer, touch hers to his. His eyes, suddenly serious, seem to carry the weight of something more than play.

"This is becoming tedious!" Patches tells them.

Zelda backs off—it's too much, and all at once. But she thinks she sees what this is now, this thing she's started. They're flirt-fighting. That bit you get in the movies where two people—who are obviously into each other but pretend they're not—spar until one of them pins the other, and aggression slips away like the mask it always was, and they make out. They're flirt-fighting. She could stop it right now. If she wanted.

The cat shies away from baby Andrew Jackson. "I do question the wisdom of stirring the pot in this fashion, actually," he says. "Less surrealism and more realism is perhaps what's called for? For the time being, this is still a lucid dream."

"Oh yeah," says Zelda. She doesn't really want to talk about this right now. "Lucid dreams. You can take control of them, right?"

"Beedoh," FDR says again.

"What is he—?"

"I think he's trying to veto something."

Patches sighs. He continues stoically, as if his tail isn't being played with by Thomas Jefferson. "Lucid dreams are commonly thought to occur when a dreamer is closest to wakefulness. There are even those who hold that lucid dreams aren't true dreams at all, but instead a partially conscious state."

Zelda shrugs and twirls her sword. "So what I hear you saying is I'm on the edge of waking up already? I don't see a problem."

"Yes," says Patches. "The edge. The edge of a pool, say. And at a time when the dreamer *should* be surfacing and pulling herself onto solid ground, she is instead clinging to that edge. Clinging too long, until the edge feels to her like the only place to be. I fear she clings so long she will soon lose her grip, sinking slowly into the incoherent deep. The shifting, muddled waters of the subconscious. Do you see?"

"I see," says Langston. "Cats really don't like water, do they?"

"Quiet." Patches locks eyes with Zelda. "Do you *see*?"

Zelda pauses. "The dream is getting weirder," she says. "Because instead of getting closer to waking, I'm getting further away."

"I fear it's true."

"Or," offers Langston, "dreams are just like this. I've woken right up from dreams that are plenty strange. I've woken *because* they were strange."

"Taft, put that down," scolds Zelda. He's sucking on a rock. "*Taft.*"

"Perhaps. I am a poet," says Patches, "with a poet's interest in the cartography of dreams. That is all."

Well. Zelda's sword feels heavy in her hand. Langston's hangs limp. They stare, each holding the other's gaze, which isn't quite as electric as before. Patches has been a bit of a buzzkill.

After a moment, Langston says, "Do you want to get going?"

Doesn't she? Isn't she trying to rush to the end of the dream? Here her life has an actual ticking clock, but it's like she's asked the ambulance driver to circle the hospital a few times because one of the EMTs is cute.

So she intends to say yes, and surprises herself when she says something else entirely.

"Oho! Giving up, are you?" she taunts Langston. "Conceding defeat?"

Langston raises his eyebrows, then smirks.

"Coward!" Zelda calls. "Have at thee!"

Maybe Patches has killed the mood. Maybe Zelda's trying to force something that was never there.

But she sallies forth once again and swings her sword in a controlled and friendly arc, absolutely aiming for Langston's shield and nothing else. In the tradition of backyard sword fights everywhere, she means to wrap this up with some lively clanging before maybe throwing herself into a hammy death scene. She'll collapse into a beautiful tableau. Langston will bend over her; he'll say, *Oh, what have I done?*

Maybe he'll think of a way to bring her back to life.

That's the plan, anyway. But when Zelda strikes Langston's shield, it splits and crumples, and her sword comes a lot closer to doing him real harm than she'd like.

"Yaa! Langston? Was your shield always cardboard?"

He looks at it with alarm.

"I've made up my mind!" says Patches. "Zelda, your sword will be called Nerdslayer."

Something changes in Langston's posture. He closes up. He barely has what you'd call a shield anymore, but Langston hides behind it anyway and backpedals up a hill, a scabrous hill that's all loose shale and fallen branches with a dead tree on top. Zelda follows after him.

"Hey," she says. "Sorry about that."

He's still retreating. He's still retreating, and his ruined shield is growing larger, inflating like a life raft. He can't see her lower her sword, which suddenly feels soft in her hand.

"No, not 'Nerdslayer,'" says Patches. "Pool Noodle. No—Yoga Mat. Bouquet of Roses. Roll of Wrapping Paper. Zelda, I can't name it if you keep changing it."

"I'm not changing it!" Zelda shouts, frowning at the wrapping paper—no, feather duster—and wondering if that's true. Is she changing it? Did she change Langston's shield? It doesn't feel like she's in control, but what about her dream life ever made her think she'd have real control?

She chucks her sword aside—it's useless, insomuch as it's now a toilet brush—and tries to grab the lip of Langston's shield. To stop him. Comfort him.

"Hey, c'mon, Langston, it's me."

She can't control him, either. His shield is an actual life raft now, huge and yellow, and when he drags it back across a dead branch it pops. There's a tremendous *bang*, and both combatants are thrown backward onto their haunches.

"Ow," says Zelda, "my haunches."

She takes a moment to catch her breath, blow her hair out of her eyes. Her own shield is a big melting Popsicle. She only takes two bites and throws the rest away.

"Langston!" she calls. She can't actually see him—he's lying under a deflated life raft. "What the hell was that?" Patches joins her, pressing close to her shin. Charcoal clouds roll in. The landscape has forgotten what it was wearing and now looks as blasted and cold as a dead volcano. It has that manic look a place gets when the ground is brighter than the sky.

"That's never happened before," he says quietly, from beneath the raft. "I think . . . for a second I forgot it was fake?"

It was fake? Zelda had thought it felt real. Wait, what was he talking about?

She pulls the thick rubber blanket off of him. There he is, lying on his back in the shale, wincing and blinking like it's his first morning in a strange bed and he doesn't know where he is.

Zelda feels embarrassed. She feels ashamed. Possibly he's not even as into her as she thought. He probably would have teleported in to save *anyone* from a car crash. He probably imagines *all* the girls he meets in prom dresses.

He squints up at her. "I panicked," he says.

"Because . . . why? Do you think I'm going to hurt you?"

Langston shrugs. "Because I'm afraid of getting hurt."

Zelda studies his face. She isn't positive they're talking about the same thing. What she does see, if only for a moment, is another paper doll who's too quick to let the dream carry him away.

"You're just the same as all the people in town," she says plainly.

"I'm not!" he protests. Thunder cracks, and lightning pinballs around the sky. "You lost control, too, okay? How's your sword?"

She looks for it. There's a didgeridoo over by the big Popsicle—that's probably it.

"When I was a kid, I used to make a lot of cardboard shields," Langston says. "Duct-tape handles. I guess my mind wandered."

"Did you also play with a lot of yellow rubber life rafts?"

"Yeah, no," Langston says. "I don't know what that's about."

He smiles, a little. Zelda tries on a smile, too.

"I'm sorry," he tells her. "It's the dream. I swear I'm not really like this." Then he can't meet her eyes. "Actually . . ." he adds. "Actually, I'm afraid I might be exactly like this. But this place . . . Everything feels a little bigger, doesn't it? Everything's turned up. It's not real."

Most of the baby presidents have wandered out of sight. One of them's crying.

"Baby Harrison's running a fever," says Patches.

It's not real, Zelda repeats in her mind. *These big feelings.*

She holds out a hand and helps Langston up. His hand is just his hand. It doesn't have to mean anything that she's holding it.

Stars wink on in the dark. Scarcely a second passes before they begin to fall, dragging neon furrows, dividing up the sky.

ELEVEN

ZELDA LOOKS BACK NOW AND again, and her little town is always where she left it. Should she really still be able to see it? The jagged line of houses and buildings narrows until it's just a thin zipper between earth and sky, but not as thin as she thinks it ought to be.

To the blackened west (if there is a west), the landscape sweeps upward into a colossal rise—sharp ribs of dark stone, brutally thick, sheared to a crisp, flat top and crowned with gold where the sun burns aglow a thin vein of clouds.

"Look at this place," says Langston, breathless. Zelda feels strangely proud.

The trees around them are growing shorter, and lean. Scrappy little trees that grasp at stones. Each one makes a wiry birdcage of its branches. Huge, dreadful birds stare silently out at them.

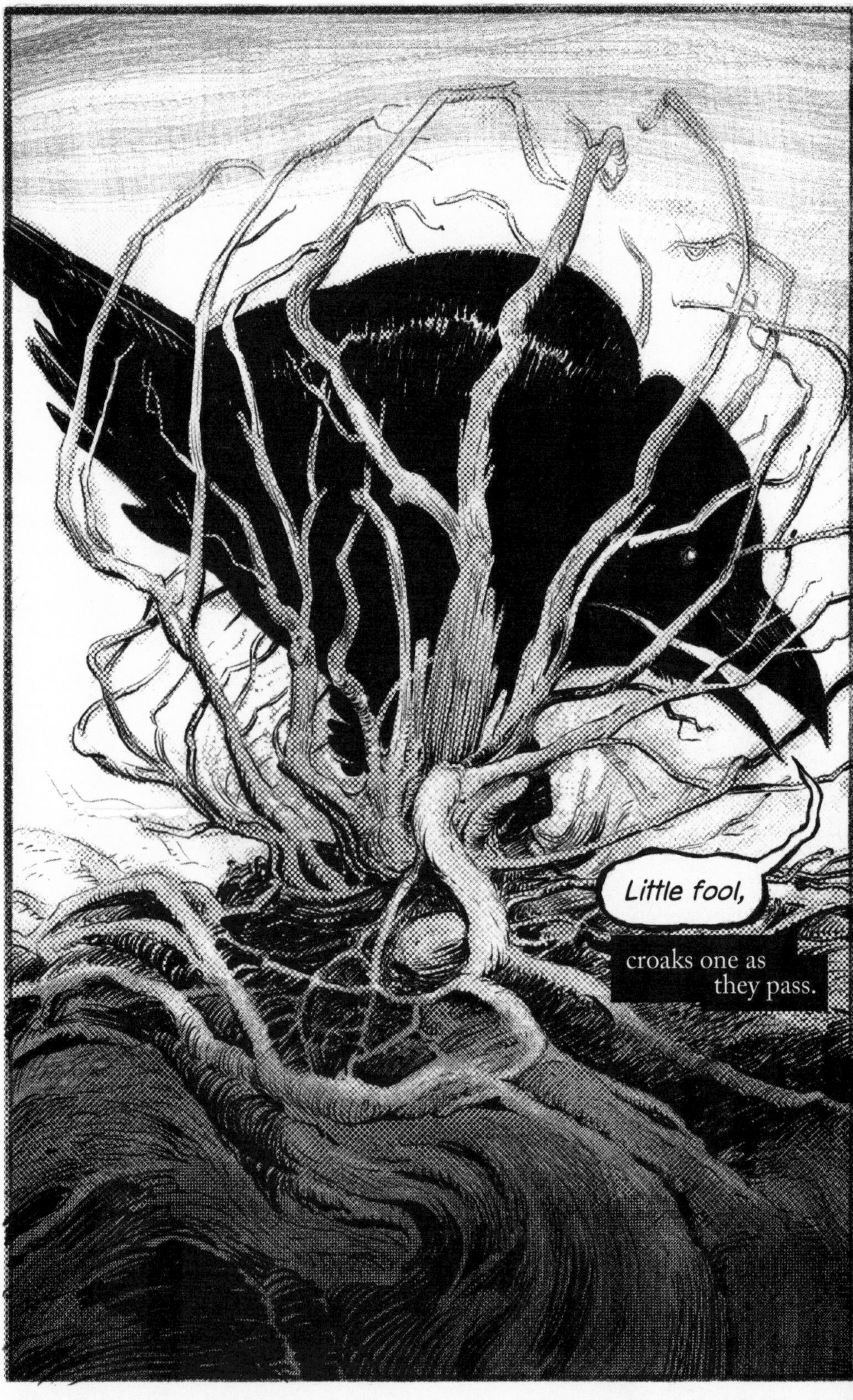
Little fool,
croaks one as they pass.

"Quiet," whispers Zelda.

It's cold comfort when even these meager trees give way to scrub—spiteful bushes of briar, fractals of thorn on top of thorn all the way down. It hurts to walk. Patches has to be carried. In time, the scrub turns to sterile tundra. It's as pink as a tongue.

The sky can't seem to decide what it wants. Zelda has wondered more than once about navigation, and the moment she thinks to steer by star-lines, she notices the star-lines aren't there anymore. Now all above her it's as teal green as the ocean. A massive blue cloud noses across the sky, slow as a whale.

She and Langston have barely said a word to each other since the sword fight. Patches is telling them stories from his life. Zelda's only half listening. Against the hum of his baritone, her anxious mind reels from one little fire to the next. How vast *is* this landscape? Does it go on just a little farther or for ten thousand miles? Why can't she wake? And if she's really so worried about waking, why was she trying so hard to kiss a boy?

She gasps. What if it's like *Sleeping Beauty*? And kissing Langston is the only way to get the dream to end?

But no, she glances sideways at him and reminds herself that none of this feels much like a children's story.

". . . and that is how I spent my sixth life," says Patches.

Except maybe the talking cat, Zelda thinks.

"My seventh life, now, that was *very* short. Ate a penny. And once my eighth life started, I was missing Zelda terribly—"

"*Aw*," says Zelda.

"—so I came home, and found her in her geography classroom yesterday morning. And the rest you know. I only get one more life after this one, so I'd like to settle down, maybe keep a blog where I review books I like. Do people still blog?"

"Not really," says Langston.

What it almost feels like, to Zelda, is the dream trying to lead her astray. Just as she starts feeling dissatisfied with her precious little town, a wholly original character runs across the street in front of her and falls into the bushes. And that would make sense if Langston's sudden appearance—and disappearance—hadn't been the apple that spoiled the barrel in the first place.

Zelda looks backward again, expecting her town to definitely be too distant now to see. It's still there, though. Like it's following her.

Anyway. The dream isn't some living thing. It doesn't have wants. If it *is* trying to lead her astray (and it isn't), it could only be because the dreamer herself doesn't really want to wake up. Right? And what a monstrous thought that would be. Impossible.

Meanwhile, the subtle slants and slopes of the earth have been for the last twenty minutes nudging Zelda and Langston closer together.

An unevenness beneath their feet happens to tip Zelda one way and Langston the other. They bump shoulders.

"Whoop," says Langston.

"Ha." Zelda's arm erupts with goose bumps. Which probably aren't as noticeable as she thinks they are, but still she weakly adds, "It's chilly."

"I wish I had a jacket I could think about offering you, selflessly," says Langston. "Or, like, a coat, a big fur coat."

Was that flirting? Are they flirting again? Or just friendliness?

"I have a fur coat," Patches says, "but I don't like to lend it out."

"Would you say you're *attached* to it?" Zelda asks, her voice getting too loud for this dismal landscape. She sounds like a car alarm. "Get it? *Attached?*"

"I get it and have gotten it, yes. Now I must suffer with it, like the flu."

"So to speak. But wait—so you'd have to *think* about offering me your jacket?" Zelda says to Langston. "Really?"

Langston's face is hard for her to read. A lot of things have been hard for her to read, lately. He says, "I just don't know if we're there yet. Plus if I let you wear my jacket, what would I use to cover mud puddles and whatnot?"

Zelda thinks. "In TV and movies, you always know a person cares about someone because of a jacket, or a blanket. Like, if a character falls asleep and another character covers them with a blanket? They are going to get married."

"*Exactly,*" says Langston. His eyes are playful. He adopts the kind of fake look of disinterest people use when they're haggling over a car they are definitely going to buy. "See, I just met you. We're nowhere near jackets and blankets yet."

Zelda laughs and breaks off from the pack a bit. *Thank you for the successful conversation*, she wants to say. *Let's wrap it up before it gets to be too much again.* Never has she thought so hard over every word she says and every word said to her. It's like she's speaking a new language, one of the Romance languages, and every sentence has to pass through a translator and two fact-checkers on its way out the door. It all feels a little jovial anyway, considering the setting.

The way this place looks, they might as well be walking across a colossal tombstone. Maybe there was birdsong, before. There might have been the buzz of bugs, but she only notices them now in their absence. It is perfectly, perfectly quiet. The sky is going gray again. Gray but for these black ribbons running through it in the distance, like ink suspended in water. The Northern Lights in photonegative.

It *is* chilly here, and smells like a matchstick. The ground is dotted with smooth pebbles, strange little swirling stones. Zelda imagines that one of them looks like the shell of some crustacean, and then she sees it's so. As if she made it so.

It wobbles up onto a bristling clutch of awful legs and dodders past them. Patches hisses at it. Then more movement catches Zelda's eye.

"Langston?"

"Yeah, I see 'em."

They're everywhere now—nautilus shells, claws, and pincers. Some the size of softballs, some big as spare tires. Patches flicks his tail and darts about until Zelda scoops him up again.

"Foul lobsters," Patches mutters.

They clack and scuttle, teetering and top-heavy, so many legs, each one like a team of pallbearers carrying its own curling coffin. An unbroken line of them stretches all the way to the horizon, where the black borealis twists and roils.

Langston has his sword out, and he and Zelda mince around until it's clear that the horrid things don't mean any harm; they don't even seem to know the three of them are there. Now Zelda's embarrassed for dreaming up anything this revolting—it's like she's been caught picking her nose.

Langston says, "You win; you're definitely the dreamer."

"I probably just went to the beach in real life," Zelda mumbles. "Or ate crab recently. Or something."

Then, *CRACK*. The sound whiplashes through the landscape.

The crustaceans all curl up like roly-polies and dart in different directions. The three travelers turn every which way, trying to see what's spooked them.

The thunder echoes and winds down.

And there's a shape, far off in the borealis: a teeming many-legged thing.

"Another weird crab," says Zelda.

"But big," says Langston.

"And flying," adds Patches.

Dark and writhing, it barrels toward them through the sky.

Langston steps in front of Zelda and Patches and raises his trembling sword. Which is sweet. Stupid, too. Zelda cranes her neck over his shoulder and squints.

What appeared to be one gargantuan thing with too many legs is now looking more like four merely Very Big things with a slightly more sensible number of legs.

"What is it?" Langston whispers. Zelda raises her hands to her eyes and encircles them like binoculars. The approaching things, magnified, come into shimmering focus.

"It's four horses," she says.

Four dusky horses, wispy of body with contrails of dark vapor, gallop madly through the ether. Each horse bears a rider, each rider bears a fierce countenance—like a William Blake painting come to life. But not exactly like a William Blake painting.

"Are they wearing gym shorts?" asks Zelda.

They're huge—titans. Titans wearing gym shorts. The lead horseman holds aloft a dodgeball like he wants to crown someone with it, and all the while the wind flaps his mustache like the wings of a terrible eagle.

"It's . . . *gym teachers!*" says Langston.

Zelda squints. "Okay, well, could be worse."

"How? *How* could it be worse? If we run right now, I don't think they'll follow us into town."

The horsemen are drawing near. Langston is still in front, and he's obviously regretting his position like a kid at the top of a water slide. Zelda grabs his wrist and pulls him along after her as the horseman with the mustache unfurls his ropy arm and lets the dodgeball fly. It rockets down with an eerie whistle and, *BOOM*, craters the ground where they'd been standing.

Now a hundred balls rain down, a meteor shower of organ-red rubber. *WHAM*, and the air's peppered with loose stone. *WHAM*, the sound clatters through the earth and knocks Zelda's knees, rattles her bones. She stumbles, and leans on Langston's arm, and looks up just in time.

"Duck!" she screams, and pulls him down as a wailing red comet soars overhead. The ground shudders them both onto their backsides.

Then there's a lull. The dark horses have galloped overhead and begun to recede, but now they trace a sharp curve as they turn to make another pass.

"GET READY, LADIES!" howls one of the gym teachers.

Patches rights himself and turns to face them. "Two of us are gentlemen!" he answers.

"They know, Patches," says Zelda as she scrambles to her feet.

"Are you certain? People can't always tell with cats."

"Are you okay?" Zelda asks Langston.

"*Gym*," he says. He looks like he swallowed a bug. "God. What is even the point of it?"

The horsemen have really caught them out in the open. This

tundra has no cover anywhere Zelda can see. "I don't know," she says distractedly. "A little fun and games in the middle of the school day, I guess?"

Langston looks at her like she just defended waterboarding.

The gym teachers and their horses have finished their bank, and now they're stampeding back toward them.

"STOW YOUR KNITTING, LADIES: HERE COMES THE HAMMER!"

"I am a tomcat!" Patches calls to the swiftly approaching disaster. "And the boy is a boy!"

"They know you're not a lady, Patches!" Zelda adds. "It's meant to be insulting."

"Oh, good lord." Patches frowns. "How is that insulting?" He turns and shouts it to the horsemen: *"How is that insulting?"*

The horses' manes and tails billow all around as they snort and thrash, but the gym teachers rein in their steeds and pause.

The leftmost gym teacher answers, "IT MEANS YOU'RE A BUNCH OF SISSY LITTLE—"

"WHOA!—WHOA THERE, DALE," says the lead horseman with his hand raised. "WATCH WHAT YOU SAY."

"YEAH, MAN—YOU DON'T WANT TO END UP LIKE KEVIN," says the heavyset one. The other coaches shake their heads at the sad memory of what happened to Kevin.

"ADMINISTRATIVE *LEAVE*," the leader explains, with a grimace like it's the worst phrase he's ever heard. They all exchange glances.

"What's happening?" whispers Langston.

"My friends're excused today!" shouts Zelda. "They have doctors' notes! And I'm . . . having female troubles!"

The gym teachers blanch. One of them almost falls off his horse. They're obviously terrified of female troubles.

"WELL . . ." says the horseman in sweatpants. "I WANT TO SEE THOSE NOTES!"

They all sit a little taller in their saddles when he says this, and nod. The sky flashes. One of them toots his whistle.

"Imagine up a couple of notes," Zelda mutters. "Quick!"

"Um," says Langston. He's breathing kind of hard. "Right. A note. A doctor's note—"

"Hurry!"

"I can't . . . I can't even remember what one looks like," Langston says. "My mind's a blank."

Patches pulls his out of nowhere and pushes it forward across the rocks. It flutters and sails up and into the lead gym teacher's hand. He stares at it while the other horsemen lean in. The black aurora blooms behind them.

"OFFICE OF TOM GREENBLATT, M.D. . . . EAR, NOSE, AND THROAT, BLAH BLAH *BLAH* . . . HERE WE GO: PATCHES IS TO BE EXCUSED FROM GYM ON ACCOUNT OF HE IS A CAT."

"HMM," says another teacher with a nod. They give Patches a quick inspection.

"YEP," says a third.

"WELL, WHERE'S *HIS*, THEN?" shouts Sweatpants.

Langston has something in his outstretched hand now, and this, too, flaps and flutters upward into the burly hand of the horseman.

He reads, "DR. . . . SICKWELL?"

Zelda winces and starts looking for an exit strategy.

"WHAT IS THIS SQUIGGLY BIT HERE?"

"I THINK IT'S SUPPOSED TO BE THAT MEDICAL SYMBOL? WITH THE SNAKES."

"WAITAMINUTE—'MICHAEL IS TO BE EXCUSED BECAUSE HE HURT HIS . . . *FACEBONE*'?"

Zelda screws up her eyes at Langston. "That's not even your *name*," she tells him.

"Can't do improv under pressure," says Langston through gritted teeth.

"FORGERY!" the gym teachers bellow, and lift high their dodge-balls, and kick their horses' haunches. "FORRRGERRREEEE!"

"Duck!" screams Langston as the first missile comes flying.

Zelda snatches up the cat and pulls Langston across a barren embankment as impacts boom all around. They leap off a rocky shelf, Zelda cradling Patches to cushion him as he looks backward over her shoulder.

"Behind us!" Patches calls. "Shelter!"

Zelda turns around and squints against the dust—the rocky shelf is an overhang, so she drags Langston toward it until a dodgeball cracks the earth at their heels. They tumble forward and skid across the hard ground. Clambering to their feet, pant legs torn and palms skinned, Zelda looks frantically for Patches as she chokes on dirt.

"Here!" says the cat, already safe beneath the overhang. "Hurry!"

"Fun and games, huh?" Langston says as he wobbles onward.

"Well, obviously not this specifically!"

They scramble toward the shelter as more balls shatter the ground—a high-bouncing tumult of rubber and flint and shale. Finally, they duck and tuck close their bodies, and in the tiny hollow they wait out the storm.

"WHERE?" calls one of the riders. "*WHERE?!*"

Zelda can scarcely see three feet beyond the mouth of the cave, for all the soot in the air.

"A proper smoke screen they've made us," whispers Patches. Then he sneezes a little cat sneeze.

Langston's arm is pressing against Zelda's. It has to be, really. She feels the heat of it against her. More important, their pinkie fingers are touching. There. All of time and space is flooding through her from that warm little spot on her finger. She could just about pass out. The earth shudders, and so does she.

Langston is breathing kind of hard. He says, "This is nice."

"I'm having a really good time," Zelda tells him.

"This is exactly the kind of quality time that all my first dates can expect," says Langston. Then he seems to regret it. "I didn't mean—"

"You two would obviously prefer to be alone," says Patches. "I'll just step out into the hullabaloo, shall I?"

Zelda hugs the cat close and shushes him.

The dodgeball impacts feel farther away now, and quieter.

There's a voice. Zelda senses it's been speaking for some time, but only now have the surroundings gotten quiet enough to hear it. It's the voice of God again. The voice of God is back.

"*I know you feel safe in there,*" says the voice, as if from a great distance. "*Peaceful. You're taking time to rest up, and that's good.*"

"Are you guys hearing this?" Zelda whispers.

"*But you have to come out of it,*" says the voice. "*Soon. It's time to fight.*"

The three of them are being utterly silent, holding their breath, but God or whoever seems to have said his piece. It's quiet.

"I heard a voice," says Patches. "I could understand little of what it said."

"I didn't hear anything," says Langston.

"Okay," says Zelda. "I think we should make a run for it."

"What?" Langston chirps.

He still has a two-handed grip on his sword, and he's holding it out in front of him like a divining rod.

"Don't you think we should go?" Zelda rises on creaky legs and pokes her neck out to take a peek at the sky. "Before all the dust clears?"

"Might I suggest we wait until we're certain that Death, War, Famine, and Athlete's Foot have left?" asks Patches.

"I think maybe they already have," says Zelda.

Then a voice booms behind them. "I SEE YOU!"

"CUTTING CLASS!"

"PLAYING HOOKY!"

"I AM GOING TO BUILD YOU SO MUCH CHARACTER!"

Zelda cringes and shunts her self back into the cave. The gym teachers orbit around, one after another, and stop to face the entrance. Hovering like horseflies in the distance.

"Sorry," Zelda hisses.

"We should have stayed in the cave," says Langston.

That stung. "I know," says Zelda. "A voice said . . . I shouldn't have listened to the voice. I don't even know who it is. I'm *sorry*."

"So . . . I guess we're going to find out what happens when you die in a dream."

"In this sense, I suspect dreams are like tarot," says Patches. "The Death card need not denote real death, but rather a change in one's life: the end of one phase and the beginning of another. It could mean waking."

"Or the opposite," Zelda mutters. "It could mean sinking deeper into the pool." It's not a card she feels like turning.

Now the hooves churn the air; now the riders raise their ammunition. Zelda gets up into a crouch. She huffs and puffs through clenched teeth, trying to psych herself into the bad decision she's about to make. The lead horseman blows a pterodactyl shriek through his silver whistle, and the man on his left whips his arm. Here comes the ball, big as a washing machine.

Zelda runs out to meet it. Langston drops his sword and reaches for her, too late.

"Zelda!"

She raises her hands, plants her feet, grimaces and sighs.

"Fun and games."

And the ball pounds against her palms. There's a jolt in each fingertip that chatters her teeth and courses through her like electric eels. She has it, and the force of it skids her backward as her heels rake the earth. She has it in her trembling hands. There's a high trill as the dust settles around her.

There's a horseman without a ball now, and he looks like he's about to throw up.

"I . . . I'm out," he says; then—*POP!*—he's gone.

The leader's face is pink and sweaty, like a hot dog. He blows that furious whistle again as Zelda runs away from the cave. The balls rain down.

The one in Zelda's hands is so big, so heavy. *No it isn't*, she tells herself as she runs, *it's only a dream*; and the ball feels manageable for just a few seconds before sinking in her arms again.

BANG BANG BANG BANG BANG, and the ground begins to break into immense pieces that pull apart. "Bats!" Zelda shouts, so a flock of vampire bats swarms from one of these new fissures, clouding her from view. "Tornado!" she screams, but now she's gotten her tornado too close to her bats and that's a whole mess. Still, a dodge-ball that should have had Zelda's name on it hits the twister instead and makes a bat-covered U-turn back at the horseman who threw it.

"YEEEEK!" he squeaks. He barely dodges it in time.

Langston will come out of the cave any second to help, Zelda figures. He might not be much for premeditated heroism, but he once ran into traffic when he thought she was in danger, so. *Any second now.*

Zelda leaps over a brand-new cliff, lands ball-first on the ground below, and bounces into sort of a nice roll. It looks like she meant to do it, and she's briefly proud until she sees the heavier gym teacher right above her. He throws, she throws, and the balls collide in midair.

And apparently, when two dodgeballs collide, they turn into confetti and bees? Zelda's foggy on the rules, but that was definitely what happened.

The whistle toots. "BEE BREAK!" shouts the leader.

The three remaining gym teachers turn around in their saddles and cover their eyes with their hands. Zelda doesn't know what she's supposed to do.

"Zelda!" calls Langston from the cave. "Bee break! You gotta go back to base!"

Zelda runs, frowning. "I don't know as much about dodgeball as I thought I did," she mutters.

She's nearly to the cave when Patches yells, "DUCK!" and she slides on her thigh across the scaly ground as a ball sails overhead. Apparently, bee break is over. She catches another ball off the first bounce and sends it back at the horseman, but misses.

Whenever you're ready, Langston.

The fault lines of this place continue to grind like teeth, mak-ing a low groan Zelda can feel in her chest. Wide walls of earth are rising ahead of her—short, then taller, and taller, stair-stepped like gym bleachers, so Zelda climbs. The dodgeballs ricochet in strange ways off all these planes and corners, and on the eighth step one of them bounces right into Zelda's hands. She leaps off the top and hits a horse in the face with it.

"CHAD!" shouts the leader. Chad vanishes quite slowly, beginning with his tennis shoes, and ending with his terry-cloth headband, which remains some time after the rest of him has gone.

"Feather feather feather feather," whispers Zelda as she falls. Perhaps she doesn't hit the ground *quite* as hard as she would have otherwise.

"Yeah!" Langston shouts at the horseman from some distance away. "You're all having female troubles now, ain'tcha?" He grabs a nearby ball and gives it a throw that he probably hopes afterward nobody noticed.

Here he comes, thinks Zelda. *Good.*

Then Langston says, "Whoop—" and hunches back toward the cave as the balls come.

Oh well.

There's a high noise squealing, not from the leader's whistle, but from every sweating pore of his horrible, ham-faced, furious features. So many balls—where are they coming from? Zelda knows the men are conjuring them out of thin air, but she never sees it happen—she's always watching the wrong hand.

All the world is cracking open. Shards and shale and the sky looks like a black eye. She can't take it anymore, and all things considered, it's not the best time to hide in a cave, but that's what Zelda does—she tucks herself in with Patches and Langston and hugs her bleeding leg.

The two horsemen close ranks like a firing squad outside the cave. They take their time—they won't miss.

Patches rubs against her. "Sorry," Zelda says. "I tried."

"*You* . . . were amazing," says Langston.

She smiles and lifts her chin. He's looking her way. She's felt the warm light of his eyes before but this is something else entirely. A reverence. Like she isn't just his girl but his hero, too. Their pinkie fingers find each other again in the dark, and intertwine, and all the breath in him escapes with a shivering sigh. They hold each other's gazes long enough to know what's going to happen—it might be their only chance. She almost tells him she's never really been kissed. *Nah, don't spook him*, she thinks as they both incline ever so slightly inward. *He's not a first-man-on-the-moon kind of guy.* Their noses touch.

From the lip of the cave, Patches shouts:

"DUCK!"

Zelda jumps and hits her head and glares at him. "Duck?! Duck *where?* Oh," she says, because a colossal duck has just toddled into view, and eaten the gym teachers, and waddled off into history.

The sky clears. With tumultuous grinding and glacial slowness, the ground settles back into place.

"Did either of you make that?" asks Zelda. "The duck, I mean."

"I feel foolish admitting I did not," says Patches. "In retrospect, it's an obvious solution."

"It just . . . It ate them," says Langston.

"She," says Patches.

"What?"

"Not 'it'—'she.' That was a lady mallard; the males have green heads."

"Oh."

They watch it awhile. Finally, Patches sniffs and turns.

"So. Should we get going?"

TWELVE

THEY CAN'T SAY FOR CERTAIN which direction they'd been walking. In the blasted tundra, there aren't any landmarks, and now there's a fog rolling in.

But they're expecting the way ahead to get weirder. They have a spirited debate over whether that's more likely to be where the duck came from or where it's heading. Finally, there's a two-to-one vote in favor of following the duck.

"Probably walking right back toward town," Langston grumbles. "Fine with me."

She wants to kiss the corner of his grumbly mouth. Where it buttons to his cheek—she wants to kiss it. Like an itch that needs scratching, like a bell that's never been rung. Instead she takes deep breaths and says *what is wrong with me?* in her head with every exhale.

She needs to think this through, doesn't she? Before she rushes into anything. Like, there's a question of agency. Freedom. She tries to imagine how she'd feel if their roles were reversed—if Langston were the dreamer and Zelda just a dream girl, made to love him. Incapable of *not* loving him, maybe. It would be about the dirtiest trick she could think of, surely. Surely, it would. She knows this, but she can't feel it.

The clouds are alive, here, and they're swishing about in the upper atmosphere, eating one another.

She knows these might only be excuses for the mistakes she's already decided to make, but she thinks she could make her peace with it. If their roles were reversed. A dream person is not quite a puppet, even if he is a figment of your imagination. A dream doesn't have to do everything you want it to. *Clearly, it doesn't*, she thinks as she stubs the same toe for the third time.

Just to prove her point, Zelda thinks, *Look at me, Langston!* It's a front-page headline in her mind, a neon sign, the brassy name of a new hit musical.

And he turns and looks at her, right away. Oops. Now they're staring at each other.

"Hey," he says.

"Hello."

She expects to see that same reverence in his eyes. Or maybe an anxious, *we should talk about what happened in the cave* kind of thing. But this looks more like concern?

He says, "How are you feeling, after . . ."

She got pretty scraped up playing dodgeball. But she'd forgotten about that. She'd swear all her cuts and bruises are only galloping back now because Langston reminded her to be hurt.

"We should have a plan. For if one of us gets really injured. Someone might have to go back to town, bring help—"

"No one's going to get injured. It's fine! I'm fine."

Langston half laughs and shakes his head and says, "You're such a *positive* person."

"That sounds like a compliment, but I'm not sure."

Langston says, "Say, Zelda, how do you feel about gym teachers? *Oh, gee, Langston, they're great!* What about cannibals, Zelda? *Hey, as long as you enjoy other people, right?*"

"I just think the average gym teacher is probably a nice person who likes sports!" says Zelda. "And I think it's *weird* that every book, TV show, and movie acts like it's a . . . given that they're all worse than ten Hitlers."

Patches agrees. "It is almost as if the sort of child who will one day make up stories for a living is also the sort who is disappointing at field hockey."

Langston sighs. "Yeah. You just . . . spend the whole school day trying to keep your head down, do your work, not get in anyone's way . . . Then, heads-up! Here comes the ball! And now thirty guys are looking at you like your entire value as a person depends on what you do with it when it gets there."

Zelda, for her part, has a vague sense that whenever she dreams about sports, she tends to be better at them than she is in real life. That would explain her dodgeball performance, she thinks. Because apart from needing that *duck ex machina* at the end, she thought she did pretty well. Considering that any one of those horsemen looked like someone Thor should be wrestling in a comic book.

"So what I'm saying," says Langston, "is thank goodness for *you* back there, because . . . if it had been all on me . . ."

He shakes his head at the thought of it.

"Even if it *was* hard to watch," he adds.

"What? Hard to watch? I assumed I looked amazing. Like a valkyrie. Playing dodgeball at the valkyrie company picnic."

He laughs. "How you *looked* while you did what you did was . . . not the issue. Watching you *do* it, seeing you almost *die* fifty times . . . that was rough."

Okay, Zelda thinks. *Better.*

"That's how it is for us *amazing heroes*," Zelda says in a tone she hopes will convey a kind of screwball modesty. All her instincts, in fact, are telling her to play it down, prune back her pride, let Langston know what a big deal it wasn't. Screw her instincts. "We're always living on the edge, making our loved ones worry. I have a wife, and every time I put on my badge and walk out the door, she wonders, *Is today the day Zelda gets hit by a dodgeball?*"

Langston's smiling, at least. "Uh-huh."

"But hey, she knew what she was getting into when she married Sergeant Punch of Dream Force."

"Your name is Zelda Punch?"

"It's my wife's name. I took it when we got married."

Actually, Zelda cannot, just this moment, remember what her actual last name is. *Weird.*

"Anyway. Me and the duck handled that one. Maybe you'll handle the next one."

"Let us then fervently hope," says Patches, "that there is no 'next one.'"

"Nobody *wants* a next one; that's not what I'm saying. Just that maybe the next will play to one of Langston's strengths, like . . ."

Oh, damn, Zelda thinks. *I don't know how to finish my sentence.*

Langston finishes it for her. "Like sudoku. Oh man, what if there's a giant sudoku. And Zelda's about to put a nine where a nine shouldn't go, and I step up all like, *Zelda. I got this.*"

Zelda laughs. She hopes it's okay to laugh. She checks in with Langston, and he's smiling, so that's good. Not laughing, though.

Langston says, "I couldn't get up. You just ran right out there. Toward the danger, you ran. You want to hear what my plan was? The best I could manage? I was going to try to . . ." He mimes a stabbing thrust. ". . . pop the dodgeball with my sword."

And what would have happened then? Zelda wonders. *Would the coach have been out? Or would Langston? Would he have faded away? Or would the coaches have blown their whistles, called for a sword siesta or whatever: everyone spin around three times and back to base?* She really wished she could look up the rules for dodgeball.

"Whatever. You are being way too hard on yourself," she tells him. "I don't think a person ever knows what they're gonna do until they do it. Back in town? You ran out into traffic to save me."

At this, he's quiet. Zelda and Patches share a look.

"I just can't help thinking," says Langston, "that maybe giant gym teachers were a challenge *I* was supposed to face."

Even Patches recognizes this subject is best left alone. Zelda glances at Langston, then keeps her eyes on the road.

Anyway, she hates all these mixed feelings. Hadn't she saved them? She'd at least bought them some time until the duck showed up. Speaking of which:

"We need a new word of warning!" says Zelda, too loud, like she's trying to change the subject.

"A what?"

"A new word of warning. We can't shout *duck* anymore; it's confusing."

"Oh, right, because of . . ."

"Yeah."

They think a moment.

"CROUCH!" suggests Patches.

"*SQUAT!*" screams Zelda.

"*STOOOOOOOOP!*"

"Wait," says Langston. "Shh."

He's stopped and turned, and now he's squinting pointlessly at the horizon. As if you could sharpen your gaze enough to cut through all this fog. As if there'd be anything to see on the other side of it, if you could. Zelda suspects all this misty distance serves a purpose. Like certain video games—there isn't enough memory to render those places until you get there.

"Are we having a moment of silence?" asks Patches. "Should I be thinking about the troops?"

"I thought I heard something," Langston explains. "At first I figured it was the duck, but . . . it was like a *honky-honky-honky* sound."

"A what?" asks Zelda.

"A . . . sound like . . . *honky-honky*. Like that."

"Two *honkies* or three?" says Patches. "Be specific."

"Like a continuous stream of *honkies*."

Zelda laughs and remembers the babies. "What do you call every US president except Obama?"

"Anyway, I don't hear it anymore."

"A continuous stream of *honkies!*" Zelda answers herself. "You know? Guys?"

"Just the dream playing tricks on me, probably."

"Guys? Did you hear what I—"

"We heard," says Patches.

The sky loses its gray and starts to blossom slowly with color. It's very pretty, the sky, but too low—they keep bonking their heads on it. By the time it's darkened to night, the sky is so low they have to hunch to get underneath.

"Stoop," says Patches.

"Crouch," answers Zelda.

"Squat."

"Maybe . . ." Langston says, getting down on his knees to look up at the cosmos that is just brushing his nose. "Maybe the universe is a balloon? And we're inside it as it's deflating?" He takes his notebook out and scribbles something in it.

"Seems worrisome," says Zelda.

Patches says,

> *"How now, that this celestial sphere*
> *was once up there,*
> *but now, down here?"*

"Sure," says Zelda.

"It wasn't one of my better poems," Patches says.

"What do you mean?" says Zelda. "It was great."

"Just doggerel, really."

"Or catterel?" says Zelda. "Patches, did you hear me? *Cat*-terel?"

"I heard."

They're worn-out, anyway. The stars are on their faces.

"We could stop and rest. Maybe the sky will be higher in the morning," says Langston.

"No!" Zelda groans. "No rest. Let's keep going—we could be close to the edge."

Langston shrugs and makes an apologetic face. "I'm tired," he says.

And I may be slowly dying, she thinks. *Remember?*

"We don't have time to be tired," she says tiredly.

Anyway, the cat is already asleep.

"Eugh. *Fine.*"

They sit. They're close. Not as close as in the cave, but still. Langston looks like he thinks he ought to say something, but doesn't know what. Maybe he's wondering if that almost-kiss in the cave was a *we're about to die* special occasion or if it's something he's supposed to give another try. He probably wants to know if there's some word he can say—a spell to bring the magic back. He looks lost.

She doesn't feel like a good-night kiss, anyway.

Oh, who is she kidding? She totally does.

He looks beautiful in this purple half-light, all soft edges and steep curves. They're both lying down now, more or less—not lying *together*, exactly, but it's suggestive. He's propped up on one nicely shaped elbow. She's heard you can pinch a person on their elbow— hard as you like—and you'll never make them feel any pain. She bets she can pinch Langston's elbow and make him feel it all over his body.

The way he's looking at her, it makes *her* feel more real, too. Almost like she wouldn't be real without him.

She doesn't like *that*—or rather, she likes the way it makes her feel as long as she doesn't have to think about it. But she can't stop thinking about it. So she'll make him stop looking at her. She'll make him close his eyes. She'll bring her face so close to his, and they'll touch, and taste, and feel their way in the dark.

She moves, just barely moves, toward him.

"There's something I need to tell you," he says, and she stops. *No. No words.*

"Back in town, when you were almost hit by that car . . ." he says, and his voice sounds like something he has to wring out of him. There's something he needs to tell her, but he doesn't want to. "I didn't save you, because you didn't need saving. But also . . . I didn't save you because I hesitated."

He shifts just a little bit away from her, and Zelda feels herself becoming his mirror. No longer tensing forward, she settles backward instead.

Dammit.

"I found myself on that street corner," Langston continues. "I don't even remember what I was doing before it happened. I saw you, and the car, and I thought, *I have to move.* And I didn't move. I wasted a second shouting, 'Look out!' I wasted another, until I swear I could tell the danger had passed, and only then did I run. And stumbled. Right past you and into the bushes."

Well, Zelda thinks, *so what?* "You didn't even know who I was."

"I knew *exactly* who you were. I think I've known you my whole life."

He isn't looking at her anymore. He hasn't been able to meet her eyes since his confession started, so in that monkey's-paw fashion, Zelda has gotten exactly what she thought she wanted.

Patches is purring in his sleep. The night is still slowly descending, pushing out the day. A bedsheet that's been unfurled over the earth. It'll be on them soon.

"I'm sorry this bothers you," says Zelda. Her own voice sounds so soft in her ears. "It doesn't change anything. Let's get some rest—we can talk about it tomorrow if you want to."

"Yeah. Okay."

"Good night," Zelda says.

I'll kiss you in the morning.

"Good night."

"Not even tired," she whispers, before falling asleep.

The dark sky covers her like a blanket.

We fall asleep, and we fall awake.

Zelda is asleep for a second—not even a second—when she awakens with a twitch.

Maybe you know this kind of twitch. On the edge of sleep, we relax our hold—we fall. Sometimes when we fall we dream we fall, and in an instant we're awake again. Falling always takes you out of a dream.

Zelda is asleep for a second—not even a second—when she jerks, and opens an eye, and she's back in her yellow house again.

She's back in town.

THIRTEEN

HER HEART CLENCHES.

She closes her eyes again and thinks, *No. NO. I didn't fall asleep. I'm just resting my eyes. I'm still in the tundra, I'm still in the tundra.* She's falling. She bats her eyes. In her stuttering sight, she sees darkness, bright bedroom, darkness, and bedroom again. She tries to grab hold of the darkness and force herself up out of the pool of sleep.

She can't move.

Her eyes are open. Oh God, she's in her house. She's looking up at her bedroom ceiling. She can hear; she can see. But she can't move.

It's just sleep paralysis, she reminds herself as cold fear floods her body. *This is normal, you've had this before, a lot of people have this. It only lasts a few seconds. Move your finger. Just your finger—there. Then your hand, then your arm, then everything else, and . . .*

Her body returns to her. She rises up out of bed, gasping for air.

Every time she falls asleep, she wakens in her own bedroom.

She's never realized before. Normally, she goes to sleep in her own bedroom, too, so there was never any reason to notice. But just now—and yesterday, in class, right?—she fell asleep and awoke again under the plaster constellations of her bedroom ceiling.

She's abandoned them. Patches and Langston.

"Take me back!" she whispers. "This isn't real. Anything can happen. Put me back on the tundra with Langston and Patches . . . *now!*"

Nothing.

She tries to remember the feel of it, when Langston and she were forcing the impossible to happen, and it was all fun and games. "Now!" she says again, but she's still in her room.

Mere hours ago, the dream gave them swords and shields and bicycles and tiny helicopters. When none of it mattered, it was easy.

Sort of. The bicycle disappeared. The sword went soft, and the shield inflated and burst. She has to get back for real, and make it stick. But how?

Maybe there's still a wizard in her sitting room!

She nearly tumbles downstairs, sees the great big ludicrous cardboard door hanging there by the picture window. She runs up and pounds on it. Then listens. Listens for the sound of feet, or humming, or clarinet music. *Please be there*, she thinks at the wizard's door.

Then the wizard himself steps into the sitting room from her own kitchen.

"Erx!" shouts Zelda.

"Nothing!" he shouts back, spitting crackers.

He has an armful of boxes and bags and jars. "You're still here!" Zelda cheers. "Why were you in my kitchen? Are you stealing food?"

"I was just ..." says the wizard. "You see ... in the Forest of Hands and Feet it is difficult to get what one would classify as 'snacks,' and—"

"You know what? I don't care. Take whatever you want." Now they've each taken things from the other, she thinks. "But Erx! I fell asleep out there and woke up back here! Patches and Langston are, like, a day's walk away! How do I get back?"

"Oh. Um. Hmm. An interesting question."

"Yeah. You're a wizard—can you just ... zap me there?"

Erx crosses the room, opens his front door, tosses the snacks into his foyer. It sets the correct tone—if your wizard is going to be holding a bag, you want it to be velvet and full of mysteries. You don't want it to say FUN SIZE on the side next to a cartoon cheetah.

He says, "What do you suppose it means to be a wizard, here, where even the milkman can sprout wings and fly? When every pencil pusher can turn lead into gold. I have been asking myself this very question."

Zelda sympathizes, even as she feels she has rather a more immediate crisis on her hands. "Is it a depressing, *I need snacks* kind of question?" she asks.

"It is." Erx folds his hands and turns a tender eye toward her. And it is tender. Before, Zelda would have told you Erx has a face that's cold and impassive. But that's wrong—it's just subtle. He only has to twitch one stony brow for it to fall on you like an avalanche.

"Zelda," he says, "you have been swimming very much against the current of this dream, I think."

"I'm gonna drive very much against the current in a second," she answers, looking out the window. "You think I could steal a car?"

"Hmm."

"This dream current totally wants me back in town, doesn't it? Why is that? I swear Langston suggests it every five minutes."

"Perhaps. But instead of fighting against it, I suggest . . . following its current and gently steering. Relax. Let it carry you—just don't get carried away."

"Are you saying, 'go with the flow'? Is that what the ancient wizard is telling me?"

The look on his face tells her maybe even ancient people don't appreciate being called "ancient."

"Sorry," she says. "I'm worked up. What . . . what are you trying to say?"

He steps inside his front door and reaches for the knob. "I'm merely reminding you," he tells her, "of what you had entirely forgotten: that there is a door beneath the stairs behind you. Isn't that funny? To forget a whole door in your own house, and all that awaits you behind it."

The hairs stand up on the back of her neck.

"I'll be taking *my* door with me," says Erx. "Thank you for the snacks. And thank you for not attacking when you discovered an intruder in your home, and killing me accidentally, with all the character development and soul-searching that would imply."

He closes his door, which proceeds to fold in half, and in half again, and so on until it has either vanished, or has folded too small to see, or both. Her sitting room is an ordinary sitting room again.

But what about her stairs?

She thinks about what Erx said. *Relax. Don't fight, just gently steer. The wizard said there's a door, so obviously—*

There's a door. Her mind wants to object, but she steers into it and reminds herself that of course there's a door; there was always a door. Wild how you can almost stop noticing the little things you see every day.

It's about three feet high, tucked snug into the wedge of the staircase. It has a glass knob, cut like a jewel. Don't fight—steer. She lowers her eyes. Was she mistaken, or has there always been a small exit sign hanging above the door? She looks up slowly.

EXET

Close enough.

She turns the handle and pulls. A seal of old paint and dust comes unstuck with a musty crunch, and the door opens onto a low hallway. She crawls down the hallway on her hands and knees toward the dim light of a room on the other side. What she finds when she straightens again is another sitting room, like a mirror image. Almost a mirror—none of the corners here are square. The light in this room is of a different color.

This is not what she wanted, which is fine. She is going to relax, even as her heart thumps in her chest. Even though there is something moving in the corner of her eye, unspeakably shuddering in the corner of the room—she's not here for that. She doesn't need to know what it is. She is following the exit signs

XSIT

into her second kitchen, to the basement door. Her heart—her heart is beating too fast. Her breath.

EXZXXWVXTTTT

EXZKKKK

EXXTTT

EXIT

now through the door, down the unlit stairs. This isn't her same basement, of course. All these old houses have two basements—it's fine. And old staircases have doors, she remembers, as she carefully reaches the bottom step and feels her way around the bannister in the dark. She gropes until she finds the lines of it: the little door beneath the stars. Stairs? Stars. She crawls through the little door beneath the stars, through a hallway soft and low.

Soft and low and dark. But with stars.

FOURTEEN

AS SHE MOVES, THE HALLWAY droops like a blanket. It's a cold starlight all around, a thousand tiny pricks on her skin. Then it changes, the feel of it, like she's leaving one place and coming to another. When the time feels right, she slows her crawl and rolls onto her back.

Does she wake?

No, she was already awake.

She's panting, and awake, with the night still softly upon her. There's a slight chill where it touches her forehead, her nose, her chest and knees and toes.

She isn't in town anymore. She can feel this. She isn't in her house. She opened a small door and tunneled back through the world to this place where the sky is a bedsheet. She can hear Langston breathing. He's lying close by, just where she left him, his warmth rolling off him in waves. She can feel Patches at her feet. She's here; she steered her way back. Okay.

Okay.

That sucked.

She got the dream to bring her back, sure, but it felt like a heart attack. She doesn't want to do it again. She doesn't even know if she could.

I can't go to sleep, Zelda thinks. *Not if I want to get to the end of this dream. I don't get to. If I do, I'll just wake up back in my damn house again.*

She grits her teeth and wonders if the dreaming Zelda is trying to tell her something. Some stupid symbolism. Like, that she's the only one with her eyes open. She's the one looking at all of this squarely. Patches is here for the poetry. Langston, for all his talk about scientific exploration, is (possibly) just along for the company. Only Zelda has her eyes open. And she has to keep them open—open always, apparently—or she's going to lose everything she's gained, and never get to the end of the dream.

She feels like crying. *What am I going to do all night?* she wonders. *I can't even stand up and walk around—the sky's on me.*

She's still breathing quickly, greedily. The drumbeat settles in her chest. Under the sheet of sky, her humid breath has mustered into a nest of clouds all around.

She stares cross-eyed at it. The stars are pinpricks—actual pinpricks in the fabric of the sky. They twinkle with the light and movement of something on the other side. She shifts. She turns her head until a star's tiny aperture is centered directly over her right eye, and she closes her left. Her lashes flutter against the night's blanket as she squints through.

The star is a pinhole camera; a view through the wrong end of a spyglass. She can see tubes of paint, jars, a coffee can full of brushes—but all of it upside down. In a bright upside-down studio, two easels stand side by side, one tall and one small. Two people stand side by side, as tall and small as their easels. The little boy, maybe four, makes a self-portrait—the face he paints is as round as a button. The man beside him paints something astonishing on a big stretched canvas.

She shifts to the light of another pinprick star. There's an upside-down canyon, and a little upside-down girl stands alone at the rim of it, looking at the panorama. She has windswept dark hair; her bare shoulders are pink from sun. She fidgets with a paper bird in her fingers until the wind steals it away and sends it soaring. The girl races to catch the bird, arms stretched, until the light burns out.

Next. A pretty woman is trying to teach the same little boy how to ride a bicycle. He looks like an astronaut in his huge helmet, knee pads, elbow pads. He has sofa pillows stuffed under his shirt. The astronaut doesn't want to go to space today—he wails silently, his mouth a black hole, as his mother tries to set him on the bike seat and an older boy in the yard laughs with theatrical gusto.

(This house is yellow, too.)

Now high above a public pool, gazing down the length of a tall diving board at a girl standing at the tip. Her dark hair is dry—this is her big entrance, and the aspect of the pool, the pitch of the clouds, the angle of every shape and thing seems to center her like an altarpiece. Some kids hesitate; some burn with shame as they climb back down, but not her. The girl, with zinc-white skin and a yellow swimsuit, steps forward and points herself at the world.

Another light—this is a view from an upstairs window. A crabapple tree, a tall fence, a backyard sandbox.

Zelda shifts. In an upside-down bedroom, the boy lies fully dressed atop a queen-sized bed. The man, the artist, lies beside him and holds him close. An old woman stands beside the bed, talking. There's no sound to go with these pictures. At last, the old woman tries to take the little boy with her—but the man won't let him go. She stops trying. After a still moment, she gives them each a kiss on the cheek and leaves the room.

In the gauzy air of a one-car garage, the boy's bicycle is half-hidden behind a bag of mulch. The bike chain lolls like a tongue. A spider has made its home amongst the spokes.

One dim star offers a view of the studio at dusk. The little boy is spying from the door as the artist takes a wide brush and drags turpentine across an unfinished portrait. The faces of the woman and the older boy were just beginning to take shape, but now they smear and melt, their fine features weeping down the tall white canvas.

Zelda can't sleep. Instead she keeps her eyes open, and looks at stars all night.

FIFTEEN

THE SUN RISES AND HOISTS the sky like a flag. Now that she's free to move again, Zelda stands and stretches, paces to keep herself from sleeping. She's tragically tired and feeling very sorry for herself—the starlight picture show of the previous night seemed to want to tell her a sad story, but she couldn't make sense of all the pieces. Some of them felt out of order. Some of them felt like nothing at all.

She's turned another wide circle around their campsite and returned to find the boys awake and waiting for her.

"Whoop, okay," she says. "Lemme freshen up and we'll go."

"You got up early," says Langston.

"I . . . couldn't sleep," says Zelda. She feels about a thousand pounds, saying this. She somehow felt lighter when she had the entirety of the night sky resting on top of her.

She doesn't mention Erx, or doorways in stairwells, or all that gentle steering. She may need to try a little more gentle steering, and it won't do if everyone knows they're being steered.

This part of the tundra is as flat as a parking lot, pebbled here and there with rocks shaped like things. Sandwiches. A shoe. She brushes her teeth behind a school bus boulder. Patches follows her around, sticking his head between her hand and whatever it's doing.

"If you want a pet, you can just say, 'give me a pet,'" says Zelda.

"Hmm? Were we talking about pets?" Patches answers, butting her fingers. "If you like, I suppose."

Langston is pointing as Zelda and Patches emerge from behind the boulder. "I think it's this way," he says. "Before we went to sleep, I set my shoes in the direction we were walking." He seems pretty proud of this. "So unless my shoes moved in the night—"

"Which is totally not out of the question," says Zelda.

"—then the edge is this way."

"Well, anyway, I'm glad you thought of that," Zelda tells Langston, and he stands a little straighter. It's like she peeled a gold star and stuck it to his chest. "This weird landscape," he adds. "We never would have known where to go."

Patches indifferently cleans a paw. "I would have known," he says.

They set off toward a rust-colored horizon. Gradually, the land starts to step down—great scalloped steps a hundred feet across, painted with a swirling iridescence. Cherry trees crowd the edges.

"Did you guys notice, last night?" Zelda asks. "The stars?" She eyes Langston. *Did you see what I saw?*

"What about them?" asks Langston.

"They were holes. Like little holes in a blanket."

"Holes?" says Langston. "Are you sure?"

"I woke up briefly, and when I stretched I put my claws through the blanket," says Patches. "So if you see a new constellation tonight, that's mine."

"Did you know the stars are so far away that their light takes years to reach us?" asks Langston. "So when we look at the stars, we're seeing the past."

Zelda considers each pinprick scene.

"The past," she agrees.

The landscape gets more perilous, dropping off abruptly into sharp

cliffs like something from a cartoon. Like all good cartoon cliffs, each has a single spindly branch growing out of the face of it. Something to reach for if you fall. *That's friendly*, thinks Zelda. *Sort of.* She's lost in these thoughts as a coyote accidentally runs over the edge.

Patches has joined her, and they watch the coyote fall. "Poof," says Patches at the appropriate moment.

It's dicey terrain, and they have to help one another. It's difficult getting down the rocky shelves, and circumventing the cliffs, and avoiding all the falling coyotes.

"That one had roller skates," says Langston.

They descend to the rim of a canyon of iron-rich peaks and plateaus. Like a dry red mouth, full of teeth. The rough stone steeples ache upward, frostbitten in the frozen sky.

It's very, very big.

Zelda's standing at the edge of a pretty magnificent drop, and the temperature is falling fast. Her breath is dry ice; she sucks it back in. For a moment, she feels like she can't trust her legs to do what they're supposed to do, so she takes a sizable step backward and bumps into Langston.

He sets his hands lightly on her elbows. His body spoons her, for just an instant. Zelda regrets that her back is not a sensitive enough instrument to make sense of all those fleeting connections, but for a moment they hold the cold at bay with the warmth between them. A second later, they're two people again.

"Hey, sorry," Zelda says.

Langston nods at the view. "It's like the Grand Canyon."

"Is it?"

"Hm. Bigger, maybe."

Once, when she was a little girl, Zelda's family drove for five hours to go look at the Grand Canyon. But when they got there, it was full of clouds. So she has to take Langston's word on that.

"Do you suppose the dreamer is trying to tell us something?" Patches asks as he weaves a figure eight around Zelda's legs.

"What do you mean?"

"I mean that we three wish only to be on our way, and yet *in* our way the dream has placed no less than the world's most famous hole. Deep, treacherous to cross but too wide to circumvent."

"You're saying the dreamer's trying to keep us from getting to the edge of the dream." It's the same worry she had herself, the day before.

"I am merely saying that if the dreamer *were* to try such a strata-gem," Patches says with a stretch of his claws, "it would look exactly like this."

Langston is nodding. "We never should have left Erx's. We could have found the solution to everything without ever leaving his workshop. That place was stuffed with magic—even *he* didn't know what he had."

He knew he didn't have snacks, Zelda thinks. *He knew he needed to come to my kitchen for corn chips.*

"If we cut our losses, head back to town and keep studying the problem—"

"Naw!" Zelda hollers, hopping to get her blood pumping. "C'mon . . . this canyon isn't that bad! Right? I mean it could be worse."

"It hasn't any lasers coming out of it," says Patches, "if that's what you mean. It isn't filled with poisonous lava."

"That's the spirit!"

They search the rim, looking for a path. There's no path.

Zelda can't help feeling responsible. Like last night, she's somehow taken her eye off the ball and a new setback has come galloping in. *Stop it*, she tells herself. *Stop dreaming up new problems for us to solve.* As if the canyon might oblige by sprouting some elevators. But why not?

On a conscious level (or whatever you'd call this level she's on right now), she wants only to race to the end, confirm who the dreamer is, and wake herself up. But what does this vast gorge tell her about her subconscious? Does it reveal a deeper, more animal level that just wants to be home and in bed? She's so tired. She hasn't slept. The dream probably thinks it's helping.

"This is going to fail," Zelda mutters. "We're going to fail."

"What?" said Langston.

"I was just saying—if it weren't challenging, it wouldn't be a quest! Right?"

"I guess so. I mean, that's what it's like in stories," says Langston. "I've been thinking about the Labors of Hercules. Those horsemen were like one of those."

"Oh, right," says Zelda. "Labors of Hercules. He had to kill a three-headed dog, and a lion . . . and I don't remember what else."

"They weren't all killing monsters. One of them he just had to clean a stable. For another, he had to get a certain belt."

"Oh, like a personal shopper. *Hercules: Find me a cute top to go with this handbag.*"

Classical literature seems like just the subject for Patches to pounce on, but he's quiet as a cat. The topic lists and drifts away, and then they're all just staring absently into the canyon, their foggy breath like empty word balloons.

As if by hidden cue, they all start looking for a way down. Silently. It takes so much focus just to keep one's footing that they wouldn't have been able to speak even if they had something to say. Their fingers and paws feel vise-gripped by the cold. They search for handholds in flaking rock and rickety trees. In time they reach a level ledge and, without even a word of deliberation, stop to rest.

They watch the lightning awhile.

They're lower now, and the canyon no longer looks like a mouth of red teeth—now the mountains and mesas are like a jury. A crowd of colossi, boxed in to pass judgment on these two idiot kids and their cat. The longer Zelda stares, the easier it is to see serious features in their rocky faces. She looks away.

Patches says, "I believe I'm ready to take credit once more for this formidable panorama. It takes a *poet* to dream of such Sturm und Drang, not a pair of addlepated teenagers, no offense."

"Nothing offensive about that," said Langston. "Apart from all the words you said and how you said them."

Zelda asks, "So what do people say about, you know, what dreams actually mean?"

"A great many things," says Patches. "Freud famously believed dreams were about longing. That a dream is a stage on which we act out our forbidden desires."

Oh GOD, Zelda thinks, *don't look at Langston, don't look at Langston.*

"Freud's most famous student, Jung, had a different theory," says Patches. "He tells us that dreams are the unconscious mind's way of sorting through ideas and solving problems as we sleep."

"That one sounds right to me," says Langston. His long arm crosses to rub his shoulder. "Like, sometimes I go to bed with writer's block, and the next morning the solution's so obvious."

Zelda cranes her neck. "You write?"

Langston smiles one of his shruggy half smiles. "You know," he says. "I try to. Silly little stories."

"Oh, hey—don't do that. Don't talk it down. You *write*," says Zelda. "That's *cool.* But you say it with this . . . embarrassed shrug like you're sorry your dog farted."

He might be locked into that shruggy half smile now, like he doesn't trust what his face will do if he quits. But Zelda can see a warmth wash over him that lights up his eyes. She wants to take a photograph of him right then, with her mind. So she'll remember him after she wakes.

Patches bunts his head into her fingers, so Zelda puts him in her lap. "Is that it?" she asks. "Those two theories? I kind of thought a dream is just, like . . . the growling of an empty stomach."

"Aha, yes," says the cat as he leans his cheek into her hand. "I enjoy your metaphor. And it so happens there is another prominent theory that asserts a dream is only the random firings of a sleeping brain. Electrical shocks in a crackling box, a little gray cloud full of wonder and thunder. But random. Indeed, events so random that the conscious mind has to invent a story to bind them together after waking."

"What does that mean," says Langston as he tries on hats, "that dreams have no story at all? That they're just a bunch of disconnected nonsense? That's obviously wrong."

"It's not my theory," says Patches from deep inside a Victorian diving suit. "But I find the idea fascinating nonetheless."

Zelda catches the fifth and final softball and places it with the others inside a basket of eels. "I don't really have that strong an opinion about it," she says. "Everybody rested?" She's feeling antsy.

"Yeah," says Langston.

"I am ready to go."

Zelda rises and arches over for a glimpse of the canyon floor.

"I swear," she says, "I'm ready to *jump*." And she scares herself because it's so true. *Let the current carry you*, Erx had said, *just don't get carried away*. "Like, I could just . . . jump off this ledge and imagine myself a parachute on the way down."

"Please don't," says Langston.

She's always felt edgy on edges. Like *not* jumping is a decision she has to make, and keep making, perpetually, until she steps back at last and the fever dies.

"It's not totally crazy, though, is it?" she asks. "We'd only have to imagine our parachutes for maybe thirty seconds."

"Except young Langston will panic and imagine an empty garbage bag with the word *parachute* misspelled in Magic Marker."

"Hey," Langston says, and it's easy to imagine he and Patches are going to start grousing at each other again, but he's actually smiling. "If I'm being honest, I *am* usually more of a look-before-you-leap kind of guy. A look-before-you-leap-and-read-three-books-about-leaping-and-in-the-end-decide-not-to-leap kind of guy."

He catches Zelda's eye. He's alluding to his confession the night before—joking about it, even.

"Oh, I'm sure that's not true," says Zelda, though she's sure it is. He looks at the view. Too late, she realizes it wasn't really the right thing to say—waving away the possibility he's a coward instead of telling him it's okay to be a coward. Could she say that and mean it? She isn't sure.

She spies movement in the corner of her eye. Was it the canyon itself?

"Hey, look at that!" Zelda cheers. "Is that a trail? It's an actual trail!" It's just a short scramble down to it—Zelda slides most of the way on her butt. "I never would have seen it if I hadn't been so close to the edge."

"You could learn a lot from a cat," Patches tells Langston. "We don't shy away from life's precipices."

"You literally just got through telling us you've died seven times."

A trail, thinks Zelda. Did the dream give it to her because it didn't want her to jump?

Honky.

She frowns. "Okay, I heard it that time."

Honky honky.

"It would seem to be following us," says Patches. "This honky."

They pause to look. Above them, atop a red bluff shot through with briar, Zelda spies something ducking quickly behind a boulder.

"We see you!" Zelda shouts at the something. "You aren't as sneaky as you think you are!" The thing makes a noise. A nervous flurry of balloon animals squirts out from behind the rock.

"Oh God," says Langston. "Oh God." He turns. "Parachute," he says, and instantly he's wearing one over his backpack, but the weight of it drops him to the ground.

Zelda glances from the rock above to Langston. "Why is your parachute so heavy? Also, what is up with you all of a sudden?"

Langston wriggles free of the parachute straps. "It probably has an anvil in it—watched too many cartoons as a kid. Um . . . hang glider!"

A colorful hang glider appears, and catches the wind, and is swept out of Langston's grasp into the center of the canyon, where it is struck by lightning.

Zelda is watching the rock above. There's no more movement from the mysterious stranger, and most of the balloon animals have wandered off. Patches bats his paw at a balloon squirrel, and the resulting *pop* makes Langston start so violently that he kicks the jet packs he'd been imagining into the canyon.

Poor baby, thinks Zelda. "Here. My turn," she says. "Close your eyes."

Patches turns his back and starts to clean himself. Langston hesitates. He glances at the rock again.

"Close your eyes!" Zelda insists.

"Sorry," Langston says, and he does close his eyes. "You wouldn't know it to look at me, what with my efficient physique—"

"Dainty, frangible physique," offers Patches.

"—*efficient, space-saving* physique," Langston corrects him, "or by my astronomy T-shirt, but I have kind of a nervous attitude toward people asking me to close my eyes or look behind me."

"What? Why?" asks Zelda. "It's just me!"

"Yeah. And the *last* time one of the pretty girls asked me to close my eyes," Langston says, "her boyfriend came and pulled my pants down by the cafeteria salad bar."

It's like a smile blooms all over her body. *Pretty girls*, Zelda thinks. She's grateful his eyes are closed.

After a moment, she says, "All right, open them!" He does. "Ta-da! It's one of those dirt bikes you wanted!"

It's two of them, actually. She's not an expert, but she thinks she's conjured up a pair of pretty plausible bikes. One of them has a sidecar for Patches, which he jumps into right away.

"I want a helmet with a spike on it," says Patches.

"Can you imagine it yourself?" asks Zelda. "I'm concentrating kinda hard on these bikes."

What she's *doing*, she realizes, is forcing things. Not going with the flow and gently steering—she just forced the dream to cough up two motorbikes.

"These look . . . solid," Langston says, nodding slowly. He's trying to seem supportive, but he's conjured a thought balloon of the three of them crashing and burning in spectacular fashion. "I don't understand how these engines would work."

"Maybe they will, though!" Zelda answers. She doesn't really know anything about motorcycle engines. In her mind's eye, they're just shiny intestinal masses of lumps and hoses. Whoops, and now she's thinking of intestines. *Don't think of intestines*, she tells herself while eyeing the bikes.

You can't really tell yourself *not* to think of something.

"Okay! Hold on!" shouts Zelda. "Sorry! Oh man, gross. Okay okay okaaaaaaythere! The engines are engines again." She beams and gestures like a model on a game show.

Langston seems reluctant to get on his bike.

"Oh, come along, you big baby," says Patches, who now has his spiked helmet and a studded leather collar.

"This'll be, like, insanely dangerous, though."

"Says the guy with the hang glider," says Zelda. She straddles her bike, nearly booting Patches in the head, and hits a snag—she doesn't know how to start this thing. Is there a pedal, or something with the handlebar grips? But never mind—it's started itself, apparently. The bike clears its throat and purrs beneath her. Then:

Honky honky honky honky honky honk.

Over the noise of the dirt bike, they can barely hear it.

Langston scrambles toward his bike, jerking his head around. The mysterious stranger is on the move again, apparently, but the canyon is so full of echoes it's impossible to get a bead on it.

"Okay fine yes, dirt bikes!" says Langston. He's imagined himself the largest helmet Zelda has ever seen, and one of those padded outfits people wear to train attack dogs. He turns the grips, and he's off. Zelda and Patches follow, hurtling down the narrow mountain trail.

It's a surprisingly smooth ride. *Oh,* thinks Zelda as she watches Langston's bike ahead of her. *Our tires aren't actually touching the ground.*

"There's so much we forget to remember in dreams," says Patches, clearly. "Don't you think?" And, case in point, Zelda realizes she can hear him so clearly because she's momentarily forgotten what a racket the dirt bike engines ought to be making. "I rather think that's why nakedness is such an issue."

"For you, apparently."

"If," says Patches, "in waking life, one has cause to think about his pants, then there they are—waiting with the unshakable patience that all real things possess whether you are thinking of them or not."

"Can we talk about it later?" asks Zelda. For a second, she could have sworn her dirt bike had feathers.

"But in dreams?" Patches continues. "The very instant it occurs to us to look at what we're wearing, it is already too late to imagine the answer. We aren't prepared. And so we discover we aren't wearing anything at all. To dream of the feel of the ground beneath our feet is to comprehend that we *hadn't* felt it before—had we? And so the only way to make sense of the discrepancy is to remember we can fly."

"This is all very interesting, but our dirt bike is an ostrich."

"A magnificent animal."

"Yes. Though not an animal with handlebars usually."

"Nor a sidecar, but here we are."

They're careening down a dusty path, and Zelda can barely make out the shape of Langston and whatever he's currently riding. It's genuinely concerning, because she's suddenly afraid if she loses sight of him he might vanish from the dream altogether.

If I fight too hard I'll crash, she thinks. *Gently steer.*

The canyon is barreling past and curling inward and rolling up behind her and folding overhead, it's over her head, she can look up and see mountains pointing down like stalactites. Now those mountains come pouring down, snapping off the roof in the sky and falling, a giant mouth losing its teeth, gargantuan fangs and molars crashing to the canyon floor as Zelda swerves and weaves.

I'm in a river. The current has me, but I glide easily around every rock and thing.

Patches says,

"The hills are shadows, and they flow

From form to form, and nothing stands;

They melt like mist, the solid lands,

Like clouds they shape themselves and go."

"Can't really concentrate on your poetry just now!" says Zelda.

"That wasn't one of mine—it was Tennyson."

Then the canyon more or less settles into its new shape, and the sky clears. The way ahead is leveling out, and Zelda is sort of float-running because apparently the ostrich disappeared at some point, and as the dust clears she sees they've arrived, all three of them, at the flat, gravelly bottom of the canyon. They skid to a halt. Zelda remembers to feel the ground beneath her feet.

"We didn't die," says Langston matter-of-factly. "So." The tremors in his legs betray how he really feels, and he takes a seat.

Not bad, thinks Zelda. It was all fantastically dangerous, of course, but that little joyride probably saved them a whole day of hiking. And just thinking about the passage of time gives Zelda a chill, but she shakes it off—they are going to get to the edge soon, she will peer through the mists or whatever you do, she will confirm that she is indeed the dreamer, and she will . . . say goodbye to these good people. This cat and this boy. She'll say goodbye. She breathes.

"It can't be helped!" Zelda announces. That cat and that boy look at her, as if to ask *what can't?*, but she changes the subject.

"Look at how far we came!" she says.

She tries to trace their path back up to the rim, just to get the new lay of the land, and instead catches sight of some pointillist cluster of colors in the yellow sky. It may in fact be someone or something hanging from a bunch of balloons and slowly descending into the canyon. Langston certainly doesn't like the look of it, and he hops to his feet again and starts speed-walking through the valley.

"Better keep moving," he says.

Zelda and Patches hang back, conspiratorially, as if by unspoken agreement they're about to talk smack about Langston.

"Sooo," says Zelda. "Do we think that thing following us is the laundromat clown, possibly?"

"I think it's safe to assume Langston thinks it is," Patches answers.

"Wonder how it got unstuck from the laundromat." She watches Langston hustling up ahead. "He's handling it well."

"Yes. What a rough-and-tumble tomcat you've chosen for your mate."

"Okay, I have not chosen anyone for my *mate*—gross. I just think he's cute. And nice. I like his hair."

"Truly a romance for the ages."

"I just like a guy who doesn't have to flex and be the strong one every second." She supposes she must like this, at any rate—she's never thought about it until just now. "I was the one who took on those gym teachers, and he called me amazing."

"He also implied he should have been the one to handle that particular situation, not you."

Zelda remembers. Patches was right—Langston had done that.

Zelda blinks it away. "You know what we talked about last night?" she asks. "When we first met, I thought he'd risked his life to save me. And he could have let me go on thinking that forever. But last night he admitted he froze, was scared. He didn't have to admit it, but he did—that's pretty brave, don't you think?"

"You're reaching."

She scoops the cat up and squeezes his fluffy body. "You don't have to be jealous, you know," she says.

"I am *not* jealous."

"You two could be friends. Should I carry you up there and let him scratch your tummy again?"

"Put me *down*, madam."

She puts him down. They walk in silence for a while.

"I would rather you not be hurt," says Patches.

"Thank you," says Zelda. "Why would I be hurt?"

"Because young love is a dream from which we all must wake," says Patches with a flick of his tail. "Yours is just less metaphorical than usual."

Oh, thinks Zelda. *Right.*

"Also," says Patches, "I lied to you."

"Lied? When?"

"Remember late when nighttide's sable winding sheet did shroud the earth?"

"Are you trying to say *last night*?"

"Yes. I said I hadn't noticed the star-holes, when in fact I had."

"What? Why didn't you say so?"

"Because young Langston had *not*—and I didn't care to gossip about his home movies."

Zelda takes a deep breath, lets it out in a puff.

"Yeah," she says. "I mean, they weren't *all* about him."

If, in fact, any of them were. Some of the stars offered a peek at the lives of the same Black family, but that didn't mean it was Langston's family.

Then Zelda remembers the young boy—his startled little face—and thinks, *That was Langston, though. Of course it was Langston.* Langston learning (or not learning) to ride a bike. Langston in church, in his little suit. Langston waiting patiently at a street corner for someone to take his hand.

"I feel weird about what I saw," she says. "Do you? It's like we were spying. Like some of those stars weren't meant for our eyes."

"Nonetheless," Patches says. "What I saw before sleeping—what I think I saw—was a boy who already shied away from the wild life, even before tragedy took from him two people he loved."

Zelda remembers watching the faces of Langston's mother and brother soften and bleed down an unfinished canvas.

"I think the dreamer dreams him a history," says Patches, "just as they have dreamed you yours and me mine. I think Langston's is a history of boyhood disaster. And now, on the precipice of manhood, huge horsemen remind him of the Labors of Hercules and I wonder, *What made him think of that? Why not David and Goliath, or Thor and the jötnar, or Jack the Giant Killer.*"

"Okay, so?"

"Do you know why Hercules needs to prove himself through the Labors? It's penance. Penance for having, by divine madness, killed his own family."

"Oh," says Zelda. She watches Langston's head bob in and out of the valley's shadow. "That wasn't in the cartoon."

"No."

"But you don't think Langston actually killed anybody," Zelda insists. "You can't really think that."

"I think," says Patches with a twitch of his whiskers, "that in a dream, memory comes together with mythology and metaphor and none of it is any more or less real. I think Langston has something to prove, and on these proving grounds he has dreams. He has dreams of rising up."

"And every one's a lead parachute," Zelda murmurs.

SIXTEEN

THE VALLEY HAS LOST ITS grit, and this stretch of it is as level as a street. It curves mildly this way and that, and as a result they hadn't caught sight of the laundromat clown for hours. Langston is more or less relaxed, and the three of them are walking together again. To Zelda, it seems as if they've fallen back into the uncomfortable silence of the previous day, though she suspects it's all in her head. *Langston's* all in her head—all the fresh mystery and unexplored depths of him. Strangely, as the boy becomes more complicated the landscape loses definition. The canyon walls that had once looked chiseled and severe are growing ever more flat and featureless.

"Bored now," says Patches.

"You know," Zelda says, "I'm totally familiar with the concept of boredom, but I can't remember a time when I was ever bored."

They're quiet.

"Yeah. I don't think it's possible to be bored in a dream," says

Langston finally. "Like, a dream can seem boring after you wake up, but it's never boring when you're in it."

"I guess that's true," says Zelda, trying to remember. "Because . . . to be bored your mind has to be elsewhere, right? But if your mind drifts in a dream, then the dream just drifts along with it. I . . . guess that means I am the dreamer, then. I can't be bored."

She doesn't feel this with quite the same verve she once did.

"Nah," says Langston, by her side. "I've never been bored, either."

Patches sniffs. "I'm a cat," he says. "I'm supposed to be bored."

At some point, the ground beneath them has become an actual street, the canyon walls segmented into the brick façades of buildings. The valley is an empty city, and in the city is a small historic district zoned for commercial use.

"This is a really cool area," says Langston. "Look at that shop. Look at all these shops—that . . . that store window has everything I've ever wanted my whole life."

Zelda looks. This is everything Langston has ever wanted his whole life? It is mostly, though not entirely, unexpected.

"So *that's* what a dirt bike engine looks like," she says.

There are some vintage comics in plastic sleeves, but also nunchucks. A bow and arrows. A hoverboard—the imaginary kind. Something Zelda can only assume is a jet pack.

"Adventurous stuff," says Patches, "for a boy who looks both ways before sneezing."

Zelda steps up and touches Langston on the arm. She says, "Don't get sucked in. It's just the dream trying to sidetrack—whoa! Look at these Collectimals cards on the curb. Are they . . . are they *all* first-edition Magnitoads? They are! These are valuable! They're every—"

"WHERE ARE ALL THESE LASER POINTERS COMING FROM?" says Patches as he chases around and around and around—

"Would any of you care to eat ice cream out of a fancy hat?" asks a street vendor who sells hats and ice cream.

"Ohmygosh, yes, of course I would," answers Zelda, and she picks cookies and cream served in a porkpie.

"I want that ice cream," says Langston, pointing. "And that hat."

"A very good choice, sir," says the ice cream man. "This is the very hat *and* the very ice cream Archduke Ferdinand was wearing and eating when he was assassinated."

"Cooool."

"What about you, Patches?" asks Zelda. "Ice cream?"

"I shouldn't."

"You get a free hat."

"I do not want a hat," Patches explains. He's still wearing his spiked helmet, and he seems pretty happy with it. The ice cream man leans in.

"You don't have to have a hat, my friend—

"Come on now, step right up.

"I have forty-seven flavors in a cone or in a cup.

"Forty-seven different ways a boy like you can spoil his dinner.

"I'll just list them and you stop me when you think we've found a winner.

"I have chocolate—"

    "No."

"vanilla—"

    "No."

"rum raisin, triple berry—"

"No."

"pistachio and cookie dough; mint chocolate chip and cherry."

"No."

Zelda winces and says, "This seems like it's going to take a while."

There's a kind of rolling glow over the rooftops, coming from some distant block. It warms the darkening sky. There's a corresponding warmth just below Zelda's rib cage, rolling and glowing as the hairs of Langston's arm feather against hers.

"It's a Ferris wheel," Langston says after a moment. He arches his eyebrows and jerks his head at it.

Zelda shakes her head, but there's no vigor to the gesture. "I think we've wasted a lot of time as it is," she says. "Haven't we?"

"Just for a little bit," Langston says. "We deserve a break."

The ice cream man is telling Patches,

"You know what? I respect that. You're an ice cream connoisseur!

"Guys like you and me? We gotta see the goods before we're sure.

"Triple ripple."

"No."

"Banana."

"No."

"Valencia sorbet. Coffee. Almond. Rainbow sherbet. Rocky road or crème brûlée."

"No."

You gotta go, Zelda tells herself. *Race to the edge. Wake yourself up—you've been asleep for days.*

But then, she reasons, if she's been asleep for days it's unlikely an hour or two is going to make any difference. For all she knows, ten minutes on from here, the ground could turn into pudding and then where would they be? Stuck in pudding, that's where, and wishing they'd stayed at the place with the Ferris wheel.

Langston nudges Zelda's elbow. He's smiling at her, and what a smile. Here's everything he's been holding back, all the heart and soul of him onstage. The curtains of his face have lifted and gathered beside his shining eyes.

Zelda points a finger. Just taps at the air in front of his face, really. "You've got a little ice cream," she says.

"On my face?" He touches his cheek. "Where?"

It's a pink pearl of strawberry, a little rosebud on his lip.

Before she can think too hard about what she's doing, she flicks her tongue out the side of her mouth and licks at the corner of her own lips. "There," she says, swallowing her own voice as embarrassment and several other fires burn her from the inside out.

He licks the corner of his mouth in the same spot, like a mirror. In a close sort of way, he whispers, "Like that?"

Zelda has no breath. She says, "Yes. Good job," with barely a voice.

Langston's eyes—does he have actual fireworks in his eyes? She thought that was just a metaphorical thing that happened in certain paperback novels.

She was going to kiss this boy, wasn't she? She'd had a plan. Not in front of the cat, though.

"Patches!" calls Zelda. She's craning her head toward him, but she doesn't take her eyes off Langston. "We're going to explore, but we'll meet you back here!" The two of them hustle off without waiting for an answer.

"Papaya. Brownie batter. Lemon. Peach. Masala chai.

"Honey. Caramel. Red velvet. Cotton candy. Apple pie."

"No."

SEVENTEEN

THEY'RE HOLDING HANDS. ZELDA CAN'T remember how that happened, but there it is. The rough whorl of a knuckle under her thumb. Fingers warm and cool at the same time, soft pillows and strong bone. Patches's thoughts on nudity and flying come back to her, and with a jolt she checks to see if she's wearing anything.

"Are you okay?" asks Langston.

"I'm fine," says Zelda, smoothing the folds of what turns out to be an off-the-shoulder sweatshirt dress over leg warmers. In the reflection of a shop window, she can see her hair is a beautiful, sticky cloud. Langston's is a hi-top fade with the word *outrageous* shaved into the side of it.

A warm evening is coming on, the horizon blushing in every direction. This is one of those close-the-streets-and-let-people-walk-around-with-ice-cream kinds of places, and the cobblestones are filling up with happy people, buskers with banjos, a magician in a tux and tails. A sign declares them to be at FUNLAND or maybe FUN LANDING. FUNNEL MAN. Zelda narrows her eyes. In that now-familiar fashion, she's finding the sign hard to read. FUNT LIVER. She concentrates and squints it down to FUN LEVEL 1. A second later, it still says this, so she decides they are at FUN LEVEL 1. Another sign down the street reads ON TO FUN LEVEL 2.

So: new information, thinks Zelda, looking side-eyed at Langston's baggy, electric yellow . . . jumpsuit? She's going to say jumpsuit. On the sleeve of it is written FRESH in a very fresh typeface.

Has the dreamer never been on a date? Do they only know about them from eighties movies? Or no—maybe the dreamer is old, and settled, and dreaming of the last time they felt the synth-pop-and-bubblegum way Zelda is feeling right now.

Just like that, she's eased into thinking of the dreamer as someone else. Not her, not even Langston. It's immensely satisfying, thinking this.

She still wants to find the end of the dream. Definitely. Obviously. She still wants to know who's dreaming. But what would she make of it if she looks out over the edge, and the clouds part, and the person she sees lying in bed is . . . some stranger? And Zelda and Langston and Patches and everyone else turn out to be supporting players. Equals.

Maybe there are two random people, somewhere else in this dream, who don't know any more about Zelda's and Langston's lives than she knows about theirs. And those two random people are having their own dramatic adventure of self-discovery. Those two people think they're special, too. Like they're the stars, and they are—because there are a billion stars in the sky, and every one of them a story.

Maybe that's how dreams work. It could be. It totally could. There are as many neurons in a brain as there are stars in a galaxy— you just can't pay attention to them all.

Langston catches her frowning. "Is something wrong?" he asks. His face betrays how devastating it would be for something to be wrong just now. He takes his hand from hers, under the showy pretense of having to scratch his nose. Zelda grabs it back with a grin.

"Uh, you have *two* hands," she tells him. "No one needs that many hands. So this one's mine." He smiles, a nearby flower vendor smiles, the whole world is smiling. It says FRESH on Langston's collar, too, in a different typeface. She hadn't noticed that one before.

"So," she says. "I guess that was the clown back there." She bumps his shoulder with hers.

"That . . . was my thinking, yes."

"But you handled it with the quiet dignity I've come to expect from you."

"Pssh. Yeah." He's smiling. "I'm a real tough customer, aren't I?"

"The way I figure it," says Zelda, "we've all got to be parts of the dreamer, whoever they are. I represent the parts that are smart and funny and interesting, and you're the part that's scared of witches and clowns."

Langston hoots at this and shoves her—but he holds fast to her hand as he reels her back in and says, "The whole clown thing started after my mom and brother died."

They lurch to a stop. Langston looks just as surprised as Zelda.

EIGHTEEN

"YOU KNOW, THERE'S NO WRONG answer. Every one is sweet and frozen.

"I'll just list a few more flavors, and you tell me when you've chosen.

"Breakfast sausage."

"No."

"Tomato."

"No."

"Experimental mint."

"No."

"Cheese danish. Jambalaya. Butter. Belly-button lint."

"No, thank you."

NINETEEN

LANGSTON AND ZELDA HAVE STOPPED, but the carnival continues to spin and stream around them as a tactless calliope plays. A clown, an actual non-laundromat-affiliated clown, comes capering up behind Langston before Zelda discreetly waves it away.

"Um. I'm sorry," she says. "You hadn't mentioned your family before, apart from your grandma."

"I forgot," says Langston. "My mom and brother—I forgot they died." He looks stricken. What a sickening thing to remember. What a sickening thing to forget.

I saw them, Zelda wants to say. *In the stars.*

"They were hit by a drunk driver on the way to the skate park," says Langston. "I was supposed to be in the car with them. Baldwin . . . Baldwin was even being nice for a change—offering to give me skate lessons. But I chickened out and made a big scene . . . so they left without me."

He takes a breath.

"My mom really wanted me to go—she was always pushing me to try new things. And most of the time, there was Dad, saying, 'Langston doesn't have to if he doesn't want to—he's a careful kid, like his daddy was.'"

Langston's lost in thought now, but he squeezes Zelda's hand as though it brings him comfort, which she likes. For her part, Zelda wonders about all this forgetting. Zelda "forgot" Patches was alive until he turned up in class. Clara would have told you her grandma was dead until she abruptly remembered she wasn't.

The truth seems obvious. There will be no yellow cat waiting for Zelda when she wakes. There will be no grandma. But all these dream grandmas and dead grandmas and giant grandmas tell her that there *will* be a yearning for one that's lost. In the deep pool of dreams, you can swim with your grandma again, but when you surface, even for just an instant, a little air gets in and reminds you that she shouldn't be alive. She shouldn't, but there she is.

When you can't reconcile the real memory with the impossible dream, you forget things that happened and remember things that didn't. Zelda wonders if Langston is doing something like that now. And if so, which.

"All these missing memories," she says. "It's scary, right?"

"I guess," says Langston. "Scary how?"

Zelda's deciding how best to put it when she's jostled by a group of kids. A colorful train of them gallop by, grinning and bonking each other with inflatable mallets. "Sorry!" a girl with braids calls. The littlest of them has a tooth missing and a fizzy laugh that gets inside you and bubbles up. It's impossible not to smile.

The kids disappear into the midway, where Zelda's eyes light on a pair of big-headed costumed characters—amusement park mascots, except that they're obviously supposed to be sort of cartoon versions of Langston and Patches. They're mugging silently and giving floppy high fives to the carnival-goers.

"Oh man," says Langston, freezing. "What?"

They watch for a second in silence. The Langston mascot is pretending to be afraid of everyone who approaches him. Patches is flossing.

"Um," says Langston. "What were we talking about before?"

Zelda doesn't remember. It couldn't have been important—there's never anything important at a carnival; that's the *point*.

They stroll into the thick of it, straw crackling beneath their feet, and an arch welcomes them to FUN LEVEL 6. Loud color and twilight. Someone somewhere is selling kettle corn, and the air is thick with sugar. Zelda steals another look at Langston. He's percolating down the street beside her with this look of incredible focus on his face like he's trying to remember a Walk Like a Cool Guy tutorial he looked up on the internet. Nearby, the big-headed Langston mascot is doing a parody of it. She decides it's charming and stifles a laugh.

He's imaginary. Zelda hasn't had an imaginary friend since she was six, and never one that wasn't a *Winnie the Pooh* character, but she doesn't think she'd have anything against being imaginary friends with Langston. He is easily as cute as a piglet.

He surprises her. Two nights ago, Zelda couldn't have told you what she wanted in a boy. You might just as well have asked her what she'll want to eat at her last meal. *Tastes change*, she'd have answered with a shrug. *I'll figure it out when I get there.*

What did Tigger eat before he met Winnie-the-Pooh? Probably nothing—he was a pristine tiger toy from some shop window, a new arrival to Christopher Robin Milne's bedroom before his father inserted him into the stories he'd been dreaming up. And so the Hundred Acre Wood got a Tigger, and the Tigger must have supposed that he had always existed, that he had a favorite color and flower and food, though he couldn't even tell you what he wanted until a jar of Extract of Malt rang his bell.

Zelda swallows and looks Langston in the eyes. So this is what Tiggers like best.

"Sooooo," Langston says, and coughs. "What are you thinking about?"

"I'm thinking this is a nice night. I'm thinking it's nice to be two imaginary people on an imaginary night like this." She notices his jumpsuit now says FRESH on each button and in cursive down by the waistline. "I guess I should thank you for dreaming it up," she adds. "If you're the dreamer."

Langston waves this off. "Who knows if I'm the dreamer," he says blithely. "Maybe Erx was right, and it's a story instead."

"A first draft, probably," says Zelda.

"Hey, speak of the devil."

She's getting used to these little coincidences, so Zelda isn't all that surprised to see Erx on the path ahead, eating a churro.

The old wizard notices them and blanches, dropping his churro into the petting zoo. "Oh dear," he croaks. He stumbles back against the fence and turns every which way in a fever.

"What . . . are you looking for?" asks Langston.

"I do not know," gasps Erx. "It could be anything. An assassin. A meteor. A giant foot descending from above." He eyes the baby goats in the petting zoo as if any one of them might be hiding a knife and a murderous heart.

Zelda winces and shrugs up her shoulders. "I agree this might be a story, but I still don't think that means you have to die—"

"Zelda, I love you like a daughter. And Langston . . . I have nothing against you, but please, both of you: stay away from me."

Erx sprints away, his weird clothes flapping weirdly.

"Jeez," says Langston.

"He loves me like a daughter?" says Zelda.

She's reminded of the thing she took from Erx's workshop, a thing so laden with obvious symbolism that she felt she had no *choice* but to steal it. She glances at Langston. How will she feel when she has to use it?

"I got you something," says Langston.

Zelda's eyebrows arch. "You did?"

"Uh-huh. You didn't take anything from Erx's workshop."

Not true, thinks Zelda.

"So I took something for you." He swings his backpack around to root through the contents, and in a moment he presents her with a small, midnight-blue velvet bag, drawn closed with silver string.

She takes it gingerly. "I remember this," she says. "It was right next to . . ." She pulls it carefully open and looks inside. It's like granulated sugar, somehow colorless and also every color at once.

Zelda draws the bag closed again. "Erx called this a bag of sand that will make you sleep forever," she says, and looks sharply at Langston. "Why did you *want* this?"

He looks like he's considering how to answer when they pass a throng of carnival-goers, all converging on the same open space between two thoroughfares. There's a strange hush here, and Langston whispers when he says, "Hey, let's watch this."

They join a ring of people circling the edges of this patch of grass, and the gaudy sounds of the barkers and carnival rides seem to almost fall away. It's dim in the center of the field, but the people are lit from behind by a Milky Midway of starlight. Each head of big eighties hair glows like a halo.

"What is even going on," says Zelda.

"Shh! Look."

A woman steps from the circle's edge to the center of the space and kneels down. She scoops dirt with her fingers and pushes it aside—it comes easily, and soon she has a little hole. She gently lays something to rest inside the hole and fills it up again.

"That was a corn dog, right?" says Zelda. "She planted a corn dog."

"Shh."

Someone waters the corn dog with frozen lemonade, and the ring of beautiful people join hands. Zelda can't tell who's the first to sing, but one unassuming voice joins another, and then everyone is singing but her and Langston—nope, Langston is singing, too. Look at that: they all know the same song. Super. It doesn't have words, as such, but still Zelda can tell it's about small towns and grandmas and falling asleep in the back seat of the car on a long drive home.

Zelda rather feels like she could fall asleep herself, right now, without even sitting down. The summer night rests its warm palms on her eyes.

Then it happens—the corn dog sprouts, and a tender reed rises up from the ground. Quickly, it widens into a stout stem, then a trunk—thick as a redwood. But short. It's barely taller than the tops of their heads, and white as a wedding cake—decorations start to swan and fan up its sides.

Then it flickers and turns on. It shines from a thousand budding lights, and the ring of people squint at it and smile.

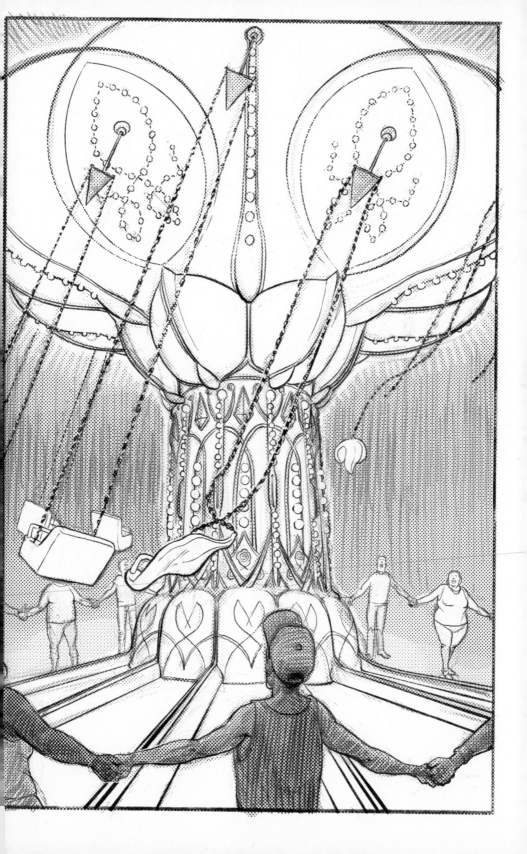

They commence singing a new song about safety and surrender, and a fresh stem grows up from the top of the trunk, forms a wide cup with electric sepals, and *pow*—a colossal blossom blooms and shapes itself into the canopy of a carousel that drops chain-link vines, which grow together at the ends into three dozen hanging chairs, and Zelda realizes, *Oh, it's a carnival ride—they grew a new carnival ride.* It costs five tickets. It already has a line.

"This place is kind of amazing, isn't it?" says Langston, his face aglow.

"When it's not trying to kill us, sure."

"The carnival is safe. The town was safe, except maybe the laundromat. It was safe to watch it all through the mirror, from afar." The new ride is up and running, swinging three dozen happy people up and around. "Just watching the wheels of it spin and turn," says Langston.

"Okay," says Zelda, "but then you're only a spectator. You don't want to always be a spectator." He doesn't answer right away, so she adds, "Do you?"

"Wouldn't be so bad if you have someone to share it with."

"Yeah, well, need I remind you that the last time you saw Erx he ran away as fast as he could?"

Langston looks at her squarely. "You know I wasn't talking about Erx," he says.

Zelda narrows her eyes.

"Langston . . . why did you take this bag of sand?"

He spreads his arms wide and pivots around like he's in a music video. He should have an open shirt and a fan aimed at him. "Look at all this! I don't think it's so strange to say I like it here. We found some islands of happiness and calm in this crazy place. The town. This park."

Zelda huffs. "I think they have towns and carnivals in the real world, Langston."

He stares a second, then hangs his head. Even now, Zelda wants to lift it up, carry it around for him awhile.

He says, "Okay, then who cares about towns and carnivals? This is the place with you. And me. Both of us, together? There is no other place."

There it is. Of course, that's what they're really talking about.

"Yeah," Zelda agrees. "That's true." She knows she has a point, but it's feeling duller by the second. "I don't like this pinch we're in any better than you, but . . . nothing here is real! It doesn't . . . it doesn't matter!"

"Yeah? Which one of us doesn't matter? We can't both be the dreamer, so which one? I feel real! I can remember my grandma. And *The Wizard of Oz*. I can remember the way my kindergarten class-room smelled, and the taste of the hamburgers in the school cafeteria. I remember the way the curtains felt in my childhood bedroom, rub-bing them between my fingers while I looked out the window."

Zelda doesn't want to talk about this. Maybe that's why she says the exact wrong thing.

"I remember my first kiss," she says. "His name was . . . Chud, or . . . Blad or something, and he only kissed me because I was the one the bottle was pointing at, but still. I have memories of him."

Langston looks away. "Right," he says. "See. That's what I'm say-ing. It's real enough."

After a fraught moment, Zelda says, "Sure, we have memories.

So does Patches. So does Clara. But maybe not everybody. What good is it, if it isn't everybody? I don't want to skate through life on Easy Mode."

Langston shrugs. "But maybe it's everybody."

"So let's test that." Zelda marches off with her fist in the air. "Science!"

Zelda steps right up to a woman standing alone by some hay bales. The fairy lights make a wide smile behind her head.

"Hello, ma'am?" says Zelda. The woman flinches and raises her head. "Sorry to bother you, but can you remember your first boyfriend? Or girlfriend or whatever?"

The woman smiles, but it's all frosting and no cake. "Yes," she says.

"What was their name?"

The woman seems to glance at the bales. "Bale," she says.

Zelda and Langston share a look. "I'm sorry," says Zelda, "did you say 'Dale'?"

". . . Yes."

"Thank you." Zelda makes a *ta-da* gesture with her hands. Langston pulls her away. "This place is full of background characters," she says as she's pulled. "The *town* was full of background characters."

"Okay, you made your point."

Zelda exhales. She feels heartsick—why did she want to make a point? Why couldn't she just enjoy the evening?

It says FRESH all over Langston's clothes—in fifteen places, with different fonts, like they're sponsoring his NASCAR team. His face looks freshly disappointed.

How did this fight even start? She can't remember how they got on the subject of dreams in the first place.

"Admit it, though," says Langston. "Earlier, you were starting to think it would be nice if *neither one* of us was the dreamer. Weren't you?"

Oh God, I forgot it was a dream, thinks Zelda. *Just for a second.* She's so tired.

"Am I wrong about that?" asks Langston. "You were starting to think it would be nice if we were trapped on this little island together."

"Answer my question," says Zelda. She feels like her heart is caving in. "The sand. Why did you take Erx's stupid sand 'that'll make you sleep forever'?"

Langston stops walking. His hi-top fade is outrageous. Bottle rockets finger-paint the sky.

"Because . . . I'm not sure I should wake up. I don't know—who even knows if it'll work—but maybe we'll get to the end of the dream and see *my* sleeping body through that fog, and we can just . . . sprinkle that sand."

Saying this out loud casts a spell on him. His face softens, and his softness looks like strength to her. He's lovely as he thinks about giving it all away. He's an angel.

"We both know I'm not a slay-the-dragon kind of hero, but I could be this kind," he says. "The self-sacrificing kind. I could save everyone."

Zelda feels helpless watching the idea of it take hold of him. "And if I'm the dreamer?" she asks. "If we see me there? What then?"

Langston's shrug starts low and climbs the whole length of him.

"I . . . really think it's me, though. The clown, and the horsemen. And . . . *you*. You're my magic mirror. You bring out every part of me, and you make it seem . . . *impossible* that I'm not a complete person."

This sounds to Zelda rather more like an argument for her sovereignty than his. But one thing at a time.

She's heard this kind of talk before, actually. The people in town would sometimes tell her quite plainly that just having her near made them feel more alive. "It's Not a Party Until Zelda Turns Up" was practically the town motto, and also the supposed message of a line of T-shirts she'd never been able to read. IT DOESN'T WIND DOWN UNTIL SHE'S GONE, said the back. The memory of this curdled once she started imagining the townspeople literally winding down in her absence: gears turning slower, slower still, until each of them stopped off-kilter, mouths slack. Waiting for Zelda to come wind them up again.

"You seem awfully sure of yourself," she tells Langston, "considering you were totally ignoring even the possibility you were the dreamer until I mentioned . . ."

Wait.

"*Hold* on," says Zelda. She makes a face at the little blue bag. "When you took this sand, didn't you think the dreamer was *me*? You were *certain* it was *me*. Did you want that stuff to use it on me?"

Langston looks rattled by the suggestion. He's got his hands up like he will literally push the thought of it away from him.

"No!" he says. "No. Of course not. Never."

He takes a step forward, and, for a moment, for the first time, it makes Zelda step back. She doesn't know what she wants anymore.

"Remember in the workshop," Langston asks her, "you tried to pinch yourself awake? When that didn't work, I learned two things about myself real quick. One—that I was happy the dream didn't end, and two—that I was *thrilled* to think all that pinching might mean you weren't the dreamer, either. I grabbed this bag of sand with no thought beyond, *Well, maybe this'll give Zelda and me a little more time together*. But now I get it . . ."

(For a moment, the carnival has forgotten to be beautifully brash, and it's so quiet she can hear him breathe. He lays a hand over her hand, and the bag.)

". . . the dreamer knows more than I do."

(His hand again—it squeezes.)

Oh boy.

"I'll do it if it's me," Langston promises. "You could do it if it's you. But that . . . that would be your decision."

His hand is the only thing holding her steady. Like he could take it away and she'd fall. With a jerk, she looks around at the quiet glow and all the happy, moonlit faces and wonders: Is that what this place is for? To make her fall?

Zelda pulls her hand free.

She shrugs off her backpack and rips it open. "Yeah . . . well . . . my decision. *Here's* my decision." She holds up the canopic jar containing the Ashes of the Phoenix, Who Will One Day Rise Again.

It's a beautiful jar, with a lid shaped like the head of a fierce bird and painted with a layered glaze that shimmers like shifting fire.

"This is what I took! It was right next to your sand. Like it *was* a decision: sleep or rise. I took this to help the dreamer wake up."

Langston reaches out to touch the phoenix head. He doesn't, though—he pulls his hand back like he expects it to be hot to the touch.

"And if it's me?" he says. "Dreaming?"

Zelda likes winning arguments as much as the next person, and she knows what it is she ought to say: *The dreamer deserves to wake. No matter who it is.* The words catch in her throat, though.

She's barely gotten a life.

She wants to live.

In that space between words, the sounds of the carnival come churning back. It's loud, and they're the quiet eye of it. Quiet, but by no means calm.

Zelda tries to hand Langston back his bag of sand. She has the drawstring of it pinched between two fingers, her arm as outstretched as can be, like she can't stand the smell of it. He doesn't move to take it, though—just leaves her to stand like that, feeling weak, her arm beginning to shake. Then he sighs and says, "It was a gift," and "Let's just enjoy the night," as he turns and continues down the midway.

So Zelda crams both the jar and bag into her backpack because she doesn't know what else to do.

God, maybe he is the dreamer, she thinks as she shuffles beside him. *He seems to have so many more memories than I do.* Zelda can hardly remember anything. Or, rather, she can remember everything, her whole life, but the last days and weeks blend seamlessly into the eighteen years before that, and she has no idea what's real and what isn't. She recalls a family trip but no family. A visit to a canyon full of clouds but no hands holding hers at the rim. A first kiss but never a boyfriend or girlfriend. She can picture a whole school full of classmates but none of their names.

There's a boy walking beside her, named Langston. She knows him.

"Can . . . you remember your first girlfriend?" Zelda asks. "Or . . . current girlfriend, or whatever?"

The boy thinks a moment.

"There *was* this girl," he says.

Zelda watches her feet. "Cool."

"She wasn't my girlfriend in the sense that we ever went out or . . . ha, had a real conversation or whatever. But. She worked at a coffee place where I used to live. I rode the streetcar there every day, for her. Not for the coffee—I don't even like coffee. I was . . ." He huffs. "I was so invisible, I think sometimes she'd forget I was there. And she'd stand at the counter and look out the big windows like she could see for miles."

He smiles, thinking about her. He straightens, standing taller.

"She was . . . You meet her, and it's like you suddenly realize who the main character is. Like she'd always been there, my whole life, and me and everyone else was just walking through her background. And I . . ."

Langston sighs. The sigh takes a little of the air out of him, and he stoops. Muscle memory of the weight on his shoulders.

He adds, "I never worked up the courage to ask her out, fine, but whatever. That's who I thought of, when you asked. So."

So.

TWENTY

"MELON. HELEN. PICKLE BRICKLE. CAFETERIA surprise.

"Figgy pudding. Stack o' pancakes. Cuban sandwich. Chicken fries.

"Avocado Avolcano! Now with guacamole lava.

"Jungle Jumble!—packed with mango, python, coconut, and guava.

"Dromedary camel crumble—you can really taste the humps!

"Or Jurassicles with fossil bits and stegosaurus lumps.

"Maraschino maple popcorn fudge with crunchy walrus topping . . .

". . . in a microwaving waffle cone that keeps the popcorn popping."

"No."

TWENTY-ONE

SHE'S STOPPED HOLDING HIS HAND. She can't remember how that happened. A nearby arrow says ON TO FUN LEVEL 15, but at this point they're having so little fun it seems like a typo.

Langston is interested, so pointedly interested in every little detail of their surroundings—the funnel cake and ring toss and Tilt-A-Whirl. Each time the choral squeal of the roller-coaster train passes, he perks up and watches, so interested is he. Interested in every face but hers.

He's protecting himself. She knows this. Twenty minutes ago, they would have run off together to explore anything at all. A small hill. A cabinet showroom. They would have stood and nodded vigorously as the cabinet salesperson explained the advantages of vinyl faux-grain laminate while their bodies buzzed and their elbows brushed together. But the evening isn't going well, so Langston is pretending he's here for the carnival instead of the company.

Fine, she thinks.

"Fine," she says aloud, just to hear how stupid and wrong it sounds.

"What?" says Langston.

"Nothing."

She keeps feeling like there's something she's supposed to be doing. She doesn't say this because it seems like a rude thing to mention, but maybe it's the reason things are going so poorly—she's distracted by this mysterious thing. Doesn't she have a cat that needs picking up? Doesn't she have a geography final?

She has the strangest sensation she's falling.

Everything smells like cotton candy. Her head feels like cotton candy. Pink and fuzzy, like it's not focusing on anything. Why is that metaphor familiar? Who cares. Who cares about metaphors. She takes in a deep, candy-coated breath, lets it out again.

Everyone here is smiling and walking close, and it really is joyous. There are thousands of tiny lights, and it really is beautiful. Lights on the Ferris wheel and the concessions and draped from tall poles to enchant you and make real life feel far away. She pulls off her glasses and lets the lights swell and spread their bright capillaries into the air. As she walks, they orbit and mingle, spilling color into one another—each one a lacy nimbus, intricate and divine.

She can't even remember what she was upset about. She can't even remember if she *was* upset. The lights and sounds of the carnival are working their magic, and it all feels like another country now.

Fine, she thinks again. *If he won't look at me, I'll look at him.* At his stupid angel face.

There's been something needling her, a thorn in her side, but it can't prick a melted heart. He turns his face to her, finally, and she forgets herself and grabs his arm. His breath catches. He looks so painfully hopeful. She pulls him toward the midway and says, "C'mon, I'm gonna win you a bear."

They practically dance across the straw to a bright booth twined with lights and ripe with prizes and topped by a sign that reads FAMBULUH.

FAMBULUH? FLAM . . . BLAM. She doesn't know why she can't read the sign, but it doesn't matter—she throws baseballs at milk bottles, one-two-three, and now it's Zelda and Langston and a stuffed pink bear.

"Hey, bear," says Zelda.

"What is up?" says the bear.

A flight of glam-rock Xanadu stilt walkers pass over and around them and are gone. Every phase of moon lights the sky at once, encircling the world like charms.

Zelda tosses Ping-Pong balls and wins a goldfish in a plastic bag, which she gives to the bear, and rings the bell on the strength test to win an inflatable mallet. Langston is looking at her with stars in his eyes.

"She is wonderful," the bear tells him.

"She is," Langston agrees. He smiles, then doesn't. "I should just let her keep playing all the games, right? She seems really happy. I shouldn't ruin that. Plus, you know . . . she's really good at them. Maybe I wouldn't even be as good." He takes a breath. "I'm good at other things."

The bear has been listening patiently. "I am stuffed with shredded newspapers," he says.

There's a game where you spin a bottle so Zelda spins the bottle. Around and around it turns with a tickety sound, until finally it slows and stops and it's pointing right at Langston. They face each other, breathless.

And then the bottle spins one last tick, and actually it's pointing at the bear.

"BEAR'S THE WINNER!" shouts the carnie. Zelda shrugs and kisses the bear on his stuffed cheek. He smells like a book of carpet samples.

The roller coaster stretches its spine like a cat. Cotton-candy snowflakes turn on the breeze. Zelda wins a hacky sack key chain and a cowboy hat and a confusing mirror printed with a photo of Hulk Hogan playing the guitar. The bear examines his reflection in a gap between Hogan's arm and torso, and considers his goldfish and inflatable mallet.

"I have a plastic bag filled with water," he tells himself, "and another filled with air. In the former, a fish; in the latter, only a dream of cartoon violence. A hammer fit for a god because it is like a god: garish, and allegorical, and empty. I have a key chain, but no keys; the hat of a horseman, but no horse; and now, alas, I have my own reflection. A tragicomic sense of self."

"Also this alien with dreadlocks," says Zelda, handing the bear a plush alien. "I won him while you were talking."

"Now you have everything you need to start your new life," Langston tells the bear.

"Thank you, my friends," the bear answers. "I will never forget you." He leaps atop a ticket booth and sings the first note of a big musical number, but Zelda and Langston have already run off to the haunted house.

They're put into a car shaped like a couple of bicycles and sent inside through big, flapping doors. And the haunted house is scary at first, with a blaring horn and a pair of headlights that zoom right at your bike. But then the second scare is a car accident, too. So's the third, and so on.

"Eh, that was a letdown," says Zelda as they exit through an archway like a screaming mouth.

Langston is quiet.

"Spinfunger!" shouts Zelda.

"What?"

"Spanflang!"

"I don't know what that is."

"Ach, the sign keeps changing. That thing! Over there!" She pulls him toward a ride that looks like a circusy centrifuge. A giant hub turning spokes capped with love seats that are each spinning independently on their own herky axles.

"Oh!" says Langston. "Cool. That is . . . definitely a thing I can do."

They jostle through the snaking line, bumping pleasantly off of each other, and when the love seats empty they're given one that has the name SIEGE PERILOUS written across the backrest. They sit, and the carnie pulls a bar and roll-cage over the top of them.

Langston says, "So, what if I'm usually the kind of person who gets really motion-sick?"

"What?" asks Zelda as the ride starts moving.

Later, when it's over and Langston is breathing deeply on a bench with his head between his legs, Zelda's thoughts catch up with her.

"I forgot something," she begins.

She sits with this a second.

"I forgot something important," she says. "I keep . . . forgetting that I forgot it."

It's coming back to her. Coming up slowly, as if through a canyon full of fog.

She sees movement through a sliver of a gap between two concession stands. One of the costumed mascots is sitting down on a milk crate to take a break, supposing themselves to be out of view. It's Zelda. That is, it's a grinning, top-heavy, carpet-headed Zelda costume. It's wearing the same clothes she's wearing. It reaches up with fat hands and lifts its fat head up off its padded shoulders.

"No," Zelda whispers. "I don't want to see."

The head is removed. It's Langston. The person inside the Zelda costume is Langston.

Zelda flinches and turns to look at the boy sitting beside her, the boy that should be Langston but instead is just a fidgeting cloud. A cloud, in vaguely human shape, sits beside her on the bench with its pink head between its pink knees.

No. It's Langston. She thought she saw something else for a second. She's dizzy from the ride. She checks on the mascot again just in time to see someone—someone who might be a cloud—finish replacing their big, empty head and get back on their feet. Break time is over.

She wonders, briefly, if she might have fallen asleep. Just fallen asleep for a second on this bench. She's so tired. That would explain it. She has to think about this.

But then the roller-coaster train jumps its track. At the peak of its tallest curve, it launches when it ought to dive, and all the cars of it sail through the air over the carousel. The passengers cheer as it crashes and careens along the ground, carving a deep trench across the midway. The rumble of it knocks loose the Ferris wheel, which drops and trundles around like a spun penny, causing a water tower to spill its contents into the freshly carved trench while a nearby sign, which *had* said ON TO FUN LEVEL 24, drops letters across the opening of an unrelated mine shaft until they rearrange to read TUNNEL OF LOVE 4 2, and the whole thing seems like kind of a setup.

"Oh," Zelda whispers. "Right. None of this is real."

All but a single car of the roller coaster eventually comes to some noisy exit through the other end of the mine shaft. That remaining, empty car—dislodged from the rest—floats like a boat in the trench at the tunnel's mouth. Somehow it already has a teenager in a hat waiting to load passengers into it.

"I forgot I was dreaming," says Zelda. "I forgot it's a dream."

The Ferris wheel swivels lower, lower, faster, faster, finally drilling down to a shuddering stop that sends a purr through the air and shivers everyone's shoulders. Every last little thing that's going to fall and break, falls and breaks. It's quiet.

"Maybe we should . . ." says Zelda, struggling to hold her thoughts above the fog. It isn't fair—everyone got to sleep but her. "We were on a quest. We're wasting so much . . ."

She looks around. Everyone, literally everyone, at the carnival is watching her. Her and Langston.

"Um," says Zelda.

Langston appears to have recovered. He takes Zelda's hand and nods toward the tunnel.

"C'mon. Let's get away from all this."

Zelda can't see the blush on her face, but it blooms in the sky— slow fireworks of dusky pink. They walk together, stiffly, trying not to look at a hundred faces that have turned like flowers to bask in the glow of them. It's like a wedding, almost. It feels like a decision.

They settle into the floating car and give the ride operator a coin. He tells them to keep their hands inside at all times. He smirks as he says it. And the boat is moving into the tunnel.

There's no lurch—it's like it's always been moving, like it's the boat they've been in all along. Langston twines his little finger around hers.

This is a dream, Zelda reminds herself.

Or a story.

A dream is just a story you tell yourself, thinks Zelda—*a story you tell yourself about yourself.*

Probably all stories are secretly like that.

So what is this story trying to tell her? Nothing so straight-forward as a beginning and a middle and a moral at the end. But this dream's been asking the same questions for too long to ignore them. Do you want to grow up? Do you want a life that's easy or a life that's real? Do you hide in a cave or go play dodgeball—scrape your knees, stick your head out, risk your heart? Ride a dirt bike or read a dork book? She's maybe reaching a little for that last one.

The answers—to her, anyway—seem obvious: *yes, real, dodgeball,* and *both.* There's something she isn't getting. And she needs to get it, because it's going to be her decision to make.

That mascot has shown her the truth. Just as she was beginning to wish for more equal footing, the mascot lifted the veil and reminded her that Langston is only in her head. An idea, living inside her.

She glances at Langston and thinks, *I made him*.

Of course she had—her dreaming mind was making everything here—but specifically and in actual fact she had made *him*. No wonder she likes him so much—he is her literal dream guy.

That's weird.

And romance—oh, *jeez*, she'd just been thinking about the utter lack of romance in her life, and now the dreaming Zelda has apparently gone and invented herself a boyfriend. Just like Shellifer or Chinny or whatever her name was, in fifth grade.

Zelda made him. Well, so what? She doesn't control him. She still doesn't know what he's going to say or do, so that makes him a person, doesn't it?

She made him. What does it mean?

It's dark in the tunnel, but up ahead on the curved tunnel wall there is a flickering projection. It's a view of town, like a magic mirror; Zelda can see her house. It isn't twilight there, it seems—her front garden is gilded by sunlight. The willow sways to the music of the wind chimes on the porch. It's taller than Zelda remembers.

As the boat passes, the projector goes dark, just as another comes to life on the opposite wall. A mermaid parade is crawling up Main Street toward the courthouse square. Zelda doesn't remember hearing about any parade, but her town is frequently up to things like this. All the classic cars have been rolled out of storage and hitched to shimmering floats. There's a girl of maybe twelve on one of these floats, waving through a fizzy bubble-machine breeze. She wears big glasses and seashells. A dazzling rainbow tail. On her face is a joy undiluted by any other feeling.

Another scene—oh, there's Clara. She and her grandmother

have come out for the parade. Both women look older—Clara's going gray. She leans in and fixes the line of the old woman's collar. She kisses the crepe of the old woman's cheek.

The next vignette is a darkened puppet theater matinee. Light leaks in through gaps in the curtained windows. Up front, there's a big felt duck onstage, vamping around. Some tiny puppet-men on horses get too close and are eaten—the kids in the audience think this is hysterical. One child in particular. He laughs and laughs, and Zelda can't take her eyes off him. He looks a little like her, and a little like Langston.

Now this fades and the inside of the tunnel lights up like a paper lantern—red and warm. They could be drifting through an immense heart; they could be navigating a valentine. Langston scooches closer.

They could just stay here. Make a nice little home for themselves in the Tunnel of Love and drink the water and forget. Coursing along with the current. Getting carried away.

He isn't dressed like 1989 anymore. Neither is Zelda—she's back in her running clothes, actually. Good. If she's going to kiss a boy, and it seems increasingly like she *finally* is, then she ought to kiss him as he is, who he is.

Who is he, though? Really. He's a character. One of many in a story she's telling herself, about herself. She's a character, too.

All those people in town, and Langston and Patches and her and everyone. Parts of the whole. *We're all the dreamer*, she thinks, excited because it sounds true. Or, rather, because it's the sort of grand, blameless idea that would be true, in a story. It would be *easier* if it were true.

So does she want a life that's easy or a life that's real?

She's been staring at him too long, and he at her. *Here it comes*, she thinks. And then, only half jokingly, she wonders what's going to interrupt them this time. A startling confession? A hurricane. The sudden appearance of a colossal parade balloon. But there's nothing here. They're all alone. Oh God.

His face softens, finally. His lips part, finally, finally.

When the tunnel light changes abruptly from red to green, Langston goes for it. He leans into that no-fly zone that exists between all but the most friendly allies.

She's supposed to lean into it, too.

She's not supposed to, for example, jerk backward, and tip the boat, and dunk herself like a tea bag in the water. But that's definitely what she does.

"Aaahsorry!" says Langston.

Her butt's wet. It feels like a shocking revelation. Like the revelation of wondering who's going to spoil your kiss only to discover, *Okay wow, I guess it's me.*

Langston has managed to stay in the boat, which is rocking, and when he lunges forward to offer Zelda his hand and she leaps up out of the chilly water, they accidentally knock foreheads in the middle.

"Sorry!"

She's sitting in the water again—he's leaning backward in the boat.

"I thought," he says.

"I just," he adds, a few seconds later.

"You know," he tells her, and the light dies inside the tunnel. "I just thought you wanted me to. You know I'll do whatever you want me to."

She hadn't known that.

Dammit, she still doesn't—she doesn't know anything. She's wasting time puzzling over this question when she could just flip to the answers at the end.

She gets sloshingly to her feet and tramps over the boat.

"Sorry," she says. "We can't . . . not until . . . sorry. Sorry! But I have to know. Patches!"

The tunnel walls are flimsy curtains and she rips them apart.

"Okay. You made me do this. As a one-time-only favor

"I am giving you a chance to try the forty-seventh flavor.

"In a tomb in ancient Egypt there's a prehistoric scroll,

"and the legend it divulges tells the story of a bowl.

"It's a bowl carved out of diamond in the center of a fountain

"that is housed inside a temple at the summit of a mountain.

"After seven years of searching, I unearthed it in the Andes.

"In the bowl there lay an ice cream . . . made of starlight . . . topped with candies.

"And they say this frozen treat will choose a single cat to try it—

"just one cat in all the world, and all he has to do is buy it.

"For the one who eats this ice cream, all his wishes will come true.

"Look: It glows with starlight radiance—this ice cream's chosen you."

"No."

The ice cream man sits down on the sidewalk and stares for a thousand miles. Patches sniffs.

"What was the second one again?"

"Vanilla?"

Patches gets the vanilla.

"Patches!"

He flicks his ears and turns. "Zelda?"

The carnival and countryside are swept away with a sound like a sword unsheathed and he can see her, distantly, stomping across a stormy plain.

He drops his vanilla ice cream on the ground and hurries after her.

"Patches!"

"Coming!"

She flings her arms and pulls the empty plain apart—behind it is her high school.

"Nope," she says, and sweeps this aside to reveal a roller rink, a basement, a hoard of gaudy treasure. "Nice try," she says. She huffs and puffs, and it's gone.

Patches falls in step with her. "Where are we going?"

"To the *end*. Did we all forget? We are going to the edge, and we are going to *see*."

Before them is a dark forest. Again, she reaches for the gap in its curtains, tries to brush it aside.

It won't budge.

She tries again and again, but the forest won't budge.

Night falls like it was pushed.

TWENTY-TWO

"THIS IS THE THICKEST FOREST I've ever seen," says Zelda, if only because neither she nor Patches has said anything for a while. The tallest trees here are titanic: thick and gray as city streets, too tall to even glimpse the upper canopies. Smaller ones pack the gaps between, their needles as dark as iron. "Like a forest from a fairy tale," she adds, and wishes she hadn't when it seems to cause a wolf to howl in the distance.

"Will young Langston not be joining us, then?"

Zelda's heart moves like a bird. She can feel it trying to fly back to him. *Simmer down, heart.*

"Young Langston just . . . needs to cool his jets until I see what's what," she says after too long.

Patches shies away from a fallen branch, a rotten and tumorous limb, and pads closer to Zelda. He tells her, "While I have private reservations about the boy's fitness—"

"*So* private," Zelda agrees. "I've been like, *When is Patches gonna let us know how he feels?*"

"*Despite* my private reservations," Patches insists, "I do understand what the poet Emily Dickinson understood."

Zelda frowns. "Hope is the thing with feathers?"

"That the heart wants what it wants," Patches answers. "Or else it does not care."

Zelda holds her arms close against the chill. "Langston wants some girl in a coffee shop," she grumbles. She tries to really put some stink on "coffee shop," but she's forcing it. She sighs. "No. I know what he wants. I know what everyone wants," she says, "I just don't know *why*."

"'Twas ever thus."

The air is still on the forest floor, but something is knocking the high branches. Something creaks and groans. They pick their path gingerly through red ferns and blue mosses that cover the earth like a bruise.

She's forgotten what the wizard told her. How foolish is that? She doesn't know if this is a dream or a story, but either way—one thing you obviously never do is *forget what a wizard told you*. She was doing a lot of forcing back there, sweeping the landscape aside, being pushy. So the dream pushed back. Now she has her hand out in front of her like she can feel her way through this witches' wood. Like she can gently steer them to a yellow brick road.

"I stole something from Erx," Zelda says.

"I saw. A jar, yes? What was it?"

"Erx said it contained 'the Ashes of the Phoenix, Who Will One Day Rise Again.'"

"I see. You're expecting it to be symbolic?"

"Isn't everything here?"

"Perhaps. You will spread those ashes in the right place or at the right time, and the psychic trigger of it will wreak some useful havoc in the world beyond."

Zelda hunches her shoulders. "Sounds stupid when you say it out loud. I *also* have some sand that'll make a person sleep forever."

Patches's tail flicks, hackles raised. "What? Why would you want such a thing?"

"That's what *I* said! Langston took it, not me. I guess he thought it'd be good to have options."

"Options for whom?" Patches wants to know. "To what end?"

Again, the wolf howls, long and low. Every tree cracks its knuckles; the wind condescends to sting their eyes and wend, wormlike, through their hair. Everything stirs.

"I think he'd rather keep living here. I think he'd rather I keep living with him. He probably wants us to get a little place together in the Forest of Hands and Feet, binge-watch other people's lives through the Magic Mirror."

"Then we are fortunate to be rid of him."

Zelda is quiet. Patches twitches his ears.

"This is you agreeing with me silently, I trust?"

Zelda blows her hair out of her face. "Do you get the impression the dream is trying to make a case? Like it wants us to stay here."

"And what a compelling case it is. Just look at this tempting vacation destination."

Which is fair. Still, she may be imagining it, but as she gently steers she could swear there's something warm, ahead, in the heart of the place.

"Yeah," she say to Patches. "But what do you bet it's like this because the dream wants us to give up and go back to town? It's trying to keep us from getting to the end of the story. And . . . it almost got me, back there. It almost got me with the rides and the cotton candy and the . . . company. It still might. There is a whole *world* here. A whole world of people. Sure, some of those carnival-goers seemed a little two-dimensional, but the folks back in town? Clara, and the Mayor, and . . . and my classmates, whose names I can't remember just now . . ."

Patches sniffs.

"Fine," says Zelda. "But *you*. You're a person. A cat person. And I already said Clara, and . . . even the laundromat clown seemed to have an inner life, you know?"

"And Langston," says Patches.

Zelda bows her head. "And Langston."

Langston codders through the dark forest, flashlight in hand. He was clever to think of bringing a flashlight, he tells himself, and resents the way the light of it gathers like frosted breath around its mouth. There's a compass in his other hand, but the needle is only turning drowsy circles. "I'm . . . I'm worried we're going to get turned around in here," he whispers to himself, because this is a whispery place. He whispers like the forest itself might be sleeping—he has the skin-crawling feeling he's walking across the needly hide of something lying prone and patient.

The ground here is covered in mushrooms. The mushrooms seem to be respiring. The gills quaver under every cap, and each stem shrinks and swells, shrinks and swells.

Langston pockets the pointless compass and reaches into his pack. "Bread crumbs," he says, freeing a loaf of white bread from a plastic bag. Soon he's tearing it into snowflakes, letting them drop to the forest floor. "I find Zelda, I tell her how terribly sorry and wrong

I was for whatever I'm supposed to be sorry about, and if we have to, we can follow the trail of . . ."

His stomach goes sour—the mushrooms are eating the bread crumbs.

He watches one mushroom gorge itself on a hunk of bread, its stem swelling fatter and fatter until the whole thing shrieks and pops like a balloon. He can hear the sounds of other mushrooms shrieking and exploding behind him.

So Langston keeps throwing the bread crumbs. If they have to, they can follow the trail of exploded mushrooms.

"Did you hear something?" Zelda asks.

"It sounded distantly like a mushroom exploding," says Patches. "You were talking about the townspeople."

"Right." She breathes. The air here has weight. And texture. It goes in and out of her like a chimney sweep. "So. Erx said maybe this was all a story. Well, if it *is* a story, then I guess Langston thinks it's a saving-the-world story. Save the world and get the girl. Who cares if it isn't the real world—it's the only world he knows."

"He's been doing a bang-up job."

"I know. He hasn't really stepped up yet."

"And so, what?" asks Patches. "If young Langston finds the edge of dreamland and confirms he himself is the dreamer, then he plays sandman and sprinkles the contents of that bag . . . where? Over the edge? In his own eyes? Enlighten me. You must have a similar plan for the ashes."

"I don't know. I'm hoping it makes sense when we get there."

"Ah yes. Such is the hallmark of our quest thus far—it makes more sense as it goes along."

"Ha."

"So what does Langston do if the dreamer is me?" says Patches. "Does he pour sand in my eyes? Mix some in my kibble?"

Zelda sags. "No offense, but I really don't think you're the dreamer. And so I don't think the sand or the ashes would even work on you, because . . . everything here? Everything in this whole crazy dreamworld? It's all just different pieces of the dreamer's mind. Different . . . conflicting ideas. Stuff she's working out. Right?"

"I agree."

"So sand or ashes: It's really a choice. It's just a choice the dreamer hasn't made yet, and so they were waiting back at Erx's for Langston and me to find and take. Or not take. Because I want to leave, and Langston thought maybe this is a place worth saving. I've been wondering if he's right."

Patches hunches as some weeping spirit sails over their heads, and asks, "Are you still wondering it now?"

Zelda frowns. It's a good question. Maybe it's the overall gloom, maybe it's the litany of tiny mushroom screams, but this forest is starting to get to her. You can see it in the curve of her back, or the dying embers of her eyes.

"If you'd asked me when we were leaving town," Zelda breathes, "I felt I *had* to be the dreamer. Because all the puppets in town had gone and shown me their strings, and I was feeling like I must be the only real girl in the whole world."

There's a rasp in her throat. She coughs it loose.

"So I was going to be the dreamer, and I was going to wake myself up, because . . . shouldn't I get to be challenged? And take chances and . . . screw up, even? And maybe have to earn the love I take, sometimes. I wanted it all to *mean* something.

"And then, it's funny—out beyond the town, it's like everything got less realistic but more *real*. So about the time we got to the carnival I'd started playing around with a different idea: What if the dreamer's some stranger? The dreamer's a stranger, and so we're all equals in here. And maybe the dreamer just sleeps forever—that's not any of our faults."

Her head droops. "Now I've got it all messed up in my mind." She sucks in air. "If I was able to believe in myself as a real person *and* a figment of someone else's imagination at the same time, then what about everybody else? You, and Erx, and Langston. You're people. If I'm the dreamer *and* Langston's a person, am I making him love me? Am I making you?"

"Zelda."

"What?" she says. "You don't know I'm not. So . . . at least Langston's quest is noble, or whatever."

"The noble death is but a paper crown on the head of he who does not wish to live," says the cat.

Zelda says, "Huh." She's too tired to work out what this means. "Anyway, he wants to save everything. Meanwhile, the only quest I'm on is to find the air lock and take all the oxygen with me. You know if I succeed, you die, right? Everyone dies?"

"If you are the dreamer," says Patches, "then each of us is a part of you. As you've said. We are all of us, you. Your fate is our fate."

Zelda knows she won't be able to see the carnival from here, but she looks all the same.

"So why is one of my parts a cute boy who wants me to fail?"

The forest floor crackles. Something moves. What Zelda mistook for a nearby boulder rises and pulls its head out of the earth like a tick—exactly like a tick; it rises on rickety legs. And runs. Other boulders shoulder their heavy backs and scurry after it, and what Zelda can't see, she can hear: a thousand spider legs chattering in the darkness.

They're running. Every one of them is a monster, and they're running from whatever monsters fear.

"I want to be carried," says Patches. Zelda lifts and presses him to her chest, kisses the top of his head.

Langston has a look like he wants to be carried, too. He has his sword drawn but he may be trying to hide behind it.

He's being followed.

He can't even tell you how he knows, but he knows. He's being followed. Something has entered the forest after him.

Then the forest floor crackles, and the ticks rise, each the boss monster of its own domain. But they're running from something; something worse. The *snicker-snack* of their legs is all he can hear for a long minute, but when that sound fades, another comes from behind him through the trees:

Honky.

Patches moves to higher ground, stepping up Zelda's arm to perch on her shoulder. "Don't feel right," he tells her.

Zelda doesn't feel right, either. She tries to answer, and is only half-surprised to discover she can't find her voice. That when she tries to speak, the only sound is the stifled hiss of something slithering inside her.

A dream is like a story you tell yourself about yourself, she thinks. Sure. But it isn't just any kind of story, is it? It's a fairy tale. One of those messed-up old-world fairy tales that's all about fear and want. And fear of wanting. A story you can't understand with your head because it comes from the gut, passed from mothers to daughters, one belly to the next. Our primordial inheritance, Zelda thinks, because at this moment she can't remember ever having had a sunny dream.

She'd been telling herself she was steering toward something good in this forest, something yellow and bright. She's sure now she was mistaken.

Patches is stiff and perfectly still on her shoulder. She can't see him, but she can hear him—he's hissing, too—and feel his needle claws sink into her flesh.

There are so many trees—it's been like moving through a crowded room. But now Zelda could swear the trees recede, make way. Because something is about to happen.

There is blackness in the lean spaces between the trunks—thin glimpses of a vast nothing far, far away.

No, there isn't.

Zelda sees the truth—what she'd thought were two faces is a candlestick. What she'd taken for woods and distant darkness is actually a close ring of sharp black slashes before a backdrop of painted trees.

Every slash is a witch.

One by one, the witches turn and show their faces, and dip their bobbin hats, and shake their spindle arms.

"*Daughter,*" one says to Zelda.

"*Daughter.*"

"*Daauughhter.*"

Honky honky honk.

Langston scrambles over and through the mushrooms and ferns, pinballing off trees, trying to shuffle-step backward and stumbling and almost impaling himself on his own sword.

Honky honky honky-honky-honky-honky.

He pinwheels to his feet again, runs. It's harder—the trees here are packed tighter, even the black sky once again seems too close. As if it's all going to draw closed like a velvet bag and he'll be trapped with the laundromat clown and his own stupid heart.

He'd never see Zelda again.

He'd never have to face her again, though, either.

He feels a confusing unwinding, a sense of relief. He doesn't have to ever talk to Zelda again if he just stops here and lets his childhood catch up and eat him. The laundromat clown is scary, but you don't have to puzzle over what it wants. You don't have to wonder if it thinks about you, cares about you. It cares about you very much and thinks of nothing but grabbing you and eating you and twisting your guts into balloon animals. And isn't that love?

Honky honky honky honky honk.

Unconditional love would be nice, too, obviously. Mothers and grandparents and the love of a coffee-shop girl that exists only in his dreams. Childish love, that's what he wants, without fear of rejection. Doesn't everybody, though, really? Why not admit it?

He squeezes between two stout trees and is met with a brightness that makes him squint. He turns to it and shields his face with his hand.

"Look at that," Langston tells himself.

His eyes flutter and adjust. He puts away his sword. "A clearing," he whispers.

There *is* a clearing—the first he's seen since entering the forest—and it's a pillow of lush green grasses and wildflowers, surrounded by saplings. A singularly sunny glade. And in a shaft of buttery sun stands a little yellow house as appealing as a child's drawing. A square and a triangle, extruded into three dimensions. Four windows and a door; gables and a single chimney sitting just so.

"That's the house I grew up in," says Langston, and you can hear the smile in his voice. You can see his shoulders slacken, his spine straighten, as he walks toward the clearing. "There's the chip in the siding where I crashed my wagon," he whispers, as if he's forgotten he's alone.

"*Langston?*" Zelda breathes, a hundred miles away. She could have sworn she heard his voice. She glimpses something fine and yellow beyond the trees.

"Is . . . is that a house?"

"*You look frightened, Daughter,*" says a witch, and they all take a step toward her.

Zelda doesn't want to offend them. "I thought I heard a wolf," she whispers. "Before."

"*You did hear a wolf, silly. You heard* the *wolf,*" says one witch, or maybe another. They step closer.

"*These woods* are *a wolf,*" says another, or the first. "*His strong back is the ground beneath our feet.*"

"*We are ticks. We are nothing to him.*"

"That's . . . probably not true," says Zelda. They're so close now.

Patches has stopped hissing, but he's still stiff as a nail. She's worried about him. So, though her head weighs a thousand pounds, she turns it to look at him, and she's paid for her trouble with a swipe to the cheek.

Zelda gasps.

Patches scratched her. Scratched *her.* Now he leaps down to the forest floor and crouches behind the hem of a witch's robe.

"*He's ours now,*" the witch says.

"He belongs to us," says another.

"They all belong to us."

It doesn't occur to Langston to knock—this is his house, isn't it? He just strides up the yellow brick walk and tries the door. It comes open easily, airily. Before him is all the old furniture, its arrangement as familiar as a map of the world. He weaves through it, touching a finger to an armrest, along the mantel, between the ears of a cast-iron Scottie dog. Past the kitchen and the dining room, and now he's returned to the foyer and the base of the stairs.

There's a framed photograph here, a Sunday-clothes kind of family portrait from a portrait studio. Langston and Baldwin, Mom and Dad. This photo strikes a chord—Langston's seen it before, but it's been a long time. Why would that be? There's a glare on the glass, and it's masking the faces of his mother and brother, so he takes the frame off the wall to see them better—but the glare stays put. He tilts the photo this way and that, but try as he might, he can't see them. Nor can he quite remember how their faces would look if he could. It occurs to him that here, in a dream, this is really just two ways of saying the same thing.

"They still live," his dad said, after the accident. "But only in our memories."

In his mind, Langston's wearing that same little church suit, the one from the picture. "They're imaginary," he had answered. He'd had imaginary friends before—he could have two more.

"Yeah," said Dad. "All right. Imaginary. And you and I, we have to go on being real. Without them. We have to stay safe, so their memory will last."

He knows that he nodded then, and made some worthless five-year-old's promise. Now that he can't even remember their faces,

Langston figures he has finally failed his mother and his brother in every last conceivable way.

He wipes his eyes.

There's another photo on the wall, up a step. His family's trip to the Grand Canyon. The four of them standing stiffly with a pink panorama behind them. Here it's like Mom and Baldwin must have moved—they're a blur. His own face is clear, though, and gleaming.

"Look at this little idiot," Langston whispers.

You'd never guess it from his smiling face, but the thing Langston remembers most about that trip was the spotlight of his father's fear. Fear that his boys would make some deadly mistake at the canyon's rim. Over Mom's objections, he'd told them the cautionary tale of a little girl he'd read about, a girl who'd chased after a toy and fallen into the canyon. And later, at the rim, near a trailhead called Bright Angel, Langston saw her. He saw the girl.

No. Obviously not. Langston had seen *a* girl, and his five-year-old brain had taken pieces of the story and the memory and mixed them together—a little bit of dream-logic creeping into a waking brain that was too young to always know the difference. This was just a girl, a little girl with dark, windswept hair looking out over miles of canyon, all alone. He lost his whole heart to that girl, instantly, falling utterly in love like only a five-year-old boy can.

That was the first time he saw her.

The finial on the bannister feels *warm*. He doesn't wonder about that. Instead he wonders, suddenly, whether his old bedroom looks the same up there on the second floor. He climbs the stairs, opens the door with the poster of a frog saying *This is my pad* that he never understood as a kid and only narrowly understands now. All his old models are there, still smelling of glue, their decals curling at the edges. His bed is his bed, covered with stuffed animals. It *is* a stuffed animal, strong-legged and soft-backed and faithful. He could pass out from all the nostalgia radiating off the periwinkle wallpaper.

Patches growls at Zelda. It sounds to her like the pitch of a drill touching a tooth. His eyes are sheathed in their milky inner lids. Zelda's cheek feels red.

"*It's good you came,*" says a witch; maybe one, maybe all.

"*We need a thirteenth.*"

"*You'll stay; we'll eat houses and children together.*"

In a panic, Zelda looks to the yellow house in the clearing—did Langston go there? The witches *snick* and *snack* their fingers together.

Zelda knows what they're implying: that the house in the glade is like a gingerbread cottage, covered in candy. A witch's house, a trap.

But.

She squints at it.

She would have walked right in. They could have let her get caught. If it *is* their web, then what are all the spiders doing out here?

"That house," she says. "It looks nice."

"*It looks however we please.*"

"Right," says Zelda. "Right. So . . . change it. Right now, change it. Cast a spell, or whatever you do. Make it look like *anything* else."

The witches are quiet. Zelda doesn't think any of them have so much as glanced at the glade since they arrived.

"Are you . . . afraid of that house?" she asks them.

They cry like cats. They step back, and put on a great show of laughter, but laughter is something they've only read about in stories.

Zelda's limbs feel looser. She looks all of them in their Halloween faces. "You're afraid of a *house*," she says, and picks up a stick.

TWENTY-THREE

LANGSTON IS LYING FACEDOWN ON race-car sheets. This bed is just right.

He rolls on his back and smiles up at the ceiling, the stucco patterns. There are pictures in the plaster—he discovered them as a boy. Sometimes on warm nights, a breeze would move his curtains, and in the shifting light his plaster pictures would almost seem to move.

He realizes something: that whenever he dreams, if he dreams of a house, it's this house. The house he lived in when he was five, and new, and still making the map of all his mind's monuments and milestones. Still separating the world's parts into the concrete and the allegorical. Back when certain things could be both.

No matter if he's dreaming of his grandma's house, or a friend's, or of any one of the rentals and apartments he's lived in since— irrepressible dream logic always shapes it into this little yellow box. His original packaging.

This was the place where he could feel safe without having to always be safe. Here he could take his tiny, five-year-old chances. Then they lost this house, Langston and his dad did. After. They lost it for real, so Langston moved it into his dreams. And to go on feeling safe, Langston tucked himself inside new boxes that were less easy to see.

A little movement catches his eye. The swaying curtains framing the window above his headboard look authentic, but Langston feels them to be sure. Yes—they're gauze-thin and pilly. He rises and kneels on his pillow, half expecting the window to overlook a crab-apple tree and the Smithsons' backyard sandbox.

Instead he sees forest, and fungus, and Zelda swinging a tree branch at some witches. Langston clambers out of bed and races downstairs with his backpack and sword.

"*Daughter.*"

"*Dauughhhterr.*"

Zelda's keeping them at bay. Or they're toying with her—she isn't sure. The stick in her hands is slow, heavy.

Anything is possible, she thinks. *Gently, now.*

"I don't know why I thought this was a stick," she says aloud. "When it's obviously a shining sword with a golden hilt and a jewel-encrusted . . . you know, thing."

The witches hang back and stare.

"The butt end of the handle," adds Zelda.

"*Pommel?*" offers one of the witches, right before Zelda cuts her in half with her pretty new sword. Right through the witch's middle, which feels no more substantial than cobwebs and ashes. Her torso topples off dead legs and lands near where Patches lies bunched up and growling.

Zelda swings again, and again, smiling as the witches back up to the edge of the trees. The half-a-witch crawls to a safe distance and spins out a new pair of legs.

"Go away," Zelda tells them. "You're gonna lose—you're not even real."

"*Said the pot to the kettle,*" says the half-a-witch, and she spits. Or tries to—she's dry as salt.

"You're made of cobwebs!" Zelda tells them. "Plus you're the bad guys. So, sorry! Bad guys don't win in the end."

"*Daughter,*" says the bravest witch, the only one moving closer while her sisters move away. "*You are mistaken. This isn't a story.*"

"*It's a nightmare,*" another witch agrees.

Now they all step closer and speak in turn.

"*In nightmares, the bad guys win. The bad guys* always *win.*"

"*Never a happy ending in a nightmare.*"

"*Not true, sister. Consider: How do* all *dreams end?*"

Now they all look at Zelda.

Zelda whispers, "And then she woke up." She's beginning to feel the cold.

"*So wake up, Daughter,*" says the bravest witch. "*If you can.*"

Zelda can't, of course. For reasons. She swings, and the witch steps back. "It's complicated!" she shouts. "Also, shut up!"

"*Poor paper doll, thought she was a real girl.*"

Zelda lunges and cuts this witch's arm off at the elbow. But whatever lives in the cobwebs is already knitting a new one.

"*How could she know, when all she can see is the paper?*" says another.

Zelda lunges again and cuts off its head.

But the head rolls to a stop in the mushrooms, mouth agape, and makes a clicking sound in its gullet—and now Zelda's sword is a snake.

She cries out, tries to will it to be a sword again. She whispers to it—"Sword sword sword sword sword"—but it goes limp, and she drops it. Her sword slithers its golden body, shakes its jewel-encrusted rattle, and slips off through the gasping mushrooms.

"Bats," Zelda whispers, but the bats she conjures dissolve with the wave of a witch's fingers. "Tornado," she says, but there's no wind left in her. And now the sisters are closing in, knitting the air with their needle fingers.

Their mouths aren't holes, notes Zelda as she curls up on the cold earth. They have the pocket-mouths of puppets. She's trying to decide if this makes them more or less terrifying when one of the witches explodes into dust.

The others turn and hiss, and there's Langston.

"The Sssword of Omensss!" shrieks a witch as Langston swings again, and whiffs.

Patches is suddenly at Zelda's side, his eyes clear and bright.

"I'm sorry!" he says. "I'm sorry!"

"Forget it," says Zelda.

"Would that I could turn back time—"

Zelda gives him a perfunctory pat and gets to her feet. "Weren't yourself," she says.

The clicking noise comes again as one witch crooks her slim fingers, drawing sinister ciphers in the air. And the sword in Langston's hand wavers, but there's no overcoming its ThunderCat magic. Langston has whiffed again, however, and fallen on his backside. Zelda dives in.

"You saved me," she says, smiling and grabbing his sword. "Now gimme."

"Be careful," says Langston. "That might be a spell or something."

"It's not a spell. It's not even good poetry." Zelda points at her head and shakes it at the witches. "I'm impervious to poetry! *I only read magazines!*"

They snipe at her, one by one, swooping close and coughing with false laughter as she pivots and swings. The tatters of their black shifts crackle and flap. Sometimes she slices only the air, but even that feels like some kind of victory—she *hates* the air here. Sometimes she connects, trimming a leg or giving a broom a haircut.

"Maybe . . ." says Langston. "Maybe I should try? Let me know when you get tired."

Zelda happily punctuates his sentence with a roundhouse swing that slices right up the center of a witch's broomstick and sends it sprawling into the crook of a tree.

But she has no time to celebrate—she's left her flank exposed, and another witch dives in close enough to rake Zelda's backpack with her needle fingers. Zelda feels it tug and rip. She feels herself get lighter as something slips from her backpack and breaks to pieces on the forest floor.

"No," Zelda whispers, and turns. The urn is smashed, the ashes of the Phoenix coughed up in a pile. She swings the Sword of Omens like a mad pinwheel to keep the witches away and shouts, "Langston! Save them! *Please!*"

But there's already something happening with the ashes. A glow. A ribbon of smoke. Then Langston has to back away as they burst into brilliant flame and the Phoenix rises again.

It's a beautiful bird—like some mix of rooster and eagle and living fire. Zelda doesn't have long to look at it because the witches pounce on it, and pull it apart, and gobble it up.

"*NO!*" Zelda cries, but it's entirely too late.

It's a terrible scene, but she can't close her eyes to it. They're like frenzied crows, and she tries to beat them back, but there's always another, and another, diving and picking and lifting off again with shreds of the bird in their teeth.

Now the witches are full of fire. Their bellies glow like embers, and their heads become hooded in a black smoke that seeps out of their ears and eyes. Now they draw away. Their necks are like dry hinges; they pitch back their heads and make a keening trill.

All the forest quivers.

Shadows answer the call. Every patch of darkness is given form and crawls out from under rocks and roots. Soft-bodied, misshapen things hobble and lurch. Sliver-thin worms by the thousands wriggle their black bodies free of every minute cavity in the forest floor.

Patches skips every which way to avoid the creepers, but soon there's nowhere for him to go. They slither through his fur. Zelda swings her sword and stamps her shoe squarely down on a little inching slick of a thing; she thinks it's vanquished until it slinks from under her sole and slides up her ankle. When she tries to slap it off her thigh, it clings instead to her hand; when she tries to shake it off her hand, it slips through the fork of her fingers.

There are more of them—so many more. She can feel them on every inch of her back, knitting themselves together. Zelda dusts another witch with a swing of her sword, but soon her arm's gone black, and it isn't working right.

She can't see Langston anymore, but she can feel him close. Zelda forgets the sword and reaches with both arms for the boy, the only warm body in the world. The creepers want to cover him completely, but they can't. They can't have this place where her cheek presses his cheek. Where her hand squeezes the nape of his neck. They won't have her where he reaches up the tail of her shirt to cradle the small of her back, skin against skin. They're going to claim all the pieces of each other they can and hold tight, even as they're covered in pitch.

And they are—they're covered completely.

Zelda wakes up.

TWENTY-FOUR

"OH MY GOD, DID YOU fall asleep?"

For a second, Zelda doesn't know who it is, where she is. A girl is standing under fluorescent lights in a magenta polo shirt and hat and candy-striped shorts. *A ridiculous getup*, Zelda thinks, before noticing she's wearing the exact same thing.

"The gross break-room couch isn't really for napping," says the girl. "Or sitting on or touching in any way if you know what's good for you."

It's Caroline, Zelda thinks. *I'm in the break room at work. I fell asleep at work.*

"C'mon, hup hup! Your break was over a long time ago," says Caroline. "And I'm all alone out there."

Early September at the Build-A-Buddy Factory is peaceful—a person has time to think.

The rest of the mall is buzzing with back-to-school shopping. But nobody really needs a back-to-school Buddy Bear, despite the store's efforts to convince you otherwise. Everything is 20 percent off, and there are little plush apples sewn into the paws of every little plush animal.

"Come get a stuffed octopus, shoppers!" shouts Caroline at no one. The store is empty apart from her and Zelda. "He has a graduation cap and a little diploma! He has graduated from Octopus University!"

This would ordinarily be Zelda's cue to join in. She's almost required to—Caroline is her assistant manager—but she isn't feeling it today. Her silence is awkward, like she's forgotten her line in the school play.

She is struck in the head by a tiny hippopotamus. She doesn't even look at Caroline, just picks the toy up and puts it back in the hippopotamus section.

"What's with you today?" Caroline asks. "You're boring."

"Sorry," says Zelda. "Didn't get a lot of sleep last night."

"Aw, poor baby. Poor little sweet little *angel*."

Zelda smiles despite herself and punches Caroline in the arm.

"Shut up."

"Nobody ever gets a lot of sleep. You think I got enough sleep last night? Talking about how much sleep you didn't get is also boring."

"I just had this . . . terrible nightmare," Zelda tells her. She assumes this is true—she doesn't really remember it. Anyway, there must be something very true in Zelda's expression, because Caroline doesn't take this gift-wrapped opportunity to make fun of her again.

She feels . . . *so sad*. She feels like she just watched her house burn down.

Caroline gives her a bear hug and a loud kiss on the cheek. "Mwah. Go get a pretzel," she says. "It's not like we have customers."

Actually, that's a lie—here's a customer now. A girl of maybe six or seven has come into the store, alone.

"It's my turn," Zelda says.

"Oh, who cares? I can take her."

"No, this is good. What better way to cheer myself up than to help some li'l sweetheart find the teddy bear of her dreams?" Zelda says with a smile. It's the sort of syrupy language they use in fun, but she thinks she might actually need this today.

The girl is walking slowly past the Little Me dolls, touching each one lightly on the top of its head. These are the most customizable toys in the shop—there are dozens sitting out for display purposes, but the whole point is to make a doll with *your* skin and *your* eyes and *your* hair and some bangle or accessory that denotes your six-year-old soul. A skateboard or paintbrush or maybe a stethoscope if you want to grow up to be a doctor. A lot of six-year-olds didn't really have their lives figured out yet, so you eventually pushed them toward a soccer ball just to get them out of the store.

"Good choice," Zelda tells the girl. "The Little Me dolls are my favorite. We can make one that looks just like you, or your best friend, or anyone you want!"

The girl doesn't reply, but she nods carefully.

"Where's your mom?" asks Zelda. "Or dad?"

"Getting glasses."

"At the eyewear place a couple doors down?"

The girl nods again. This sort of hands-free parenting used to surprise Zelda, but it happened more than you'd expect.

"Do you want to see how we make a Little Me?"

The girl nods again and offers her hand. They aren't supposed to touch the children, especially when their parents weren't around, but Caroline isn't going to write her up. So Zelda takes the girl's hand and leads her to the Imagination Station.

"I'm going to make a little boy," Zelda says. The girl's sour expression tells Zelda exactly what she thinks about that. But the boy dolls don't sell very well—if Zelda messes one up, the store owners aren't going to care. "Which one do you like?"

She shrugs like Zelda has asked her which booster shot she wants first. Finally, she points at a doll with plush skin as pink as hers. Zelda grabs the brown-skinned doll next to it instead and picks out a pair of dark eyes.

"This is the fun part," she says. "You put the head of the doll in here, and the eyes in here, and . . ."

She lets the girl pull the lever that rivets the eyes in place. The hair goes on with velcro and just a few threads—Zelda has to do that part. She chooses a dark 4C wig with squiggly little tips. Then a Velcro sword in his Velcro hand, and he's nearly done.

"The last part is the most important," Zelda tells the girl. She turns the doll around and waits for the girl's full attention. "Do you see this flap in his chest? We have to give him a heart." She picks a soft gold heart from the bin and holds it between her fingers. "And here we say . . . we say, 'This heart is *my* heart, and my heart belongs to you.'" She's supposed to let the girl put it in, but Zelda does it herself. Then she closes up his chest and has a good look at him.

He doesn't look like anyone particularly. How could he?—he's floppy and soft-headed, fabric and plastic and thread. The genius of these dolls is that any configuration looks just enough like a hundred thousand people. A million.

His attributes—his hair and eyes and blunt little sword—she picked them at random, certainly. She looks into his dead plastic eyes and expects to feel only dead plastic feelings.

Oh, wow, she's crying—how did that happen?

"What's wrong?" the girl asks her.

That's when Zelda remembers her dream.

All of it—the forest and carnival and canyon and horsemen and failed geography tests. First it comes in pieces, then a flood.

"Noooo," she whispers. "Ohhh, no no no. Oh God."

The girl steps away. Zelda tries to lean on the riveter for strength, misses, falls backward onto her candy-striped shorts.

Her face is tingling, hot. She tries to catch her breath and wails. The girl screams, too, in sympathy or in fear.

"Whoa!" says Caroline, somewhere. In a second, Zelda can feel her by her side. "Kid! What did you do to her?!"

Zelda can't see much through her tears, but the sound of running feet tells her the girl has decided to leave the store without paying for what she's broken.

Patches. Erx. Clara. Zelda lost the townspeople. She lost the town. She burned her house down.

Langston.

For a while, Caroline sits on the floor with her, a strong arm around Zelda's shaking shoulders.

When the worst seems to be behind them, Caroline asks, "Man, what is with you? Normally, I like messing with the kids a little, but if that girl tells her mom, I'm gonna *have* to write you up."

Zelda swallows her grief and crosses her hands over her chest. It's all gone. *He's* gone. Her eyes have cleared, and she looks down at the little Langston in her lap. Nothing left but a souvenir. She's visited a magic kingdom and exited through the gift shop. She squeezes its middle and feels the soft heart inside.

Great: Here's her whole dilemma, buttoned up into a flagrantly obvious symbol. She made Langston. The one in her lap but also the one in her dream. He was her toy. Her puppet. And you can't pull a puppet's heartstrings and tell it to love you.

This was probably the best way it could have gone, really. What if they had made it to the edge (as if dreams have edges—how stupid) and discovered the truth? He was a smart boy—he would have figured it out. And she would have had to watch him do it: watch his face, see it dawn in his eyes that he wasn't his own man, that he'd never made a choice in his life. So he didn't love her because he couldn't love her—not in the way he thought he did. He'd turn away from her then. Or try to.

Or even worse—what if he didn't?

What if he couldn't?

Well. It's not a problem she has to solve anymore. She thought she was the dreamer, and she *was* the dreamer. She needed to wake up, and she woke up. She got real life.

She looks around—around at the dreary bits and pieces of everything she wanted.

Caroline takes her arm, and Zelda gets to her uncertain feet. "I lost so much," she says. "I left my home and let it die. I was holding a friend, and I let him go."

"Yikes. I let you fall asleep in the break room and you wake up talking like a YA novel."

"I don't know what to tell you. I don't know how to make you understand. All my imaginary friends died. I burned their bodies. I let the light in, and they turned to dust."

"Uh-huh. Were they vampires?"

She should feel better. She woke up, and she's fine, isn't she? Even better—she had somehow only been sleeping for an hour, not days or weeks. But her quest was supposed to end at the edge, with discovery and understanding and hugs, probably. Maybe a click of her heels. Not like this. Retched up into reality with nothing more magical awaiting her than the promise of a fifteen-minute coffee break and a pretzel.

"I . . . think I will go get that pretzel," Zelda says.

"I'll walk you. I kind of want to get fired anyway."

On the threshold of the store, they're met by the same little girl and her mother. The girl points.

"That's her! She cried and fell down."

The mother is wearing showy new glasses and an equally showy expression. They were probably both selected in the same mirror. If you're the sort of person who's ever said *I have never been so outraged*—even once—then you're probably the sort who says it once a week. And this mother looks like she's going to be that sort of person.

"I have *never* been so outraged," says the mother.

Caroline steps protectively between them. "I'm her manager," she says, "and she's going to be disciplined for . . . being sad in front of your daughter."

The mother jabs her finger at Zelda. "You *terrified* her!"

Zelda tears up again, and hugs little Langston to her chest. "I'm sorry," she says. She isn't really saying it to the mother, so it comes out sounding true.

She almost forgot him. Well. She won't now. She has this toy in her hands—she'll buy it with her employee discount! He'll live on as a toy and a memory. A memory and a toy—that's . . . all he ever was, really. And Zelda will go on being real without him.

The mother looks a little disarmed by all this penitence. "Well. You've probably given her *nightmares*, you know that."

Nightmares. Zelda starts crying again.

"All her friends just died," Caroline explains.

The woman straightens. She doesn't know what to do with this information. She was really enjoying her high horse, but the ride is ending quicker than usual.

Caroline nods sadly. "They were vampires. It's a really big deal."

"Um," says the mother. Her face does a lot of different things at once. "Is . . . there someone above you I can talk to?"

"Nope, I own the whole franchise. That's my name up there: Caroline Buildabuddy. Caroline Buildabuddy-Factory. I hyphenated."

Reflexively, Zelda looks up at the sign, the sign for the store at which she works. A sign that's rendered in miniature on her own name tag, on her paychecks, on the hem of her candy-striped shorts. A sign she knows very, very well.

It takes her three tries to read it correctly.

Her heart leaps in her chest.

"Okay, we're gonna get a pretzel," Caroline tells the mother. "Feel free to steal something while we're gone."

Caroline pulls Zelda away before the mother can think of a

reply. Zelda cranes her neck to read the names of all the stores they pass. GIMFER'S. HORNSHOOLIUS. A clothing store named HAMFUH. A coffee kiosk called SMOF. She's beaming, teary-eyed, at every one of them.

"I gotta go," she says.

"Yeah. That's cool. You okay to drive?"

"Not like that," Zelda answers. "I left some friends in the middle of something. I have to go punch some witches."

Caroline raises an eyebrow. "You mean those kids that hang around the Cinnabon?" She has a look like she might also like to punch some witches.

"Not mall witches—real ones. I'll come find you, Caroline. After this is all over, I'll find you, if I can. You're a good friend. I mean, it's possible you were really only born from my subconscious twenty minutes ago, but you're a good friend nonetheless."

She stops next to a big planter in front of the FURT LOCCKER. Caroline turns to watch her.

Zelda gazes down at the little toy boy in her hands.

"I'm holding on to you," she tells Langston, trying to get back that feeling. The pink fuzzy feeling of being carried along a forking river, hand on the tiller. "I'm holding on to you, and I never stopped. In the nightmare forest and the worst possible moment—I'm still holding you," she says.

Zelda closes her eyes, and everything is black.

TWENTY-FIVE

NOT THE BLACK OF NIGHT. Not the darkness you see when you close your eyes. This is the utter nothing inside the black tar of the witches, she knows it.

"NNNNNNNNNNGFF!" Zelda screams into the hardening shell. She strains every fiber of her body against the tar and the nightmare and the forest and the muffled keening of the witches all around her.

I am the DREAMER, Zelda screams inside her mind. *And if I am all up to my eyes in witches and goop right now it is probably because deep down I think I DESERVE it or something, which is STUPID—I deserve GOOD things and I get to change my mind if I'm not feeling it and I am going to get all this gross metaphor OFF of me and stab those OTHER metaphors and then I will march directly out of ALL this symbolic nonsense right . . . NOW!*

She pushes, and something gives. It starts with her little

finger—there. *Just your finger, then your hand, and then everything else.* A shiver trembles up her arm, shakes all her bones. Fissures form in her shell, and even the dim light of the forest looks like little glimpses of springtime through the cracks.

"Not a nightmare!" she announces as she frees her jaw. Or she tries to, anyway—it turns out her face is numb. Scabs of black plaster crack up and drop to the forest floor. "Novva nahmah!" she tries again, and then she stops trying. Whatever. Her trap is coming undone, and so is Langston's. Zelda's body is hers again.

But she can see enough now to know the witches are closing in.

They're leaning close with their moldering vegetable faces. They're worrying the air with their fingers. Zelda glares at them over Langston's shoulder with her one good eye.

"It's not a nightmare," she tells them now that her mouth is working again. "It's a love story. And I always read to the end of the book, no matter how dumb it is."

"Zelda?" calls Langston. And the sound of his voice rings her rib cage like a bell. They're still more or less hugging each other like a couple of cutesy-poo figurines. A black ceramic glaze is holding them together, but now it's falling to pieces all around them. "I was having one of those dreams," says Langston. "Where you think you've awakened but you haven't."

"We should run to that house," Zelda whispers to him. "The witches don't like it. Where's Patches?"

She can turn her head enough to see a black, lumpish Play-Doh version of him near her knees.

He looks like he was trying to huddle close to her when the black tar took him.

Now Zelda has a witch all up in her face. She and Langston

disentangle, and crawl backward like hard-shell crabs on their hands and heels.

"*Never will you get to the house,*" says the witch.

"*We'll cut your strings,*" says another.

"*Cut all the ribbons and mincemeat of you.*"

"*We have lonesome knives for blackbird pies.*"

"I am seriously so sick of your deal right now," Zelda tells them.

They *do* have knives, though. Long and bright.

"*Pretty girl. It's midnight.*"

"*Pretty things turn to pumpkins here.*"

"*Pumpkin girl—I'll carve you a face.*"

"HELP!" shouts Langston. "HELLLP!" he calls.

His call spreads itself thin and dies. It's quiet again.

Then, something answers.

A looooong, dry creak.

Every witch goes stiff and turns her head to look at the clearing. In the clearing, the yellow house creaks. The creak echoes and takes its time dwindling away. One of the witches twitches.

Then the house groans like a hundred loose floorboards; it whinges like a hinge. The muffled whump of a furnace and the castanets of a half-dozen ticking radiators seem to rattle and peck at the witches' old bones. They flinch and shiver. Then the little yellow house rocks once, twice, on its foundation, and the roof yawns open. The gable levers up on a pistoned neck.

They can't get to the house, so the house comes to them. It transforms and pivots on flat feet; dashes out of the glen, uprooting trees to clear a path. The witches try to react—there's no time to react. The house is here. It pinches witches between fingers of aluminum siding and tosses them clear of the forest.

Zelda shakes off the last of her shell and cracks Patches out of his. He has big, sad eyes. He looks like the cover of a three-ring binder she had when she was eight.

"Zelda—"

She can feel the hot welt on her cheek where Patches scratched her.

"C'mon, we should help the house," she says, not looking at him.

The witches are circling on their brooms, trying to look scary. The house flicks one so hard she probably lands in a completely different dream. Then it empties its water heater on another, and she melts.

"YES!" Langston cheers. "WOO!"

Another tries to sneak around to the back door, but Zelda gives her a harsh editing with the Sword of Omens. The house seems to creak in appreciation, so Zelda smiles skyward.

Then the earth beneath her feet begins to stir.

The earth beneath her seems to breathe, and the remaining witches lift up on their brooms. They retreat, buzzing off into the darkness, but cackling as they go. Then a shiver ripples over the land, sending the house and everyone else backward onto their foundations.

"An earthquake," says Langston.

But it's not an earthquake. The forest itself is waking.

The robot house scoops Zelda up in its long-fingered hand—

"Whup," she hiccups.

—and bowls her through its own front door and across the hardwood floor. She slides to a halt against the stairs and Langston and Patches appear in similar fashion a moment later.

Zelda gets to her feet and crosses the floor of the nearly empty parlor—being a robot seems to be hard on the furniture, which has mostly slid into the same corner by the fireplace—and she opens a window.

The robot is all folded up and house-shaped again, apart from its legs and feet, and it starts jogging them through the forest. The sudden lurch sends Zelda onto her bottom again, and Patches rushes to her side.

"Are you all right?" he asks.

She actually thinks she might have broken her tailbone. "I'm fine," she says.

"I'm sorry!" Patches says, stretching to steady himself on her knee. "About before, when—"

"I know you are!" Zelda answers, getting up. "It's fine!"

Everything abruptly pitches forward. The house has found itself suddenly sprinting down a steep hill that was recently level ground.

"Watch the furniture!" warns Langston. A chandelier drunkenly swings. The wide drawer of a secretary coughs up office supplies— Post-its flap and fall; pens and markers log-roll across the floor. The house is really hoofing it now, and it has its head up and its arms out again for balance. The dark sky is pumpkin-orange with dust.

The room keeps redecorating itself, but Patches crosses it like he's been training for this his whole life. He heads for higher ground and ends up on the fireplace mantel—stable except for a smooth marble top that his fluffy belly skates back and forth on a bit.

The slope is too steep. The forest rises as if on its own unlikely legs. There's a hitch in the house's stride—a tottering, just shy of calamity. It's about to fall.

Patches says:

"O tragedy, tragedy!
Failure and fie!
Erelong we cursèd three will die
When we're dashed on the rocks
And the chorus has chorused:

'Alas, they were shipwrecked
Whilst crossing a forest.'"

Always with the poetry, Zelda thinks. *The witches liked poetry.*

Zelda avoids slipping on a marker and sidesteps a sliding otto-man, only to be sacked by the couch. She rides it into the front wall.

"Oof." She hooks her fingers over the windowsill to watch their progress. There's more light ahead. At the very moment when it's too late to do anything about it, she realizes they're about to go off some kind of cliff. Is it the edge? Is it the end?

The house falls. The fall only lasts a second, maybe two, but they're weightless. For a weightless moment, there's air between Zelda and the couch, air between the couch and the floor.

Zelda closes her eyes. "Fly," she whispers.

Nobody flies. But the house settles lightly as its big robot feet reach solid ground again. Zelda strains to look through a window on the other side of the great room. She sees the forest of the witches, rich and loamy black, still rising up behind them.

"Go!" Zelda tells the house. "Keep going!"

The house doesn't have to be told twice. It ramps back up to a brisk pace, huffing and puffing chill air through its chimney. "It's following us!" calls Langston from his perch atop the dining room table. "But we're faster! I think we're gonna lose it!"

They just might. The house is finding it easier to run in this new forest, where everything's thinner and brighter. Faster and faster still. Too fast, maybe—the house stumbles over some low tree and wob-bles worryingly before finding its footing again.

"Careful now," Zelda mutters. Her knuckles are white against the windowsill.

The trees look different here—trunks like flat palms with stout branches that splay like fingers. Or else trees that look like feet. Hands and feet.

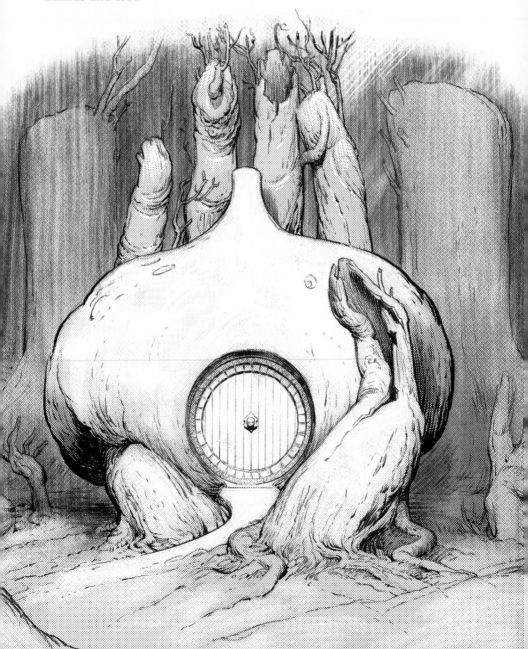

Oh dear.

Far ahead of them Zelda can see a little lamplight, maybe some smoke. It's a red clay hut built into the hollow of a massive hand-tree, and it has a familiar circular door.

"HEY!" Zelda shouts out the window. "HEEEEYYY!"

"What are you shouting at?" asks Langston. He's at the rear window. He doesn't see it.

"HEEEYYYY! LOOK OUT!"

The red hut with the circular door is getting closer. It's getting too close.

"RUN!" Zelda screams. "EVACUATE!"

There's a tree shaped like a foot, with knotty toes and a hooked ankle, growing almost sideways out of the cracks of a rocky tor. The foot trips the house.

"Oh, that's dumb," Zelda whispers. The house staggers every which way and fights to stay on its feet. "LOOK OUT! RUN RUN RUN RUN RUN!"

Erx pokes his raisin head out of the distant door. He's heard her. He sees what's coming. Zelda thinks the house sees it, too, but nobody really has time to react. Erx gives her a look. A weary look, a look that says, *Called it.* There's a crunch.

"Ohhhh no," Zelda says. "Oh boy." She hugs her knees as the sofa pirouettes away from the window. "It was . . . so *fast* . . ."

It could all end anytime. The dream, her life. She knew this, but did she really *know* it? Langston knows. He has memories full of loss. Zelda never lost so much as a baby tooth that wasn't placed on a pillow and sent around town on a parade float.

It's good Langston didn't see. What would it do to him, losing someone else? Surely, it would confirm his every instinct to keep life small, stay safe, watch others have bigger lives from afar. And yet.

And *yet*, didn't Erx decide to stay home, let adventure be something that happens to other people? What good did that do him in the end?

"It really makes you stop and think . . . think how precious . . . Oh man, I think I'm having some character development."

"Who are you talking to?" calls Langston.

"No one! It isn't about anything! We gotta stop."

"Stop? Now? We can't—"

But they *have* to, it would make no *sense* if they didn't, so Zelda screams it with all the lucid dreamer authority she can muster:

"STOP!"

The house skids to a halt.

She scrambles up from the couch and grabs a black marker on her way out the front door. The house has time to kneel just enough that she doesn't hurt herself dropping to the forest floor. Then she turns and hoofs it back to the ruins of Erx's atelier, with all the horizon ahead of her darkened by the wicked black wilderness shambling toward them.

Erx's house is utterly crushed. Pulverized inside a big hole shaped like a foot. She looks away before she goes and recognizes something in the rubble. Something other than the front door. Because the door is still standing on the lip of the hole. The circular door is the only thing upright and intact, just as Zelda knew it would be.

It's hard to concentrate when there's an angry landmass grinding slowly toward you, but Zelda breathes and takes hold of the doorframe, gently turns and pushes like she's folding a tent. It's easy this time, she thinks, helping the dream decide what to do, and soon she has a sphere, an icosidodecahedron, an octahedron, a cube. She fumbles it a bit and clamps the cube under one arm while she uncaps the marker with her teeth. She addresses her package:

and looks around for Erx's mailbox.

The ground shudders at the forest's approach.

Maybe the mailbox was there before she thought of it, and maybe it wasn't—who cares. She stuffs the box inside it and runs, knowing it'll work because it already did.

Langston is hanging his head upside down from the front stoop of the house, and he calls to her as she arrives.

"What were you doing? What was that back there?"

"A hole," Zelda tells him. "A plot hole."

The thing that pursues them howls.

The house kneels, and Langston helps her back up. The tide of furniture goes out again, but Zelda stays here with Langston in the foyer, which has the advantage of a bannister one can lash oneself to and ride out the storm. She stumbles up to the stair beside him and seizes the railing.

"By the way," she says, "your sword is by the fireplace, in with the . . . poker and all that. You see it?"

He sees it. The rack of fireplace tools is bolted to the hearth and as such is just about the only thing in sight that isn't sliding around.

"Not sure I should keep claiming it's *my* sword," says Langston in hushed tones. "You know, you keep saving me when I'm in the middle of rescuing you."

"Oh, what, the witches?" asks Zelda. "Team effort. You loosened them for me," she adds, like they were a jar of pickles.

"No. It's okay. I mean, there's a kind of guy . . . he says he likes tall girls, and he believes it because, in his mind? He's a giant. Then he finally sees what a real tall girl looks like standing next to him, and all he can think is, *How do I cut her down to size?*"

"Uh-huh," says Zelda, trying to listen over the drumbeat of the house's feet, the unspeakable sound of the thing that followed.

"I used to worry I might be that kind of guy," Langston continues, "but watching you . . ." He leans into her, his face so close she swears she can feel him without touching, like it's the sudden gravity of him, drawing her in. "I *like* looking up at you."

They hold fast to the rails. Zelda shivers, and tries not to sit too square on her tailbone.

"And I know you're the dreamer," adds Langston. Zelda starts.

"No, it's true. I've been kidding myself. I thought the dream was trying to tell me something, but . . . if it is, it's saying, 'The smart money's on Zelda.' You lost the ashes, but I'll bet you find some other way to wake."

She rests her head on his shoulder.

"I think I will, too," Zelda admits.

Langston takes a slow breath. "All I ask," he says, "is after you've woken . . . come find me sometimes. When you sleep. Maybe you can, right? If you remember. Then . . . grow up, meet someone real, marry them if you want to. But don't tell them about me. I can be your secret, always waiting for you, every time you close your eyes."

Zelda lifts her head to look at him.

Patches calls from the mantel.

"Our pursuer!" he says. "It is the forest, but it is also a titanic beast. Like Fenrir! Oh!"

Patches scrambles into the foyer.

"It's leaping. High. It's about to land—"

It *is* an earthquake. They're once again weightless. The sky is falling.

It's everything they can do to avoid flying up to the ceiling as the robot tucks itself into a house, and rolls like a die, and slides to a stop on its foundation.

TWENTY-SIX

SHE'S LYING WHERE SHE LANDED, diagonal on the carpeted stairs. Tomorrow she'll have a bruise for each stairstep, marked out on her like a ruler. If there's a tomorrow. Zelda opens her eyes and examines the house. Everything appears to be damaged, apart from a piano that's rolled in from another room. Every tabletop is splintered; all the legs are broken. Zelda's own legs seem basically fine.

The house is panting, its front door swinging open and closed.

She whispers, "If I . . . could just fall asleep—right now—I could wake up back in my *own* yellow house. Safe. I know I could. I might do it if I knew how to take you both with me."

"But that would be like giving up," says Langston, beside her.

Zelda takes a deep breath.

"I know," she says. She wobbles upright, finds her shoe.

"Patches?" she calls.

"Ever faithful, I remain," he groans from the next room.

Zelda slips on her shoe and steps out the front door, squinting into the wind. There's a lot of wind. And not much of anything else.

The ground is smooth and white. The sky is white and smooth. This is the blank paper. The *I can't think of anything to draw.* There's nothing here.

Except a cliff. Up ahead is a cliff.

She looks left and right. The cliff seems to extend infinitely in both directions. The lip of a circle, maybe.

"This is it," she says. "We made it."

She can hear Langston behind her. "I wondered if it might be something like this," he says. "A big drop, I mean. A fall."

The sky looks bigger here. Zelda hurts her neck, looking at it. It seems to arch higher, yawn wider.

It's a struggle, what with the wind, but she staggers to the cliff and peers over the edge. There's nothing down there but pink clouds. A thick, swirling, fizzing, pink fog. Like the cloudy Grand Canyon of her childhood.

She remembers another circle, hastily-drawn with dots in it—a map of the whole world.

"It's the edge of the map," she whispers, and she can't help but laugh. "That stupid map." And here, at the edge, is the sort of Great Unknown where mapmakers used to stick the compass rose and a drawing of a weird dragon. The fogbound, howling, medieval ends of the earth.

It churns, a turbulent sea of clouds. A groggy basin. There are occasional flashes, but instead of lightning Zelda feels certain they're more like ideas, gasping for air in a sleepy head.

She squints—there. She saw something. A splash of color, a whisper of movement.

"The Magic Mirror was showing us this," calls Zelda. "Exactly this. Remember? All that fuzzy pink. It wasn't broken—it was always showing us the end of the dream, just like we asked it to."

Langston is still some twenty feet behind her, and really leaning into the wind. Like he's planted in place. You could draw numbers in the ground around him and make a sundial, if there were any sun.

"You know what it means that you can walk to the edge and I can't, right?" he shouts, his voice catching. Zelda doesn't answer. She just strains to part the clouds and catch a glimpse of the real world. "It's like . . ." Langston continues. "It's like you're the only one who can leave. If you wanted. Falling always takes a person out of a dream. You could jump, and fall, and the moment before you hit bottom, you wake."

People don't just jump off cliffs, Zelda thinks, knowing that's not strictly true. People probably jump off cliffs all the time. And each step off that edge, over that line, is the end of a world, if only for the stepper. But *this* line. This literal end. She can feel the closeness of it, buzzing in her brain, exciting her skin.

And in a flash, she understands why she's so anxious—she's worried she'll actually do it. She takes a step back, then a half step forward again as Patches calls out from the rooftop.

"What are you two whispering abou—AAH! SQUAT!"

Zelda turns and gives him a look. "What?"

"DUCK!"

She sees it.

"Langston!"

Zelda grabs Langston's shirtfront and pulls him to the ground with her as a jet of white flame whistles like a kettle overhead.

"Ow," says Langston. "What . . ." His voice fails him as he turns.

Behind the house, impossibly large, is the wolf.

"Oh," whispers Zelda. "So the witches weren't kidding about that."

It's the wolf, and it's the forest. It's both. Its body is dark—night seems to cling to it like a scent. It stands, the forest does, on lank legs of sodden black soil, wormy and shaggy with capillary roots. The trees are hairs on its back. Its long, dark mouth hangs rabid, full of white nothing. No tongue, no tunnel—just white. Its eyes are utterly empty.

It doesn't so much breathe as spit flame. Zelda slides into a skid and drags Langston with her and they narrowly avoid another salvo. Her instinct is to hide behind the house, but the house is kind of a personal friend now. It ratchets up on its legs and springs free its arms. It turns to square off against the wolf like a boxer. It looks *so* small.

A little corner of the roof is missing. It must have caught a bit of the wolf's white fire, and now that part is gone, erased. But the brave little house stands its ground, does that *come at me* gesture with its fingers. And then the wolf howls, and that howl smashes the house to pieces.

Zelda gasps.

Every little part of the house, every shingle and nail, scatters and clatters across the white plain.

Langston whimpers. Whimpers but tightens his brow. And for a moment, he steps forward, fists clenched.

The wolf hunches low. It pads backward as storm clouds brew around it. They watch one another. Then, after a few lifeless moments, the wolf seems to . . . unfurl.

Serpentine shapes ripple from its dark body. Horn and bone push forth from its face, its snout, bifurcating again and again into new mouths, new teeth.

The wolf is a curling tangle, a Celtic knot, iridescent and scaly silver and elsewhere as blistered as a burnt tree. A face that is every animal's face. A shaggy scruff; limbs and claws without reason or symmetry.

"A weird dragon at the edge of the map," Zelda whispers. "Why do I keep giving it ideas?"

It's an obstruction. A congestion. Literally, it is a blockage between them and where they've been, but it also seems to Zelda like a clog in the pipes—a coming together of every bad thought.

It destroyed the house.

Zelda looks at the house's robot legs lying splayed on the white. Bricks and boards and aluminum siding in a jagged pile. There's something stirring, and Zelda remembers with a sick heart that the last place she saw Patches was atop the house's gable.

"Patches!" she calls. "PATCHES?!"

"I'm here!" comes his muffled baritone, secreted away behind a hot water heater that's toppled on the white plain.

Zelda's folded herself like a wallet in search of a pocket. Langston is trembling beside her. He makes a noise in his throat, looking at the ruins of his childhood home. They're still stirring, these ruins. Look— that's the front door lying on its side, opening and closing, gasping like a fish. More movement now—beds and ottomans and a claw-footed bathtub crawl free of the wreckage and hobble about. A chair takes a loose board in its arms and joins it to a window frame. The upright piano has lost its teeth—*That happens a lot in dreams*, Zelda thinks—but it's gathering them up and filling the gaps in its smile.

"Those floorboards just hammered themselves in a row—did you see?" Zelda cheers, taking Langston's arm.

But at the sound of her voice the wolf expands. Its head, its neck, stretch toward them, uncoiling slowly like a loose spring. Its mouths hang slack, glistening, a bone-rattling purr traveling the length of every tube and valve of its impossible body.

The rumble shakes something loose inside Zelda. Her heart flutters, her eyes wet. She has to look away as she whispers,

"Did it . . . did it just say my name?"

It's so *close*. She can feel its breath. If she turned to look, its teeth would be all she could see.

"GET AWAY FROM HER! YOU DEVIL!" bellows Patches. "SERPENT, AWAY!"

Zelda risks a peek and sees that the great beast has turned to look at Patches, who is out in the open and quivering and staring it down.

"VILLAIN! YOU HAVE MADE AN *ENEMY* OF A *CAT*!" says Patches. "QUICK AND MAKE PEACE WITH YOUR GODS!"

Then he pounces.

He manages to sink his front claws between two fishy scales of the wolf's long train of a neck, and scrabbles up. The wolf lashes backward to strike, but Patches is not where he was, and the monster nips its own flesh.

Patches is a dervish. He rakes and claws, swiping, leaping, howling, hair on end and three sizes bigger than usual. Scales and fur flutter like rose petals to the ground: *She loves me, she loves me not.* The wolf whips about and strikes again, but now it has Patches on its head. The cat plunges his claws into one huge, burning eye.

But the monster has a lot of eyes.

It shakes its heads like a rattle, and Patches is thrown free. He sails over the ruined house and lands on his feet, but tumbles and rolls. And where he stops, he stops completely.

"Baby!" screams Zelda.

She remembers when Patches got hit by a car. She was coming home from school on the first day of the third grade. He was in the street. He was lying in the street. She knew right away. He didn't look like he was sleeping.

Before she can think, she's racing across the cliff toward him. She bargains as she runs: If she can just get to him, he'll be fine. If she can only apologize for how she's acted, he'll be all right.

But she can't reach him. Suddenly, the wolf is blocking her way, and she hasn't even a sword. Where is the sword? The monster possibly grins. Its breath is a hot graveyard. Then:

Honky honky honky honky honky honky honky honky honky honky honky honky honky honky honky honky honky honky HONKY HONKY HONKY HONKY HONKY HONKY HONKY HONK.

The laundromat clown attacks it.

TWENTY-SEVEN

ZELDA HAS NEVER SEEN THE laundromat clown angry. In town, it always wore the same smile—handing out dryer sheets, making change with the coin dispenser on its belt, always smiling. It's still smiling, but it's a fishhook smile. And it is trying to hug one of the wolf's legs and bite one of its ankles with its teeth. But the wolf's leg is like one of those giant sequoias you can drive your car through—the clown can't so much hug it as flatten itself against it.

The wolf doesn't even lift its paw. Instead it lowers its barnacled head, opens all its mouths at once.

"AW, COO COO COO KISSY *COO!*" the clown exclaims. It seems like it might be a real stirring battle cry in whatever language the clown speaks. It leaps backward and commences to furiously twisting a balloon animal army—little dogs and horsies and a lot of snakes to save time. These charge into battle, and the air fills with stuttering *pop*s as they burst against the wolf's nose. Then the wolf spits forth white-hot fire, and there's nothing left of the clown but shoes.

"NO!" Langston erupts, leaping to his feet. He rushes forward, actually rushes forward for a second, through the rattling mess of house all around him. And the wolf flinches.

It flinches, and Zelda thinks, *That's twice now, isn't it?*

"That was . . ." Langston says, and falters. He considers each of the animal's horrible faces. "That clown . . . was MY nightmare! It . . ." He looks confused. He looks like a little boy. "It cared! It wanted to eat ME, personally! It's wanted to eat me my whole life! Who are *you*? Who are you, bad guy? Huh?"

The wolf *hates* this. The wolf whines and minces its terrible feet. Nonetheless, it lets loose a torrent of fire from all its mouths, fire that curls and arcs every which way across the plain. Zelda drops flat on the ground, and it singes her hair. Not one lick of it touches Langston, though. He stands there, tall and trembling, and not one lick.

I know what to do, thinks Zelda.

She scans the wreckage for the Sword of Omens.

"Zelda?" groans Patches.

"Patches! Baby," she says, and sinks down beside him.

"One life left," Patches says weakly, and stirs. "DUCK!"

Zelda drops, but it's actually the duck. The giant duck is back.

"I wonder how long she will last against the wolf," Patches says, and Zelda holds her breath. Maybe hope *is* the thing with feathers? A second later, they wince. "Well," says Patches. "That's it for the giant duck. Rest in peace, feathered friend—you were linguistically confusing."

"I think I know how to handle the wolf." Zelda sighs. "And it . . . ugh, it's going to be so annoying. Have you seen Langston's sword?"

"Yes, under yonder mattress."

"Do me a favor, okay? Give Langston a pep talk for a change. He's going to rescue me."

"That . . . seems unlikely."

"Yeah. But the wolf doesn't care about my bravery," Zelda says. "It isn't the sum of all *my* fears." She realizes what she's saying, what it means. "Dammit." She starts toward the beast, and looks back at Patches. "Cross your fingers I don't die!"

"My fingers don't work that way!"

Zelda breaks into a run, slides into a twin mattress like it's third base. The butt end of the Sword of Omens—the pommel—is sticking out from a set of box springs.

"Zelda?" calls Langston. "What are you doing?"

Sword in hand, she races back out into the empty white. Then stops, because the wolf notices her. *Okay*, she thinks with distaste. *Here we go.*

She can gently steer Langston, too, in a way.

She hopes.

"Don't you dare try to hurt Langston!" she cries, and raises her sword. It's a little much, maybe—acting always seems easier in her head. The largest mouth cracks open and spits fire, but Zelda's already on the move, fighting every sensible instinct she has, running *toward* the wolf.

"Zelda!" Langston screams. "No!"

The monster sees her coming and could not appear to care less. She's dreamland's most dangerous girl, but for all the wolf cares she may as well be its most dangerous ladybug. And is it really this far away? The all-white landscape is messing with her sense of perspective, and the wolf is so big, and she's barely halfway to its paw and already winded.

One paw. One paw is so massive that soon it's all she can see. Loamy black hills make its toes. Iron outcroppings form each vaulted nail.

This dog has worms. They course through every inch of him.

Zelda swings and tries to give the wolf kind of a severe pedicure, but the sword bounces right off. She almost loses her grip. She swings again and again, trying to find something soft. There's nothing soft.

"Come on, Zelda!" Langston calls. He sounds panicked. "Come back! It's too much, even for you!"

Then a weird claw descends from above and tweezes Zelda's head between two dark nails. It lifts her off her feet, and, oh God, it hurts. Her neck pops and stretches like a bendy straw.

"ZELDA!"

He isn't running away, though he looks very much like he wants to. That's bravery, Zelda supposes. Although he might only be holding his ground because there's a literal cliff behind him.

She tries to raise her sword arm but gets a keen sense that if she does so, she'll pass out. And while waking up just now in her own bed would be a nice trick, she thinks she needs to stick around and see this through.

Good, Patches is saying something to Langston. She can't hear him, but still she's certain it's something Shakespearean, a *once more into the breach, dear friend* kind of message, and, God, now the monster has lifted her to the elevation of all of its hideous faces. Just breathing this near to it burns her chest and eyes.

"H-hey," Zelda says to the wolf, a gurgle in her voice. "Hey. You got a lot of ears, so I know you can hear me." She clears her throat. "Later? When this is done? I want you to understand . . ."

She smiles, barely.

"This was how I *beat* you."

Then she hurls the Sword of Omens to the empty earth below, and screams.

"LANGSTON, *SAVE* ME!"

She tries to follow the sword's descent but loses it somewhere before it hits the ground. Well, Langston probably saw it. Hopefully. "You're my . . . hoo . . . you're my hero, Langston!" Zelda groans. She has to pretend to be just another damsel now, trying to act sufficiently distressed so the boy can have his story arc.

"Let her go!" screams Langston, somewhere. That's a start.

"Here, boy!" calls Patches, and there's the Sword of Omens, sticking out of a cracked toilet.

Langston rushes to the toilet and pulls his sword free, holds it aloft like it makes him the rightwise king of England.

Zelda tries to call out to him one more time, but she hasn't the breath. The rank leather fingers of the black claw squeeze with exquisite slowness. The wolf's eyes, all of the wolf's growing constellation of dead white eyes, train on her. She's looking through the wolf's hundred jaws into the stark void and snow-blind death inside. She's so tired. She'll just close her eyes now. This wasn't one of her best plans.

Then the monster howls in pain.

Okay. He must have stabbed it somewhere. She's sure she'll hear all about it.

"Hey!" Langston shouts, his voice warbly but loud. "Put . . . my girl . . . down! And keep her name out of your mouth!"

The wolf rears back, but Langston presses his attack, slashing at anything within reach. Zelda normally would make some crack about that *my girl* stuff, but Langston looks like he needs the self-esteem. Also, she can't breathe.

In the shipwreck of the house, the piano has found its keys, and it's playing accompaniment—something thunderous and heroic-sounding, like in a movie. Langston swings and swings.

The monster cries out with a dozen voices—and is it possibly smaller than it was a moment ago? Zelda could swear that it is, as stars fill her eyes and an inky veil drapes drowsily over her bloodless face and shouldn't she sleep? Wouldn't it be good to sleep?

Silly. You're already asleep and dreaming.

"No. I'm really not," she whispers.

"Put her down!" screams Langston. "Carefully!" The wolf swipes with a talon, but Langston trims its nails for it and the sea of clouds flashes and flashes.

So the wolf sets Zelda down on the white plain. Then it pulls back a bit. It seems to be trying to decide what it really wants out of this situation. It's looking more and more like a proper wolf. It's looking more and more like an ordinary forest. Langston rushes to Zelda and kneels by her side.

"Say something," he says.

"Someth—" she tries, and coughs.

"Are you going to be okay?"

She wobbles to her feet. Patches is here, smiling up at her.

"Clever girl," he says.

"What do you mean?" asks Langston. "What did she do?"

"Nada," Zelda wheezes. "You did everything this time." She

yanks her backpack around to see what all this horseplay has done to her stuff. The bag of magic sand is still there. Her toothbrush is broken.

"Well," says Langston. He waggles his sword at the wolf, who is smaller and has kind of an embarrassed look on its face. "I don't think that monster's going to bother us anymore." He shrugs. *No big,* his shrug wants you to know.

Zelda smiles.

"It was your monster to face," Zelda says, and she clasps his warm arm in her hand. "But it wasn't your Labor."

He's confused, trying to decipher her meaning. Then she surprises him by wrapping his body in her arms. She hugs him tight.

"You don't have anything to prove," says Zelda. "Not to anyone but yourself."

Then she peels herself away, and Zelda and the cat walk toward the edge.

This isn't quite the bouquet of roses Langston wants it to be. "Well," he says. "I *got* this! So."

"Thank you!" Zelda calls, and waves.

In a moment, she's back at the edge, and notices that Patches has followed her only partway. He's some twenty feet back, nursing a leg, stymied by wind.

She still can't see clearly, through the fog. Not from here.

"I'll . . . I'll be along presently!" says the cat.

"It's okay," Zelda tells him. "You can't. Just me."

She was made for this. To be this. She was made to be a lot of things, really, but one of them is this.

"Zelda!" shouts Langston. "What are you going to do?"

"You know, I just realized . . ." she says softly. She isn't really talking to anyone but herself. "I swore I'd never left town before. And yet, don't I have this childhood memory of a canyon filled with clouds?"

"Zelda?"

"Probably just some dream I had."

She jumps.

TWENTY-EIGHT

SHE FALLS A LONG TIME.

Were she screaming, she would have long since lost her breath, and inhaled, and screamed, and lost it again. She's not screaming, though. This is where she wants to be—if indeed she wants anything at all. If indeed she wants. She'll find out in a minute. And if she doesn't . . . well. She's either doing as she pleases or else she hopes it's pleasing, what she's doing. Either way she feels fine.

She falls. The clouds leave chromatic dewdrops all over her skin. Her hair probably looks ridiculous. She feels like an angel, though.

The wind whooshes by her, but she senses its pleasure to see her nonetheless—they're like old friends who'd catch up if they weren't rushing so quickly in opposite directions. Below, the clouds are parting; the air is clearing. *Is this what you wanted to see? Let us just scooch out of the way, and . . . there.*

It's Langston.

But she knew it would be.

"So I'm a paper doll after all," she says to herself. "Just a dream girl." The kind of cute character who has bedroom constellations and talks to her gate.

She was, in fact, Langston's unopened toy. Sitting on her shelf, the whole town her original packaging—just a part of Langston's perpetual childhood.

She can't get mad about it, anyway—not now, as she looks down on the boy in his hospital bed. He didn't know.

He looks a little beat-up, but still beautiful. A Sleeping Beauty. There's a tube across his face, another in his arm. They've discovered a perfectly unlikeable shade of blue and made him a gown out of it. Zelda watches his chest rise and fall and rise, so slowly.

There are freshly cut flowers in a vase rising up out of a tent city of greeting cards on the hospital nightstand. There is a week-old Mylar balloon floating shyly in the corner.

There's an older man curled up in a chair on the other side of the bed. *Oh.*

He's tall and thin and covered with a blanket. His brow is creased.

Zelda could swear she's still falling, though the hospital scene below her isn't getting any closer. Not noticeably so, anyway. Zelda suspects it's all very large, and very far away.

She'll never actually get there.

There's an electronic chirp that she mistakes for some hospital sound. But Langston's father (it could only be Langston's father—she's seen him through pinholes) stirs and checks his phone.

He stares at it a long time, his thumbs twitching over the screen. In the end, he calls the sender instead of texting.

"Hey," he tells them. "Yeah, I know what I said. But some days it's like it's . . . too much to text about, you know? Like, you're trying to find the words for the worst day of your life and your damn phone keeps suggesting little frowny faces."

She knows this voice. Oh, wow, this is the voice of God that told her to wake up. To come out of it and fight. To "Come back to Daddy."

"Aha," she tells herself. "I should have figured that out."

There's a window with a view of the neighborhood across from the hospital. It all looks . . . brighter to Zelda? She has to squint. But it's nonetheless drab. Deeper, crisper, but altogether more gray. It's like a fantastic movie has ended and now she's exited, blinking, into the theater parking lot.

"No, no change," says Langston's father. "Oh, don't you worry—if I ever get any good news, you'll *know*. I'll call every number in town. Friends, complete strangers . . ."

It was never much of a smile on his face—still, it fades as he adds, "*When* I get good news. I said 'if.' But I meant *when*."

The door opens.

"Call you back—someone's coming in."

She's a doctor, wearing what doctors wear. Langston's father straightens and starts fussing with the blanket. His whole demeanor changes from weary to bright-eyed petitioner. Here's someone new: another bureaucrat of disaster who can give him his boy back if he asks the right questions and gives the right answers.

"Are you Mr. Briggs? I'm Dr. Sundaram. I'll be taking charge of your son's care while Dr. Fischer is away on vacation."

Langston's father hitches up his smile to keep it from slipping. "Vacation," he says.

"I've read your boy's chart," says the doctor, "but a chart can't tell you everything. Why don't you tell me a little about him?"

The man seems to exhale at this. His smile relaxes into something more or less authentic.

"His name is Langston," he says, "and he was in a car crash. Crossed the road on my bike when he shouldn't have."

Of course, thinks Zelda. *A car and a bike.*

"He's been like this for a few weeks," he adds vaguely, with an edge that tells Zelda that he knows exactly how long it's been. With nothing useful to do for his boy, he's become an atomic clock. "He's a good boy, a good student. Hasn't soured on his daddy yet like some teenagers do. A dreamer, always writing stories and songs."

He looks at the bed, so Zelda does, too. "It's been just the two of us for a long while now. This has ... it's been a lot. Dr. Fischer said he could wake up anytime, he just needs the right push," the man says, and he has to press a hand to his face to stifle something. "But ... she didn't know just how to push him, exactly."

Zelda looks away.

"*Push* isn't quite the word I would use," says the Doctor. "Every patient is different, but most in your son's situation just need time. Time to heal."

The father nods. "And the others?"

Maybe God is dreaming, Zelda thinks.

On the seventh day he rested, and dreamed an anxious, messed-up future for all the things he'd made. Everybody naked and unprepared and nothing working quite the way it should. Maybe God is asleep and dreaming and bewildered by the nightmare things we do, as if we aren't all little pieces of him.

He wants us to love him, too. He thinks he's giving us a choice.

She wonders suddenly if Langston was even a character in his own dream before Zelda borrowed that bike. She was the star, and he was just the audience. But then he saw her in danger, a real familiar kind of danger, and before he knew it he'd inserted himself into his own movie. It got weird. And when it got too weird, he discovered he'd made Zelda too well. If she was a part of him, then she was the part that wanted to live and explore and ask questions and demand answers. Part of him loved it—watching her work. But old habits die hard, so before long he was following her all over dreamland saying, *Maybe we should go back to town. Let's think this through. What if we just fall in love and stay here forever?*

Something terrible happened to Langston when he was little, and it took away his childhood. Maybe he thought it took away his future, too. Maybe he's been hiding ever since. So when he came out of hiding and joined Zelda, the dreamscape became an obstacle course of his fears. Silly stuff about *being a man*. Serious stuff about being a child.

There's a little bag in Zelda's backpack. Inside it is a sparkling sand that will make a person sleep forever. She takes it out and looks at it. There isn't much light here in this in-between place, but the sand gathers all of it, multiplies and refracts it. It looks pure and right. Zelda looks back at the scene below her. There's a boy in a bed, and his eyes have dark lashes. Crinkles underneath them like he's halfway to a smile.

The doctor is explaining something about outcomes. She's saying that even mild cases like these are unpredictable.

Langston is happier in the dream, Zelda thinks. She could pretend to be happy, too, for him. Forever. She could do that to make up for the terrible thing she's about to do. Because she knows she could sprinkle the sand right now into his pretty eyes, through the impossible distance between worlds. It'll work because it isn't even really sand—it's a decision. A decision Langston wants someone else to make for him.

She takes a pinch of sand between her thumb and forefinger and stretches out her arm. She holds it there, at the ready. When her arm starts to tremble, she reaches with her left hand to steady her right.

She's too ashamed to look at his father. She'd prefer to stare out the window, but with a sigh she realizes she's going to have to look Langston in the face again sometime, if only to aim, so she does. And her heart goes soft.

"You better have learned something, dummy," she tells him. "That was a long walk." She draws her arm back. "So . . . keep taking walks, okay? Get back on that bike. Don't let people step on you. Stab fear in the toe. If you wake up, we all get to live, even Erx. He hid in his house, and he *still* got stepped on. If you remember him, he'll be as alive as he ever was."

When she sprinkles the sand on her own face, she has to be careful. Wouldn't want any to go astray. It catches in her lashes and pricks the corners of her eyes. She has the bag open again, and she pours more—on her face, her neck. It covers her down to her toes like she's coated in starlight. She doesn't want there to be any left.

Won't work on me anyway, she reminds herself.

Then she feels light, and flat as paper. Then like origami. Then darkness.

TWENTY-NINE

A BELL RINGS.

Zelda stirs and slaps everything on her end table until the ring-ing stops, and finds her glasses, which are fine despite some light slapping, and blinks away the sleep that pricks at her eyes. Blinking, she takes in the stuccoed patterns on her bedroom ceiling.

They look as they've always looked: there's the Four Horsemen, and the Tunnel of Love. The Wolf. The House with Feet.

She can't remember what she'd been dreaming about. She was worried about someone, she thinks; some anonymous dream person. She's pretty sure it wasn't anyone she actually knows.

In the eggy morning light, she dresses for a run, laces up her shoes, steps out the door, and she's off.

There's no one out on the streets this morning—that's unusual. No paperboy, no mail carrier—even the laundromat is missing its clown, and that's an absence that floods Zelda with grief. Confusing, inexplicable grief that almost stops her cold. She's trying to shake it off as she turns into the park to circle the courthouse a few times, and that's when it hits her.

Or she hits it, possibly. It's all relative. There's Zelda, and there's the ankle of a yellow house with feet, and they come together in a way that isn't really anybody's fault.

Smarting, Zelda tumbles backward onto the deep grass. She touches her forehead where it got smacked and squints up at the house, and its robot legs. As she's watching, a Frisbee sails in through one of its open windows and breaks a lamp.

"Oh," she creaks. "Right." From this vantage, she can see all up into its plumbing; she looks away out of politeness.

Beyond the robot and the courthouse is white flatland, and the edge. She's still at the edge of the dream. The geography of the town has changed. The laundromat is nearest the edge, with all the other buildings and city streets fanning out behind it. Like the laundromat is the tip of an arrow, and the rest of the flock followed it here.

A crowd of townsfolk has formed near the edge—as close as the wind will permit—and is peering collectively into the foggy basin. Other people have gathered to gape up at the robot house in wonder. It's not even the weirdest thing they've seen this week, but they've forgotten. One of the Frisbee bros helps Zelda up.

"Dude," he says. "That house has legs!"

"It's friendly," says Zelda.

"Can you talk to it about giving our Frisbee back, then?"

The house has seen better days—it's missing shingles here and there, and she's not sure it has as many right angles as it used to—but it's nothing a coat of paint and a massive renovation can't fix. It tilts forward to examine Zelda, and you can hear all the furniture shift inside. And now the front door opens, and there's a boy there. A boy with a sweet face.

"Zelda!" Langston says. "You came back?"

"Yes! Somehow."

"Why didn't the dream end when you jumped?"

"It . . . wasn't time," she answers vaguely.

"How did you even . . ."

She just smiles, because she isn't clear on the details herself.

"Zelda!" Patches cheers from an upstairs window.

"Patches!"

"Downstairs, please!" he says, though it's unclear to whom. "Take me downstairs!"

The house ratchets down, and Langston runs over to her, to all of them. A moment later, Patches appears, lying atop a footstool like it's a sedan chair while the stool's stubby legs hustle him across the lawn. Zelda stoops to scoop him up, but he stops her with a paw.

"My leg," he explains. "A bad sprain; mustn't be moved."

So Zelda satisfies herself by leaning in and kissing him all over the face.

"Sorry I was a jerk."

"Only human," Patches answers.

Langston is looking like he wants a sprained leg too as he asks Zelda, "Why did you come back?"

"To say goodbye."

Clara is here. She waves. Caroline—Caroline from the mall is standing at the fringes, looking confused. Even the wolf is hanging back sheepishly. Everyone is here. Almost everyone.

"They think the . . . the laundromat clown brought them here," says Langston. "Just dragged everything behind her."

Zelda forces herself to look at all their frightened faces.

"It's been a challenge," says Langston. "You know, reexplaining everything to them—they'd all forgotten that they're in a dream—"

"But there's something about a house that can turn into a robot that expedites things," says Patches.

"Yeah. Like, someone says, 'I just can't believe that I could be living my whole life in a dream and not know it,' and then I say, 'House?' And then the house turns into a robot and the person says, 'Okay, good point.'"

Look at these two, Zelda thinks. *Finishing each other's sentences.*

"They wasted precious time trying to startle their own houses into changing into things," says Patches, "but Langston's childhood home appears to be a special case."

Which makes perfect sense to Zelda, but she keeps that to herself.

"Actually, with a little prodding, the Mexican restaurant turned into a Vietnamese fusion restaurant, but that's it."

The laundromat remains a laundromat, and its washing machines weep frothy tears.

"I feel bad about the clown," says Langston. "Like, I spent my whole life being afraid of her, but now I'm sorry she's gone. Is that weird?"

It's weird that you keep calling the clown a she, thinks Zelda, but she doesn't remark on it.

"Come to the edge with me," she says to Langston as she eyes the town. She slips her hand into his and feels the heat of it climb her like a thermometer. It's embarrassing—she didn't expect to have an audience.

"Oh. Okay," says Langston. "I'll come as close as I can. You're still the only one who can go all the way."

"Wait, so that's it?" calls Caroline. Poor Caroline. "Zelda's gonna ... what, jump? And that's it for the rest of us?"

Langston takes a step in her direction. "We have to let her go. She has a life. We're not even real."

"I have a life!" shouts Caroline. "It's ... not the life I thought I'd have, but I was gonna try community college again in the fall!" She's wringing her hands—she's had less time with the truth than anyone. "I feel real. I don't know what it's like to be any more real than this. Why do we 'have to let her go'?"

Langston says, "Because we love her."

The crowd goes silent.

"Don't we? I bet some of you barely know her, but still you love her all the same."

Zelda, who suddenly does not know what to do with her own hands, watches the crowd. The crowd watches her back. She's expecting some challenge, an indifferent shrug at least, but no one appears to disagree. Not even Caroline. Some actually smile. It's breathtaking—she may not be the dreamer, but she was always the center of the dream.

It fills her from head to toe. But watching the townspeople she's once again struck with the conviction that it was right for her to leave. The town was *her* perpetual childhood. Growing up is realizing you're not the main character. Or else everyone is, too.

"We love her, every one of us," Langston continues. "Even the wolf knows her name. Even the witches called her *daughter*," he says—and the witches bob their heads and nod reluctantly. "Because we're all a part of her. You . . ."

He waves at Caroline.

"Maybe you're her sense of justice. You don't think this is fair because *she* doesn't think it's fair. Maybe Patches is her . . . I don't know, arrogance?"

Patches huffs.

"Maybe I was here to help her find the courage to face her problems, so she's ready to wake up again," says Langston. "Or. Or maybe I was just another problem to solve."

After a moment, he smirks.

"It probably isn't as simple as I'm making it sound. *My* dreams are nonsense. Stuff out of focus, your body won't do what you want. They're . . . like that helpless, stretched-out moment when you know something bad is barreling down on you but you can't get out of its way."

He pauses, thinking.

"But this dream . . . Zelda cared so much she tamed it. She made it stand still. Zelda's heart is so big we all got a piece of it and we'll still have a piece of it when she leaves."

Zelda sighs happily as she looks at him. She's made the right decision, she thinks.

The Mayor steps forward and turns. "Citizens," he says, "I should like to say a few words. I'd like to thank Zelda on behalf of the town. I'd like to give our thanks for dreaming up such a lovely place to live. I grew up in this town. I . . . I guess I thought I'd die here, too. But won't Zelda be carrying a little of what made our town special into the real world? I think she will. Maybe that darling girl can make our dream come true."

This is a real personal best for the Mayor, speech-wise. No campaigning, and not a single mention of a local sports team for cheap applause. Zelda notices some tears in the crowd.

"I guess," the Mayor continues, "I guess I didn't really grow up here. Did I? I'm sorry, I don't understand how it works. Well, anyway, thank you, Zelda. Thank you and sweet dreams. Go Ravens!"

There's some light cheering at this, and a lot of shushing. Langston is taking Zelda's hand, pulling her to the edge before she's cajoled into having to give a speech of her own. She lets him.

His hand feels strong around hers, like it's made of stauncher stuff than before. All their talk about the meaning of dreams comes back to her now, and she decides that maybe—sometimes—a dream really is about sorting big ideas and solving problems. Getting to try something astonishing just to see how it might go—but here in this airless miniature, under glass. Maybe when it works it's like training wheels and a steady hand pushing you forward.

Go ride a bike, Langston, Zelda thinks. *Let me push you.* She wants to tuck that thought inside his mind like it could be the fortune he finds after everything breaks.

They've gone as far as Langston can go. The wind is stinging their eyes, making them blink away tears. It's the only explanation for these tears, wind.

"You're probably wondering about the Tunnel of Love," Zelda says.

"Yeah . . ." Langston admits. "Did I say something wrong, or do something wrong, or something?"

She shakes her head. "You didn't do anything wrong. I didn't do anything wrong. It's just the stupid universe, is all."

Langston laughs. "Oh. *That.* You're saying we're star-crossed, is the problem."

"The *problem*," Zelda argues, "is we're not star-crossed *enough.*"

It doesn't help that Langston is letting his mind wander, and Zelda is treated to another thought balloon picture show—like the trailer to a movie, and once again she's the star. A love story so sweet that it's all she can do to keep from wanting a taste.

She says, "You're supposed to be the main character of your *own* life, you know."

He nods slowly. "Yeah. Right." He has no idea what she's talking about, but he will.

"Hey. That coffee-shop girl you told me about—"

"Yeah, I'm sorry, I shouldn't have. You know I can't even remember her face? It's just the idea of her, the idea of this perfect girl I've been seeing my whole life—"

"Great, but shut up. I think you're ready to talk to her, okay?"

He flinches. "What?"

Then she kisses him. She slides her hands up his fine neck, pulls him close, and opens him up. Gently, she guides the dream. She guides him.

She kisses him, and the wind sighs and disappears. As she kisses him, she pulls him close (it's easy now), and they're almost weightless. They're on the moon. As they kiss, a sudden brightness causes Zelda to open one eye, and she sees the sun rise like a rocket into the sky.

Flatterer, she thinks.

They part. But only for a moment before he kisses *her*. She falls into it.

She hopes Langston will have a life full of weird kisses, awkward kisses, kisses too soft, too hard, bumped teeth. Also, good ones. Really good ones. It hurts to think about that, and it should, but she wants good ones for him, too.

Not one of those kisses in the waking world will ever be perfect, though. Not like this—this dream of a kiss that could only happen here, and could only happen now, in the last heartbeats before waking.

There.

When it's done, Zelda draws back and says, "Pinch me."

He takes a breath and nods. He's ready—it's time. He pinches her on her arm, and winces. She tries to treat him to a nice smile when he opens his eyes again.

"Should," he says with a furrowed brow, "should I . . ."

He pinches her harder.

"Ow."

"But—"

She shrugs, still smiling.

Langston staggers. "Oh." His eyes pop. *"Oh."*

"Yep."

"I was *right*."

"Yeah, yeah."

"I *am* the dreamer. But . . . why can't I get to the edge?"

He's actually nearer to the edge than he's ever been. Zelda wants to laugh as she thinks it was her kiss that brought him here, so close to waking. So. Just a little like *Sleeping Beauty* after all.

He's sure to notice any moment, so Zelda lightens her touch, and gives him her best smile, and now he's all hers. "You can get to the edge," she tells him. "Doctor says you just need a push."

Then Zelda digs in and hurls Langston off the cliff before she changes her mind. Or, to be accurate, before he changes his.

He's falling into the clouds. He's leaving her. There's anguish on his face as he sails away, kicking and grasping and calling her name.

Patches is beside her on his little footstool. "That was good," he says. "But hard to watch."

"Yeah. I wish it didn't have to be the last thing I see."

Langston vanishes into the fog. Zelda closes her eyes.

"Well," says Patches, as everything fades to white, "at least you won't have to think about it for very long."

THIRTY

LANGSTON'S FATHER PRESSES THE NURSE call button again, and gives Langston another hug—lightly at first, like you'd hug something bird-boned and newborn, but then harder and harder—and presses the nurse button *again*, and kisses his face, and isn't this button connected to anything? Finally, he charges into the hospital hallway, terrified Langston will be asleep again when he returns.

"HE'S AWAKE!" he screams down the corridor. "DR. SUNDARAM!" Then he pinwheels around and charges back again.

The doctor is not on duty, so it's hours later when she finally arrives. But the nurses have been in and out, taking vitals, asking questions. As Dr. Sundaram pushes into the room, she can be heard asking someone, "And he hasn't relapsed?" Langston doesn't hear the reply, but he knows the answer anyway.

"Langston," says the doctor from the foot of the bed. "Welcome back."

Langston doesn't answer. He's not really looking at anyone or anything in particular. The doctor clears her throat.

"Please don't be alarmed," she says to Langston's father, "if he seems a little unresponsive at first. Normally, recovering patients are in and out of consciousness for several days before—"

"He said a word. Is that a good sign? Right when he was waking up he said a word. Kind of loud, too."

"What was the word?"

"It sounded like *Zelda*. Maybe. Maybe not—I don't know about any Zeldas."

This is all very interesting to Langston. He wonders what it was that he really said—he doesn't know any Zeldas, either.

THIRTY-ONE

WEEKS PASS.

The days flicker through Langston's room. Bedsheets come in and go out like the tide. The leaves outside his bedroom window change color and drop. Langston changes his clothes, too.

"He's making a very promising recovery," says Dr. Sundaram. Today is another hospital day. Langston's wearing a paper gown. He's sitting atop the examination table in a room demarcated by a paper curtain. His clothes lie like a cow pat on the floor.

He thinks, not for the first time, that hospital days are a lot of getting stuck in things and getting other things stuck in you. He doesn't say this out loud. There isn't a lot he's said out loud these past weeks.

Langston's dad is smiling and nodding. "And the memory loss?

He doesn't remember his whole first year of college now, so that was money well spent."

Langston can tell his dad is trying to catch his eye, let Langston be in on the joke. Langston keeps staring into the same middle distance where most of his life seems to take place these days, just out of reach.

"When he returns to school, he may find the familiar environment brings some memories back," says the doctor.

The man's face falls a little. "Well, I don't know when Langston will be ready to try school again—"

"I can appreciate wanting to keep him in the nest, Mr. Briggs, but it will be good for Langston to get back to his old routine."

The room is conspicuously quiet after she says this.

"You probably see a lot of patients and their families, Doctor?" says Langston's father finally. "So I wouldn't expect you to remember every little thing I've told you? But my family has been through a lot. Langston and I have been through a *lot*."

"I remember, Mr. Briggs—"

"We lost Langston's mom and brother to a car crash. Langston could have been in that car, too. He was only *five*. We lost a *lot* of things after that. Some days the only thing we had was each other, understand?"

"Mr. Briggs, I wasn't—"

"He could have gone to any school he wanted, but he chose to stay in town because we stick together. We understand each other."

Langston's father frowns and continues. "Except . . . except I guess I don't understand why one day there's this mysterious thing he *has* to do so bad he can't even wait for a bus or a streetcar and so he drags out my old bike—which he has *never ridden*—and goes and gets himself hit by a car."

He's looking at Langston again, in case Langston picks today of all days to fill in the blank. But Langston doesn't know what he was trying to do, either.

Dad turns pointedly back at the doctor. "I've lost people. It can't happen again, you get me?"

Dr. Sundaram is slowly nodding. "That must have been terrifying. It's not my business, so the last thing I'll say about it is that a person . . . they have to be able . . ."

"A person is supposed to be the main character of their own life," says Langston.

Both his father and the doctor jerk and look at him like he's performed a magic trick. *Watch me pull a statement out of my hat.*

"That is one way of putting it, sure," says the doctor.

"A friend told me that," says Langston.

"One of your online game friends?" says Langston's dad, with a scoff that is probably meant to sound friendly. "Doctor, I love my son, but he doesn't have any *real* friends."

"I had a . . ." Langston croaks. He doesn't want to say the word—it isn't big enough. "A dream. A really *big* dream," he says, and he looks at each of them with a challenge in his eyes. "In the coma. I've been getting it back in bits and pieces for a while now. It's just starting to fit together." He hesitates, and touches his fingers to his lips. "I think . . . I think I had the same dream, nonstop, for three weeks."

The moment he finishes saying this, he feels certain it's true.

The doctor has a good bedside manner. Her face barely betrays how stupid she finds this idea. "I'm sure it feels that way, Langston, though you've likely had many hundreds of dreams since your accident."

"I don't remember a single one since I came out of the coma," he says. "I used to always remember my dreams."

"Don't I know it," says Langston's father. "He'd tell me every one at breakfast. He's lucky he has such a loving daddy, Doctor, because you *know* how boring other people's dreams are."

Langston huffs and smiles a little. "Sorry to bother you."

"A lot of witches, Doctor!" his father explains. "And wizards and astronaut clowns and dirt-bike races. Exciting stuff. You know what hasn't been exciting? Losing my mind with ... with worry these last few months, wondering if he's ever gonna ... gonna wake all the way ..."

He puts a fist to his mouth. His eyes are wet. And with that, Langston really does wake up, finally, completely.

"Dad," he says. He looks him in the eyes. He hadn't before, he realizes—not for a long time. "Dad, I'm sorry."

And he is sorry. But because he still feels a confusing mishmash of loyalties, he adds, "It was a laundromat clown."

"A what?" asks the doctor.

"Laundromat clown. I never said *astronaut*, I said *laundromat*." He realizes the one doesn't really sound better than the other.

The doctor asks about this, so Langston describes the polyester pantsuit–wearing clown, with its orange hair and frightful makeup.

"I've been dreaming about her for years. If I ever got too close, she would lurch out and pinch my cheeks," he finishes. Then he makes a sour face because his father is laughing at him. He has a whooping, gut-busting kind of laugh. Three months of brave-faced stoicism are cracking open, and this is what's spilling out. It takes a while. Finally, a falling sigh signals the all clear.

"Poor Miss Pitts," he says. "She always did wear a lot of makeup.

And that orange *hair*—don't you remember, man?" He turns to the doctor. "Old Miss Pitts owned the laundromat we went to when Langston was a little boy. Oh, she loved you, Langston—always wanted to make baby talk and pinch your cheeks."

Langston winces. He doesn't remember, really. He hasn't seen the actual woman in years, but there's a fun-house version of her that's been living in his head since he was five.

"She scared me."

"Well, all right. I get that. Going to that laundromat all the time was . . . It was right after everything. We lost Mom and Baldwin, and then we lost the house."

"She wouldn't let me forget," says Langston, and his face screws up at the memory of her. A memory that's somehow both rosy and rotten at the same time. "She was always so busy feeling sorry for me I couldn't forget and be a kid for five seconds. *You* wouldn't let me forget."

Langston's dad flinches. "Wait, I wouldn't let you forget what? What are we talking about?"

"You never let me forget, but you didn't let me remember, either. We never *talk* about them." He presses his hands into his cheekbones. "Like, we gotta be so serious and silent all the time and we never talk. You put away all their pictures, and I'm forgetting their *faces*."

"Oh. All right. You're right. I got those old pictures somewhere, in a box . . ."

"I've forgotten too much," Langston says. He rattles his head. "The clown was *real*? *For real*?"

Langston straightens. There's a wild look in his eye. Without a word, he leaps off the examination table and through the curtain.

"Langston?" his father calls after him.

Langston runs back inside a moment later.

"Clothes," he tells them.

Putting his clothes on feels like dressing a dog. Nothing's cooperating. And it's hard to concentrate with people yelling at you, but eventually the job's done.

"Dad, I love you," he says, "but you can push me without pushing me away, you know?"

"Langston—"

"And if you want to keep someone safe," he finishes, "you don't teach them to be afraid of bikes. You teach them to *ride a bike*." Then he leaves through the curtain again.

It takes him three tries to find his way out of the hospital, but eventually he's on the street.

"She was real," he says.

He runs. He's mostly got his strength back after weeks of atrophy, but he's still easily winded. *This is dumb*, he thinks. *I could go tomorrow. In a week. In a month, when I'm stronger. Making a big rush of this is literally what got me hit by a car in the first place.* He almost turns around and gives up on the whole idea when he sees Erx sitting up against a newspaper vending machine.

No, not Erx. Not really—a homeless vet with a long gray beard who always hangs around the university. A guy Langston used to see every day. But he looks exactly like Erx—if Erx wore a parka and camo pants and was holding a cardboard sign that reads COSMIC TRUTHS 98¢. It's just the confirmation Langston needs to keep going, and he's so happy he digs into his hip pocket to check if he has any money. He finds three dollars and hands them over.

"You're real," he tells him.

The panhandler smiles and says, "That's the nicest thing anyone's said to me in weeks." He waggles the three dollars. "This is good for three cosmic truths."

Langston realizes he's less than a block from a streetcar stop.

"One: You never forget your first love," says the man, raising a finger.

The streetcar will take him to within two blocks of where he wants to go.

"Two: You never forget how to ride a bike."

Or it would, if Langston hadn't just given away his only three dollars.

"Three: Therefore, your first love is a bike."

Langston turns and scowls. "What?"

"Think about it."

"No."

But there *is* a bike-share station here with a bunch of identical yellow bicycles, all in a row. He stares at them for six minutes—he doesn't have a wallet.

"I don't suppose you could loan me three dollars," he asks Erx.

"Nope."

"Why ninety-eight cents, by the way? For the truths. Why not an even dollar?"

"Marketing."

Then—finally—a woman approaches to return the bike she's been renting. Langston steps in her way.

"The last time I rode a bike, I got hit by a car," he tells her.

". . . Oh?" says the woman.

"That was months ago—I was in the hospital."

"I'm sorry; that's—"

"I was doing it for love. I had finally talked myself into trying something, and so I just . . . took off before I could talk myself back out of it again, okay? I was barely . . . *barely* taking a chance, and I got clobbered anyway. But . . . I recently fought a monster and figured some stuff out and you gotta get back on that bike, right? And you never forget your first love."

"I'm sorry, what does this have to do with—"

"I just gave my last three dollars to that panhandler, and if you let me take this bike I promise I'll return it in five minutes to the station on the quad."

Erx waves at them.

Langston coasts down the hill, wind on his cheeks, muscles weak but working. He's holding a smile on his face, barely—those muscles are weak, too.

But there—a man who looks just like the Mayor from his dream is street preaching from a box; he's roaring that it's a fallen world, but he's wrong—this world is fine. The Frisbee bros are on the college quad. A smiling yellow cat figurine is waving from the window of a Japanese restaurant. Langston glides to a clumsy halt beside another bike-share station and hitches his yellow bicycle to the post.

Now he's catching his breath. He's smoothing his shirt. He's thanking his father inwardly for making him wear nice clothes to the hospital. He's opening the coffee-shop door.

A bell rings. Just a little one, announcing his arrival. Behind the counter, she turns, and the whole world turns with her.

Zelda.

It's Zelda.

His dream girl.

"Oh," she says when she sees him. "Hey. I remember you."

She finishes wiping down the espresso machine and blows a bit of hair out of her eyes. Langston smiles. He hopes it's a smile. "Langston," he tells her.

"Right. You used to come in here every day."

"You noticed?"

She gives him a look. "Sure, I noticed. Did you go away somewhere?"

"I was in a coma," says Langston.

Zelda laughs, so Langston grins harder, until his smile feels like something his face isn't doing on purpose. It collapses like a pup tent.

"Seriously, though. Coma."

Zelda drops a mug. "Oh. Ohmy*gosh*."

Langston is shy—he's always been shy. But he keeps talking. He makes her laugh, and she makes him laugh harder. They can't tell that we're thinking about them. They'll be talking awhile, so we make our exit. They're in the café, but we're crossing the park, avoiding a Frisbee, passing a house with robot feet.

You'll remember all this for a while, but eventually it'll fade.

A story's end is always a little like waking.

ACKNOWLEDGMENTS

GREATEST THANKS ALWAYS TO MY wife, Marie, who when we married probably thought I would eventually stop reading her long passages I'd written—sometimes the same passage twice but with minute differences—all while studying her face for every tiny reaction. I haven't, though. You know when you go to the optometrist and they ask you which looks better, number one or number two, and you'd swear both choices are exactly the same? This is what I do to Marie, but with words. I'm sorry, Marie.

Thank you to my agent, Steven Malk, for his guiding hand as this idea grew.

To my wonderful editors, Jennifer Besser and Kate Meltzer, who gently nudged me into letting this romance be a romance.

Thanks to Shannon Hale, Callie Miller, Janni Simner, and Jennifer J. Stewart, who all read some early incarnation of this and gave me invaluable feedback. Some of them read it when it was a three-thousand-word short story. Some of them read it when it was a novella. I don't know, it keeps getting bigger. Next year I'll probably put out an expanded edition that has to be printed on bible paper, just to keep it all in.

And to my authenticity reader, who has asked to be called "moukies": Thank you, moukies—for your insights and advice, but also your enthusiasm for the story—it came at a time when I really needed it.

hello!

I'm stealing some space here at the end to share a little of the process of making this thing.

Zelda?

I'm shocked to realize, looking back, that I've been thinking about it for more than ten years.

Here's a page from my sketchbook with what I consider to be the first drawing of Zelda. I'd drawn a great many before it, but this was the first to feel like the woman I had in my head. Thoughtful. Watchful. Someone who looks like she might take the world apart just to see how it works.

Also pictured: A crow making pizza, I guess? I don't remember why I drew this.

My first stab at planning out pages 150-151.

Look, the art has to start somewhere. This garbage turned into a couple of my favorite pages.

The helicopters were in previous drafts, but I got the idea fairly late to swerve suddenly from Zelda and Langston to a Weird War story, shot through with the pathos of a soldier's letter to their girl back home. If it worked, it would be, in miniature, all of the comedy and heartbreak I'm always trying for in my stories, and I could imagine no better way to do it than with an abrupt shift from prose to comics— to put you in the thick of it without a single clumsy word of warning.

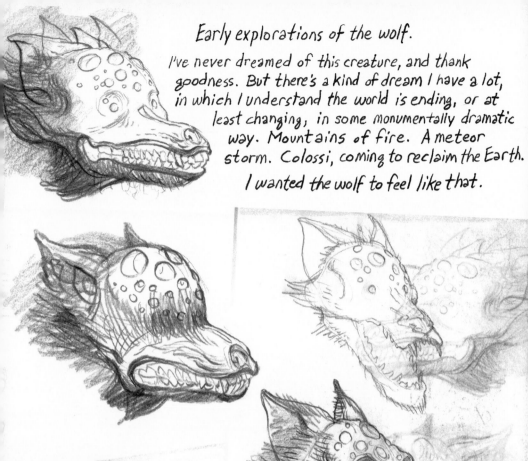

Early explorations of the wolf.

I've never dreamed of this creature, and thank goodness. But there's a kind of dream I have a lot, in which I understand the world is ending, or at least changing, in some monumentally dramatic way. Mountains of fire. A meteor storm. Colossi, coming to reclaim the Earth.

I wanted the wolf to feel like that.

I mean, most often I'm dreaming about trying to find a clean bathroom. They're not all like this.

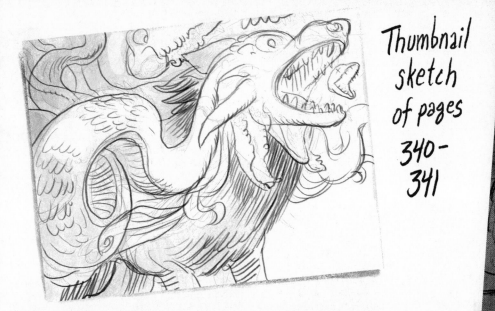

Thumbnail sketch of pages 340-341

This is the tighter sketch I proposed to my editor.

Things didn't change much between sketch and final, just got refined.

Some of it I had to invent entirely, but I looked at a lot of pictures of wolves, and took these photos of a skull I already had in my bike shed. I think it's a javelina.

Okay, that's it.

—ar